CANDLE IRON

SALLY ODGERS

Angus&Robertson
An imprint of HarperCollins*Publishers*

Angus&Robertson

An imprint of HarperCollins*Publishers*, Australia

First published in Australia in 2001
Reprinted in 2001, 2003
by HarperCollins*Publishers* Pty Limited
ABN 36 009 913 517
A member of the HarperCollins*Publishers* (Australia) Pty Limited Group
www.harpercollins.com.au

HarperCollins*Publishers*

25 Ryde Road, Pymble, Sydney, NSW 2073, Australia
31 View Road, Glenfield, Auckland 10, New Zealand
77–85 Fulham Palace Road, London W6 8JB, United Kingdom
Hazelton Lanes, 55 Avenue Road, Suite 2900, Toronto, Ontario M5R 3L2
and 1995 Markham Road, Scarborough, Ontario M1B 5M8, Canada
10 East 53rd Street, New York NY 10022, USA

National Library of Australia Cataloguing-in-Publication data:

Odgers, Sally Farrell, 1957– .
    Candle iron.
    ISBN 0 207 19755 5.
    I. Title. (Series: Master of time; bk.1).
A823.3

Cover illustration by Carol McLean-Carr
Cover and internal design by Lore Foye, HarperCollins Design Studio
Typeset by HarperCollins in 10/13 Sabon
Printed and bound in Australia by Griffin Press on 50gsm Ensobulky

7 6 5 4 3   03 04 05 06

Thank you to my friends the Scarlet Avengers (past and present) for the use of your names.

Thank you to Zara Westaway, who invented Zara the Merryhound.

Thank you to Ace and Tess, two dear dogs who lent their names to Tace.

AUTHOR'S NOTE

Candle Iron is set in the same reality as two of my earlier books, *Amy Amaryllis* and *Shadowdancers*. It is not a sequel, but for anyone interested, the events in *Candle Iron* occur some twenty-five years after those in *Amy Amaryllis*.

Most of the names of things and people in this book are pronounced exactly the way they are spelled. The main exceptions are Hasselsjo Castle, which is pronounced as *Hassle-sher* and Tace the Spellhound, whose name is pronounced as *Tar-cheh*. Trader Mohr's name is said like this: *More*.

For more information about Sally Odgers and the world of *Candle Iron*, visit the HarperCollins website at
http://www.harpercollins.com.au

SNARE

SUMMERCLIMB — 1ST MOON OF THE YEAR

OF THE HOUND

SHE was waiting by the thicket, dressed in the blue and silver robes and braided hood of a healer. From her belt hung a tapestry bag, and an ornamental knife with a hilt of bone and a blade of glinting metal. It was not of McAnerin design, but that was not surprising, since the woman was not from McAnerin either. Nor was she really a healer.

She flexed her fingers and glanced at the climbing moon. Not long now. She had set her snare. Soon it would be sprung and she would have the treasure in her hands. The lad had agreed to meet her at moonhigh, which suited her as well as it suited him. And here he came, racing his shadow across the grass. Behind him scampered a hound.

The light of the moon shone down on his face, pale and drawn beneath the gleaming hair. He was thin and quiet, and he suffered from cruel dreams that disturbed his sleep and haunted his waking hours. That was why he had come to the travelling fair. She had seen at once that this was the chance she had been waiting for all her life. The chance of power.

'I can take your dreams, pluck them out of your head,' she had promised, 'but you must pay my price.'

'Anything, dame! I cannot live like this. Everyone thinks I am going mad.'

She had told him her price, trying to hide her eagerness. He hadn't liked that, but he was coming now to pay. And when he had paid, she would take the dreams from his head, just as she'd promised. And in their stead she would leave a living nightmare.

PART ONE — SIEGE

CHAPTER ONE

BLOODLINE

WINTERWANE — 10TH MOON OF THE YEAR

OF THE HOUND

'WE can't hold out much longer, Allyso.' Merrit's voice was little more than a thread-like whisper, and Allyso had to bend close to hear what he said. 'We can't hold out,' he repeated. 'This castle is going to fall.'

Merrit was Allyso's uncle, and both of them were of the Blood of Torm. Merrit often used to say they *were* the Blood of Torm, for there was no-one else to carry on the line. The Tormblood family had never been large, and now it had dwindled to just these two: a middle-aged man and a girl.

'I used to think I might have a child one day,' Merrit would sometimes say, 'but it never happened. It seems it's left to Allyso to carry on the Blood.'

The two were alike in many ways. Both had the gilden skin and bronze hair of the Torm Bloodline, both had the same gold-hazel eyes. In colour and feature they were similar, but the resemblance between them ended there. Merrit Tormblood was as tall and strong as a stonewood tree, but Allyso was more like a honeybark sapling, very slight and skinny for a girl who was nearly fourteen. Folk shook their heads and whispered that the Blood must be weak if Allyso were the best heir it could produce.

Merrit always put them right about that. 'And what,' he would demand, 'has weakness to do with size? It's the brain and the heart that count, not the body that houses them. And besides,' he would add with a grin, 'small folk have a practical advantage. They can last much longer in a siege.'

'Is that true?' asked Allyso the first time she heard him say it. Her lack of stature had been a trial to her for as long as she could remember. Strangers usually thought she was a child of eleven or so and, thinking her so young, they tended to speak over her head or past her as if she didn't matter. That was very galling, for Allyso had ideas and opinions of her own.

'Is it true that small people are useful in a siege?' she had asked again. Even Merrit, who knew her age to the hour, was sometimes inclined to forget to answer her.

He had answered her this time, though. 'Very useful,' he had said with his lazy, gleaming smile. 'Small folk don't eat so much as their larger brothers. They can also slip away into corners and out through windows and tunnels and not be seen. Big ones like me are much too easy for the enemy to find.'

The idea that Merrit could have an enemy had made Allyso laugh at the time. Merrit was such a favourite with everyone. The castlers loved him, and even the folk of the villages thought him a better lord

3

than most. But of course she wasn't laughing now. Disaster had come to Torm, and no-one was laughing.

All her life, Merrit had been strong and proud and fearless. Now, since that shocking Midwinter of less than a moonspan before, he was helpless — weak and ailing.

Allyso fetched some food from the buttery, but Merrit refused it.

'How can I eat when my castlers are starving?'

'If you *don't* eat you'll die,' she said sharply. 'And that means that Torm will fall. *I* can't hold it, since I'm not a Mistra yet, so what will happen to your castlers then? And what will happen to *me*?'

If Merrit died, Allyso would be the last of the Blood and, thanks to the hints that Healer Hilz had dropped, she had a nasty notion of what would happen if the invaders managed to catch her.

Lord Toombs and Lord Sheels could win the castle and lands, but if one of the Blood went free, they could never be sure of holding what they had won. She was not a Mistra yet, but how could they risk what she might become and the support she might gather in years to come?

'Torm will fall, whether I live or die,' sighed Merrit.

Allyso clenched her hands. He was weak and ill, but why did he have to sound resigned? It wasn't like Merrit to be resigned. He was the one who made things happen *his* way.

'There must be something we can do! You're the one who says we must never give up.'

'Truth must be faced, no matter how ugly its visage,' said Merrit. His long face was sallow and greyed beneath its usual golden tan and his eyes were almost closed. He had given up on himself and Torm, which meant he had given up on her as well.

Allyso had never felt so lonely.

'You can make things right,' she said desperately. 'You must!'

But Merrit was in despair.

Allyso sat by his bedside and chewed her knuckles. Her heart hammered as she listened to the muted sounds of the castle. Torm was her home and her heritage, yet Torm was rotten and about to fall.

The rot had entered the castle over six moonspans before ... It was Winterwane now, as hope was dying, but the trouble had come with the bright Highsummer days.

CHAPTER TWO

SOULBINDER

HIGHSUMMER — 3RD MOON OF THE YEAR

OF THE HOUND

TORM was a Northlands castle, perched on a jutting outcrop at the upper edge of the great McAnerin Plain. The plains were rich with minerals and natural wealth, but the McAnerin people preferred a simple life. Their herds and flocks were thriving, their garnerbeast were few but carried ample flesh, their holdings bore plenty of fruit and grain, the strawcaps' nests were overflowing with eggs. There was enough to feed themselves and to trade with travellers and with the folk at the castle. The excess they stored in barns, with chinks in the wall to let the air breathe through.

High to the northwest lay the pass into the bleak land of Ankoor, and over the ocean were the desertlands of Rargon. Each was ruled by sterner laws and much more rigid customs, each had more than its share of rebels and malcontents. McAnerin, said Merrit, was fairer than either land and beholden to neither. McAnerin ruled itself by the old-time law of favour and obligation, and most of its citizens were very well satisfied.

Especially satisfied, said Merrit proudly, were the folk of Torm.

Travellers were always well received at Torm. The beds and board of the castle were open to lords and villagers, traders, herders and bards. It was said that Merrit welcomed all, bowed to no-one and feared nothing.

And that was where Merrit made a rare mistake. He *should* have been afraid, and he should *not* have welcomed the dark-eyed woman who came to the castle gates that Highsummer Eve. Later, it seemed like an omen that the soulbinder had come at Highsummer and struck her fiercest blow on Midwinter Day.

'We should have *known*,' said Allyso much later. 'There should have been some way of keeping her out.'

Yet how could the castlers have known the dame was trouble? She was drab and dour enough, but she rapped on the gate like any other traveller.

'A bed for the night, porter, and the best your kitchens have to offer!' she called. It seemed a little demanding for one who looked so shabby, and perhaps that was why Berneathy, the handsome porter, gave her a closer examination than he would usually have done.

Berneathy had been travelling for half his life and keeping the gate of Torm for the other half. He summed up most folk in a glance, then let them in and out with a bow and a flashing smile, but the sight of this woman sent a shiver down his back.

He gave her a second, more thoughtful look, for she was not like the folk who usually came to Torm. Nor was her page like others of his calling. Berneathy

7

thought most pages were cheeky brats. That didn't bother him much since he'd once been a cheeky brat himself. This page seemed to have no cheek nor any personality. He stood as solemn and unblinking as any statue, and not a statue Berneathy would have wanted to put in *his* courtyard. His dark hair was tied back in a leather thong, and his blue eyes were blank and staring. Blind? Daft? Hexed? Berneathy shivered again.

The woman rapped impatiently on the gate. A crystal flashed on her finger, and Berneathy caught his breath. The jewel was fine, but it seemed to glisten with menace. He turned away before he could be dazzled.

'Wait,' he said. 'I must ask Lord Merrit first.' He tugged the signal wire to jangle a bell high in the castle, then climbed the steps to the watchtower. He tried to move with his usual dignity, but the cold wind of dread seemed to be pressing against his back.

Merrit emerged unhurriedly from his quarters. 'What's amiss, Berneathy? You look a little ruffled.' He smiled his lazy smile. 'Has a flight of dragons come out of the North? If so, you must bid them to supper. Trader Mohr would welcome new tales to tell.'

'We have travellers, Lord Merrit,' said Berneathy, ignoring the joke. 'Come out of Ankoor, by the look of them.'

Merrit glanced down at the gates. 'A long journey for a dame and a lad, unless they have a garnerbeast,' he commented. 'What makes you think they are Ankoorian? Are they wearing those ridiculous birthchains? Or do they bear the emblem of one of the Nine Castles?'

'If they do, I didn't notice, but the dame sounds foreign, and the page said nothing at all,' said

Berneathy. 'There's something very wrong with both of them. Shall I send them away?'

Merrit hitched his eyebrows in surprise. 'Why would you send them away? Since when has Torm hospitality been so grudging?'

'I don't care for that dame,' said Berneathy shortly. 'She is pinched and mean, and the boy looks half-mazed.'

'She cannot help her face, and the lad must be tired after his journey,' said Merrit. His smile had faded, and a certain grimness came over his features. 'Stop your haivering and let them in, Berneathy.'

'But Merrit —'

'Perhaps I should hire someone less timid and less prone to superstition to hold the gates of Torm?' suggested Merrit.

Berneathy gave a slight, offended bow, and departed.

'What has ruffled my friend Berneathy's crest?' Trader Mohr, a regular visitor to Torm, had come up to the watchtower with his grey cat sprawled across his shoulders like a living shawl.

'Nothing important, Mohr,' said Merrit, relaxed and amused again. 'Berneathy mislikes the looks of that dame down there and would have kept her out. I just had to remind him, gently, who is Lord of Torm and whose opinions need to be upheld.' Flipping back his light Highsummer mantle, he pointed down from the tower.

Trader Mohr narrowed his eyes against the brightness, and his smile died. 'Perhaps Berneathy has a point, Lord Merrit.'

'What's the matter, Trader Mohr?' asked Allyso. 'Do you know those people?'

Mohr shrugged, lifting a hand to steady his cat as he turned away from the wall. 'Just one moment,' he said, and crossed to the interior stair. 'Dagg? Will you please come up?'

When Trader Dagg had joined them, Mohr nodded down towards the gate. 'Do you see that dame and her page, Dagg?'

'Stars that burn!' Dagg sounded just as unhappy about the new arrival as Mohr had been. This seemed odd to Allyso, for Traders were usually only too pleased to see potential customers, and Dagg and Mohr were a pleasant and popular pair.

'Who is that dame, Merrit?' asked Mohr. His fingers caressed his cat, and Allyso thought they seemed to tremble a little. She looked more closely and saw a dampness gleam on the cat's grey fur. A prickle of unease touched her neck.

'I haven't a notion, Mohr,' said Merrit. 'I haven't asked her name, but it seems that you and Dagg disapprove of our guests as much as Berneathy does.' He laughed. 'Do you fear they are disguised High Traders, come to snatch your profits?'

'Trade is trade, Lord Merrit,' said Dagg, offended. 'The Traders of Fielding have no fear of competition.'

'Then what is the problem? You both look as long-faced as a lamed Valourn.'

Mohr was still stroking his cat, and it began to purr down low in its throat. It should have been a friendly and soothing sound, but Allyso backed away. *Was* it a purr? Or was it more of a growl? And couldn't Merrit *see* there was something wrong? Berneathy thought so, as did Mohr and Dagg and even the cat.

'That dame is a soulbinder,' said Mohr.

'What's that?' asked Allyso.

'Mistra Allyso —' began Dagg. He stopped short and glanced at Merrit as if for guidance.

'Tell me,' she insisted. 'What is a soulbinder, and why are you all so afraid?'

'I wouldn't say *afraid* so much,' said Mohr.

'I would,' said Dagg frankly.

'*Tell* me!' repeated Allyso. She was getting tired of having to wait for her explanations.

'Go ahead,' said Merrit lazily. 'It is just one more superstition. Stars! Why must folk forever invent these shadows and wraiths? Can't they find enough in the real world to trouble them?'

Mohr sighed. 'A soulbinder is a hexmistress, my child. A peddler of charms and potions.'

'This one was driven out from Clair Village,' said Dagg. He turned his large dark eyes to Mohr. 'And well did she deserve it!'

'How harsh you sound!' said Merrit. 'Why should a dame be driven out for a matter of charms and moonshine?'

Mohr smiled grimly. 'I could tell you tales of soulbinders that would make your hair tingle on your scalp ... Tales of the real world, too. If hexes and charms don't have their effect, be sure their potions will. I've known of men whose guts were twisted into knots so fast they bled —'

'Mohr ...' Dagg's voice was low and reproving. 'Mistra Allyso will not wish to hear such things.'

'Better not, at that,' said Mohr. 'So I'll merely add that this dame wears a ring that is set with what looks like a gem of power.'

'What is that?' asked Allyso, but before Mohr could answer, Merrit said impatiently, 'Your tales are always thrilling, Trader Mohr, but best heard at the supper table! If this dame was driven out of Clair, that is all the better reason to make her welcome here.'

'I would reconsider if I were in your boots,' said Mohr. 'Or at least have a Spellhound inspect her. There was trouble in Clair, you know. Children sickened, flocks went poor ...'

'You are *not* in my boots,' said Merrit decidedly. 'You tend to your trading, Mohr, and leave Torm's welfare to me. And as for a Spellhound, there is none here and never will be.'

'It would be a good precaution.'

'And while folk wait on a hound to tell them what they should be considering for themselves, *real* evil could come and they'd be caught unwary!' Merrit must have heard his voice rising and becoming passionate, for he corrected himself with his usual laugh. 'All I really mean to say is that we at Torm will never deal in such a foolish superstition. Excuse me, Traders, while I greet our latest guests.' He bowed and left, treading unhurriedly down the steps towards the gates.

'And so we are scolded!' said Mohr after a moment. 'I have never seen our lordly host in such a spate.'

'Merrit really hates to hear about things like hexes and charms,' said Allyso. 'You know his manservant, Gregory?'

'Of course,' said Mohr. 'A pleasant lad with more wit between his ears than most his age.'

'His mother Gill was my nurse when I was a babe,' said Allyso. 'She was born in Ankoor, and so she wears a birthchain for luck. Merrit is always scolding her about it. He pretends it's a joke, but he really means it, I think . . .' She caught herself up, realising vaguely that she shouldn't be talking about the Lord of Torm to his guests. 'But never mind that now.'

She leaned over the watchtower parapet and peered with interest at the woman and her page. The boy looked about fifteen, and she hoped he might be friendly. Some pages were happy to talk to the Heir of Torm, but others ignored her, once they saw how small and slight she was. More than one had called her a scrawny lad. Corrected, they tended to be offended, as if she had fooled them by design.

The woman did not look very grand. What could such a dame have done to get herself banished?

'What did she do?' she asked the Traders. 'That dame down there?'

'It is better not to know, Mistra Allyso,' said Dagg. 'Better to keep dark things for when you are older.'

'If you don't want to explain, you shouldn't have mentioned it,' said Allyso sharply. 'And don't you call me "Mistra Allyso", Trader Dagg. I am not a Mistra yet, but neither am I a babe. Tell me about this soulbinder. Why was she driven out? Did she steal that gem on her finger? Did she smile too often at some wealthy, wedded lord? And what did you mean when you called it a gem of power?' She looked expectantly at Mohr, who was a famous gossip, but he shook his head.

'All we know,' he said, 'is that a soulbinder dame was driven out of Clair village, leaving a great deal of trouble in her wake. This one matches the description well enough to make me most uneasy.

'As for the gems of power, no doubt Merrit would call it superstition, but the tale of the gems is old and was once well-known. Some are little but luck-charms, like the birthchain Mistra Gill wears, but others command the power of the ages and work their will —'

'But what do they *do*?' asked Allyso. She could see that Mohr meant to tell the tale in full, and would probably use the rolling bardic language that employed six words when two or three would have done.

'Let me see if I recall it correctly,' said Mohr. He closed his eyes for a moment. 'Ah, I have it! The gem of time is that which gives mastery over the years that were and are to come, while the gem of truth is that which is always held by a seer who is the strongest in the land. The gem of —'

'It is time we were on our way,' said Dagg abruptly. 'My Mistra expects me home soon after Highsummer.'

Mohr smiled slightly and switched to his everyday mode of speech. 'It seems I am fated not to tell you the tale this time, Allyso. Ask me again next time we meet. Yes, Dagg, I am coming. A few heartbeats more or less cannot make much difference to your Mistra.'

The Traders left the watchtower, but Allyso remained, leaning over the parapet to watch as Merrit greeted the sinister stranger.

'I bid you welcome, Dame.'

Allyso pulled a little face. Merrit was a fine and gracious host, but his manner was sometimes *too* charming. What if the woman thought he was mocking her? What if it were not just Trader Tales and she were *truly* dangerous? She leaned a little farther, peering down.

'You are weary and worn,' continued Merrit. 'You are welcome to partake of food and shelter with us at Castle Torm.'

'You welcome us, Merrit Tormblood?' The woman's voice was strong, with a ring of metal about it, and Allyso could hear her as plainly as she heard her uncle.

'That I do.'

'And how deep is your welcome, Merrit of Torm? Is it deep and wide enough for folk from far away?'

'My welcome is deep as the great Ocean of the South,' said Merrit grandly, 'and high as the Shrouded Mountain. My welcome is wide as the Desert of Rargon and firm as the Castle of Torm. Does that please you, Dame?'

'Prettily spoken,' said the woman. 'But pretty words cannot be eaten or wrapped around for warmth. Do you really mean the words you offer me?'

Allyso drew in a sharper breath. The woman had almost accused her uncle of lying. Couldn't she understand the hyperbole of a classical Tormblood greeting?

As if she felt Allyso's shocked gaze, the soulbinder glanced up at the watchtower. Her eyes glinted like pitch, and Allyso felt cold. She stepped quickly away from the parapet and out of the soulbinder's line of sight. On any other occasion, she would have been annoyed if guests had seen her dressed in her rubbed hide leggings and a shabby overshirt, but this time, she was relieved. If the woman *had* seen her staring, she would think her nothing but an ill-mannered serving-girl.

After the soulbinder and her page had vanished into the castle, Allyso clattered down the stairs from the watchtower, across the wellyard and up to her own high chamber. Quickly, she braided her hair into a coronet. She had been doing that lately in an effort to appear her true age. Merrit had complimented her gravely, but Gregory, her friend, had smiled a bit uneasily and offered to crop it off for her instead.

A lot Gregory knew of hair and styles, she thought as she changed into a cress-green tunic and matching cap. She surveyed herself briefly in the looking glass, pulled a face at her skinny reflection and went along the passages to the main castle. On the way, she passed Mohr and Dagg, who bowed to her gravely and said their farewells.

'Aren't you staying to supper?' she asked in surprise. 'I'd like to hear the rest of that tale, Trader Mohr.'

'Not this time, Mistra Allyso,' said Dagg. 'We leave for Fielding tonight.'

'Don't call me "Mistra",' said Allyso firmly. 'I keep telling you, I'm not one.'

'You will be, when you have grown,' said Dagg with equal firmness. 'Meanwhile, you are the Heir of Torm and deserve our courtesy.'

'Tell Merrit to look for us next Highsummer, if not before,' said Mohr.

'Aren't you afraid of meeting trail-thieves if you travel by night?'

'Not,' said Mohr with a wry twist to his handsome mouth, 'so afraid as Dagg is of sharing a roof and table with a soulbinder.' He hitched his cat more closely over his shoulder. 'Greyson doesn't care for the dame either,' he added, 'and that is good enough for me, even if Dagg did not agree.' He turned and looked seriously at Allyso. 'Child, tell Merrit to have a care what pledges he makes that dame. If he offers her something, he really must deliver. Otherwise . . .'

'Otherwise *what*?' prompted Allyso.

Mohr shook his head. 'Otherwise, she may take what was offered several hundredfold.'

'We must be going,' said Dagg.

'Goodbye,' said Allyso. Mohr's warning sounded grave, but why warn her instead of going to Merrit? It was very puzzling.

Mohr gave her a slightly mocking bow. 'At your service, always, Heir of Torm.'

Later, Allyso wished she had begged the traders to speak with Merrit before they left, but on that Highsummer Eve, she had simply smiled and waved as they passed through the gates of Torm, and put the warning off to one side of her mind.

CHAPTER THREE

TOLLERMAN

HIGHSUMMER — 3RD MOON OF THE YEAR

OF THE HOUND

THE soulbinder woman seemed satisfied at first. On Merrit's orders she was given the finest guest chamber, with an anteroom for her silent page.

Gregory fetched and heated soft well-water and, with a smile and a bow and inward dismay, brought whatever else the woman asked. He and his friend Berneathy were in full agreement about Torm's latest guests.

'That dame is *trouble*,' said Berneathy, when Gregory took him his supper. But what could they do? Merrit was Lord of Torm, and it was for him to say if guests were welcome or not. It was also for him to say if Berneathy were porter and Gregory favoured man-servant, so Gregory smiled and bowed again as he fetched in the meal that Merrit had ordered, then escaped as quickly as he could. He thought he should warn Allyso to take extra care, but to do so he would have to find her alone. He knew how Merrit felt about gossip and daggering reputations. And Allyso, once his small shadow, seemed to be changing lately.

'And how does our castle please you, Dame?' Merrit asked over supper. 'Does it live up to the hospitality you expect from a place like Torm?'

'It pleases me well for now.' The woman jerked her head at her silent page. 'Tollerman, you have eaten. Go to your bed and sleep.'

'The lad must be weary,' said Merrit, 'but I doubt if he's had enough to eat just yet. See how slowly he wields that spoon! My niece must have swallowed twice as much, at least.' He smiled, but the soulbinder did not respond. 'Eat your fill,' he told the page. 'There is plenty of food at Torm.'

The page looked at his mistress and then across to Merrit. Allyso noticed his eyes, which were the same clear blue as the Highsummer sky. A bright and lucid blue, and strangely blank. She was disappointed, realising the page was not quite there in his mind. She was resigned to pages who talked over her head, but a daft one would be no company at all.

'Don't be shy, Master Page,' urged Merrit. 'If there is anything you would like, you have but to say so.'

The page said nothing, and the soulbinder chuckled grimly. 'Tollerman has nothing to say to anyone.'

'He'll talk when he knows us a little better,' said Merrit. 'My niece is just as shy.'

'The wench was bold enough when she spied on my arrival from the watchtower.' The soulbinder rose in a scatter of crumbs and left the table without farewell or thanks. The page half-rose to follow her.

'Stay and finish your supper, Tollerman,' said Merrit. 'People your age need constant feeding. You just ask

Allyso, here! She may look like a half-grown twig, but she is near fourteen and eats like any young Master.'

Allyso squirmed, wishing Merrit would not be so very hearty.

'Have some more, then, lad,' urged Merrit. 'Tell us what you'd like.'

Tollerman glanced at the pot of broth and then at his bowl.

'Serve the lad more broth,' said Merrit, and Allyso obeyed. She was not as practised as Gregory was at this, but she could manage table service without disgracing herself or Torm.

'Be careful you don't burn your tongue,' she said, and managed a friendly smile as she set the bowl before him. The boy could not be blind, so why did he look so blank as he shook his head?

She waited for him to speak. Instead, he tilted his face to the light, and opened his mouth as if for inspection by a healer.

'Do you have a sore throat?' she asked, perplexed. 'We have some tincture in the stillroom that might help.'

'Better have a look,' advised Merrit. 'If it's much inflamed, I'll send for Healer Hilz. We're such a robust lot at Torm that he seldom gets a case that's worthy of his talents. I live in fear of his leaving us for more unhealthy climes. Perhaps in Rargon, to minister to Valourns who have been lamed in competition.'

Allyso peered into Tollerman's mouth as Healer Hilz had taught her. There was no sign of redness or swelling, but she reeled back with her hands clapped over her mouth.

Tollerman had no tongue.

When the page was satisfied that she knew the reason for his silence, he closed his mouth, then dipped his spoon in the broth and began to eat, slowly and with care.

Allyso looked at the remains of her supper. It was her favourite broth, made to Gill's own secret method. It was steaming and fragrant with cresses and lean McAnerin mutton, but she pushed away her bowl.

'Eat your broth,' said Merrit.

'I think I have had enough.' Allyso nodded farewell to Tollerman and left the room in a rush. She needed fresh air before she lost the supper she'd swallowed already.

CHAPTER FOUR

CURSE

HIGHSUMMER — 3RD MOON TO MIDWINTER —

9TH MOON OF THE YEAR OF THE HOUND

'SORRY,' she said to Merrit, when he found her in the wellyard. 'I couldn't stand it. I mean, my stomach couldn't.'

'Why should the lad's misfortune turn you ill? I have seen you cosset a strawcap hen with a bleeding wing.'

'*Misfortune*! You call that a *misfortune*?' She swallowed, leaning against the coping of the well.

'What else would you call it?'

'But ... was he born like that? Or did someone ...' She couldn't say the words, but Merrit said them for her.

'Did someone cut his tongue out? How can I know? He does seem young for such a drastic punishment, but who knows what might have happened, or where the deed took place?'

'But what could he have *done*?' she wailed.

'Whatever he has done is not our affair,' said Merrit. 'So long as he behaves himself properly at Torm. Come along, Allyso. The loonymoths are out, and the lad has gone to bed.'

'He would be better off dead,' she said fiercely as she followed Merrit across the wellyard. 'How can he bear to live like that?'

'Some folk manage well enough when deprived of one sense or another. I knew a man once who had lost a hand, another had lost an eye. They used what was left, and life always had something to offer them. Life has plenty to offer to Tollerman as well.'

'Such as what?' she snapped. 'His family may have died, or they may have driven him out. He might have no-one at all except that sour-faced dame.'

'Don't see troubles where there may be none,' said Merrit. 'Most folk are good enough if you look at them in the right way. As for what life has to offer the lad, what about your friendship?'

Allyso stared. '*Mine*?'

'Why not?' said Merrit. 'Try to make friends with the lad. Talk to him, and show him around. He can hear all right, and there's plenty can be said by a smile and a friendly hand. Even without a tongue, he can probably speak in some way, though he may not like to try in front of strangers. And if he makes a friend in you, it may be easier for him in the next place he visits.'

Allyso knew she should do as Merrit said. She would do it tomorrow, or perhaps the next day, if the dame (could she *really* be a soulbinder?) remained that long at the castle. But first, she must work out a proper approach. She could never be as hearty as Merrit, for what sounded well enough in a castle lord would seem ridiculous in a skinny girl. She couldn't just start talking. The page would know she had run away from him in horror, and so now he must be feeling worse than ever. It would serve her right, she supposed, if he ignored her utterly.

She would wait until the time was right, until it seemed natural to offer him a tour of the castle. Gregory would help. He was her friend and not much older than Tollerman. And if Gregory came along with them, she would not be alone with that terrible sight if Tollerman opened his mouth.

She meant to talk to Gregory and enlist his help, but less than two days later, Tollerman disappeared.

'I hope he hasn't run off,' said Merrit, when the boy's absence became obvious with the third missed meal. 'I have no stomach for chasing children who would rather be elsewhere.'

'He isn't a child,' objected Allyso. 'He must be almost Gregory's age.'

'Then I have no stomach for chasing unhappy or unwilling servants,' corrected Merrit. 'I'd rather they left my service and found some happier occupation. But perhaps the lad will come back for dinner tonight.'

'Will you look for him if he doesn't come back, and if that woman asks you for help?'

Merrit sighed. 'I suppose so. The laws of hospitality demand it.'

'What is her name, anyway?' asked Allyso. 'We can't just keep on calling her *the dame* or *that woman*, and you don't like me to call her *the soulbinder*.'

'She has never offered her name,' said Merrit. '*Dame* is good enough.'

'And she said *I* was ill-mannered!'

24

'Folk who feel unwelcome sometimes prefer to keep their identities to themselves. Cheer up, Allyso! I suppose she won't be staying very long.'

'Oh, I do hope not.'

Allyso waited anxiously, but the soulbinder did not ask them to search for Tollerman. Nor did she seem inclined to search herself.

'I suppose she sent him south to wherever she's going next,' decided Merrit. 'She won't risk a return to the north just yet.'

'Why would she send him ahead? Surely a page is supposed to stay with his mistress?'

Merrit shrugged. 'Perhaps she has sent the lad on an errand. You might ask Berneathy if he saw him go, and if he was set for a journey.'

Allyso went to Berneathy, but he was still on his dignity. 'Tell Lord Merrit I am taking him at his word,' he said stiffly. 'I let folk in and out and scarcely dare to ask their business. Stars forfend I should give offence to a trail-thief or sleightmaster.'

'Berneathy, Merrit just wants to know if Tollerman went out and if he carried a pack.'

'Taken something, has he?' said Berneathy. 'I let the page out. It was early in the morning, but what he had in his pack you cannot ask me. I was pleased enough to see his spine and would have been better pleased to see that dame go, too. She is *trouble*.'

Tactfully, Allyso reported that Berneathy had seen the page go and that he had carried a pack. She left the porter's offended opinions to be delivered by himself — or not.

It wasn't long before they discovered what at least part of Tollerman's errand must have been, for soon more strangers arrived at the castle gates and demanded a place to stay. This was not so unusual, but their manner was mockingly familiar to Berneathy.

'A bed for the night, porter, and the best your kitchens have to offer,' they ordered, and words and tone were the perfect echo of what the soulbinder woman had said.

Berneathy was very uneasy. Merrit's comments had stung, but Berneathy knew his duty. Pages might come and go, but where large groups of strangers appeared unannounced, a porter must keep his wits. If Merrit wanted these folk in (and Berneathy feared he would), then Merrit must give the order personally.

He bowed to the newcomers, though his back did not wish to bend, then jangled the summoning bell. To the strangers he gave no answer, but said the Lord of Torm would soon come out to hear their case. And then he stood and waited.

'The summoning bell!' said Merrit. 'I quite thought Berneathy was keeping silence with me. I had to remind him of certain facts, and he has scarcely acknowledged me since.'

'In that case you'd better hurry,' said Allyso. 'Berneathy wouldn't call unless it were important.'

She went with Merrit to the gate, and stood well back as he surveyed the arrivals. 'What is your business at Torm, Masters and Mistras?'

'We are poor travellers from the North, my Lord,' whined one of the women. 'We hear there is a warm welcome with bed and board at Torm.'

'Aye, we have heard of a welcome that is deep as the great Ocean of the South,' said a long-faced man in a wheedling tone.

'High as the Shrouded Mountain,' murmured another.

'Wide as the Desert of Rargon and firm as the Castle of Torm,' concluded the woman. 'Is it so?'

'Certainly it is so,' said Merrit, with an amused tilt of his brows. 'The news of our hospitality is spreading so I would almost believe someone has been making a broadsheet. Flattering that may be, but you are a large party and the resources of my castle are not inexhaustible. Would you not rather return to the North, or travel south to Fielding? That is a Trader village, and so there are often empty beds to fill.'

'Our friend is here already,' said the long-faced man reprovingly. 'She sent for us and assured us of your welcome.'

'A welcome high as the Shrouded Mountain,' insisted a woman. 'That is the message we had from her very own page, written down in her very own words. And here she is to tell us all again.'

Merrit and Allyso turned to see the soulbinder standing silently behind them. How long had she been there, and what had she overheard?

'These folk claim to be friends of yours, Dame, and that you invited them here to Torm,' said Merrit. 'Is that so?'

'It is so,' said the soulbinder. The crystal on her finger flashed a warning as she raised her hand to greet the huddle of strangers.

'And so we may come in,' stated the long-faced man in a tone that was not so wheedling any more.

'And so we may come in,' said the others in ragged chorus.

Merrit sighed, and rolled his eyes in amusement at Allyso. 'It seems we have little enough choice in the face of such faith,' he said, and told Berneathy to let the strangers in. 'You may lodge a protest later,' he added to the porter. 'If it will make you feel any better.'

'It's too late now,' said Berneathy. His tone was far from insolence, and so Merrit let it go with a rueful smile.

His amusement didn't last, for the ramshackle party of tricksters and dark artists stayed at Torm for the span of six long moons. Clear from Highsummer to Midwinter, they stayed, eating and drinking hugely, taking whatever they wished without a smile and without a word of thanks.

A flight of leaf strippers, said Merrit with a wry expression, would have eaten less than the soulbinder's crew. And their greed was only the smallest part of the problem.

Within days of her friends' arrival, the soulbinder had set up a market stand within the gates of Torm. She did not sell vegetables, cakes, or plaited rush baskets as most vendors might, but charms and hexes, potions and wax images. These items soon found their way into almost every room of the castle, where they had a terrible effect on the comfortable ways of Torm. Small quarrels among the castlers grew into bitter rifts, as men and women tried to buy advantage or revenge.

'It's a sickness,' said Healer Hilz as he reported on injuries to three of the stewards. 'Each one is convinced the others intend him harm, and each thought he must attack them first. The truth is clouded by whatever that woman has done to them.'

'Then we must —' Whatever Merrit was about to say was lost, for a scream rose from the wellyard, and Hilz tossed away his dignity and ran.

One ugly charm led directly to another, and spite and curses thrived and multiplied. Fights and rumours flourished, and though Merrit tried to keep the peace, Allyso could see he was furious.

'How can one dame cause so much grief?' he demanded one evening. 'It all begins with her, as a poison plant begins with a windblown seed. Our castlers could stem her foolishness if they would ignore her and refuse to buy her wares. She can't force them to trade with her, and her charms are nothing anyway, nothing but leaves and spite.' He tried to smile, but it was a bitter expression. 'They are behaving more like hateful children than the folk I thought I knew.'

Allyso saw his point, but she could also see the soulbinder's power of persuasion. If she told a man that a rival had bought a hex against him, wouldn't the victim want to buy revenge?

As the moons wore on towards Midwinter, unrest and misery spread out from Torm like so many sullen ripples in a pool. Some of the herders and orchardists who depended on Torm began to deal elsewhere, and others came instead. These also fell prey to the soulbinder's evil trade.

The Summerwane harvest was poor, perhaps because the grainers had become more concerned with the gossip, hexing and spite than with looking after their crops. No-one cooperated with the gathering-home, and food grew scarce as the Winterclimb days came on. And when food was scarce for the village, it was even scarcer for the castle, for the grainers and herders looked first to the needs of their kin and gave the castle a tithe of whatever was left.

On Midwinter Eve, Merrit asked the soulbinder to leave.

'Berneathy was right, and I was wrong, and Torm has paid the price,' he admitted to Allyso. 'I have made the mistake of complacency and arrogance. See that you learn from it, Allyso, and avoid the same faults when it's your turn to Mistra Torm and its holdings.'

'No doubt I'll make other mistakes,' she said.

'No doubt you will,' said Merrit. 'None of us is wholly wise. And now you must come with me and learn the way to set things right.'

'You're telling her to go?' Allyso felt a cold twist of unease in her stomach. She wanted the soulbinder gone, but hadn't the damage been done already? Would the castlers return to their usual way when the canker of the woman's presence had been cut out? She braided her hair and dressed in her most elaborate tunic, then examined the effect in the looking glass.

A sullen child stared back.

Allyso sighed and went to meet Merrit and see how he dealt with this monstrous error he had made.

Merrit said his piece, and the soulbinder heard him out with cold eyes and a colder smile. 'And is this your famous welcome, Merrit Tormblood? Your welcome that was *deep as the great Ocean of the South*, and *high as the Shrouded Mountain*? Your welcome that was *wide as the Desert of Rargon* and *firm as the Castle of Torm*?'

'Dame, you begged a bed and food for the night,' said Merrit. 'My heir will bear witness to this.' He glanced at Allyso, who nodded uncomfortably. 'You and your crew have had the use of fifty beds for three times fifty nights, and a big proportion of the poor harvest we made this year besides. You have become a charge we cannot bear, and it is time to find yourselves a home.'

'*This* is our home,' said the soulbinder.

'There is no room for you at Torm,' said Merrit. 'There is no more food to be shared with you or with any others, and this fact stems directly from your own activities. Your trade is a foul one, soulbinder. You have abused my hospitality, and so my welcome is worn to a thread.'

The soulbinder drew herself up, and Allyso clutched at Merrit's arm for comfort. She had not done that since childhood, and it felt strange to be doing it now she was close to fourteen.

She remembered it afterwards, as the very last time she would do so.

'I hope I misheard you, Lord of Torm?' The soulbinder's words dripped like icewater down in the wellyard.

'I am sorry, Dame, but you heard me right enough. I say you must leave, and take your companions with you, for my welcome is worn to a thread.'

'Then so shall *you* be, Lord of Torm,' spat the soulbinder. 'You have spoken your doom aloud.'

'There is no need for bitterness, Dame. You have been treated more fairly than you have treated us at Torm.'

The soulbinder cut him off with a gesture. 'Your welcome was firm as Torm, you claimed, so I tell you Torm shall fall! As for you, Torm's master, *you* will be worn to a ravelling, worn to the veriest thread, and your days will be less than the crumbs that will fall from your table.'

Merrit paled at the venom in her voice, but he had the strength of purpose to persist. 'I say you must go now, Dame, whether you curse or not. Your presence has cursed us every day since you arrived, so what is one more spate of spiteful words? Leave my castle and my lands, and take your foul crew with you!'

The soulbinder spat at his feet, turned and walked to the threshold. There she spun to face the silent Merrit again, lifted both hands and made a mocking bow. Gently, almost playfully, her fingers moved in a wheeling motion, one hand circling beside the other, for all the world as if she were winding in a spool of thread. The crystal ring on her finger twinkled with deceptive gaiety, catching sparks from the Midwinter light and tossing them back to dazzle Allyso's eyes.

She finished with a tiny tug and a snap, tossed the invisible spool in the air, caught it and put it somewhere among her garments. After that, she stalked off towards the gates of the castle where Berneathy, forewarned by Merrit, was hurriedly drawing the bolts. Her friends, in a dark and muttering group, shouldered their bundles and shambled along behind her, casting ugly and malicious glances at the silent castlers as they did so. How had they known it was time to go?

Merrit watched them leave without expression, but as the soulbinder and her retinue passed beyond the gates, the colour left his face, and he staggered as if hit by a sudden buffet of wind.

'Merrit?' Allyso took his arm again, but this time it was to offer him support rather than to ask it for herself.

Merrit was breathing hard, as if he had run a great distance. 'I'll be all right in a moment,' he said. Gregory fetched up a stool, and Merrit sat down. His face was grey and drawn.

'Merrit! What's the matter?' A cold lump of fright seemed lodged in Allyso's chest, and she knew the question was useless.

She knew what was wrong with Merrit and so did Gregory.

The soulbinder's curse had taken effect.

CHAPTER FIVE

CONSEQUENCES

MERRIT did not believe in curses, nor would he tolerate superstition. Allyso clung to that belief through the uncertain time that followed.

Perhaps he was pretending to be weak, trying to make the soulbinder believe she had succeeded. Even when it became obvious that his condition was no pretence, Allyso tried to comfort herself and the anxious Gregory. Merrit was strong, and nothing could hold him for long.

Gregory brewed strengthening possets, but Merrit was too ill to do anything but sag on the stool. Soon, supported by Gregory and Healer Hilz, he took to his bed and stayed there. Hilz, who attended him almost from the first, tried every stimulant and nourishment he knew, but he could offer little explanation and no real hope of improvement.

'I can do nothing for Master Merrit, child,' he said

gravely to Allyso. She might be slight and young, but she was the only other member of the Blood, and so he could not refuse to answer her urgent questions. 'I could cure a fever, treat wounds and rashes and broken bones, but curses are a very different matter.'

'And you think it really *is* a curse that has made him ill?'

'What else do you suggest?'

Allyso gnawed her knuckles. 'Poison?' she offered. 'Perhaps that woman put something in his supper? Or could she have had some weapon?'

'There is no sign of a wound, and I think it cannot be poison,' said Hilz. 'I have treated Lord Merrit in every way I know.'

'Then who *can* help him?' demanded Allyso. She was usually in awe of the dignified Hilz, but today she was much too frightened to remember her manners. 'Since this curse was laid by a soulbinder, does that mean we need to find another one to take it off?'

'That would be like trying to heal one poison with another, or breaking an arm to relieve the pain of a broken leg. As for removing it myself, I could not even begin.'

'Then fetch a healer who knows about curses, since you do not!'

Hilz shook his head. 'There is no such person. Our guild is sworn to help and to heal; none of us would study such wicked things.'

'You should!' cried Allyso. 'How can you help if you don't understand what did the harm?'

'And how,' said Hilz coldly, 'could you trust a healer who knew the ways of harm?'

Allyso flung away and asked Berneathy. He had tried to bar the dame at the beginning, and so she hoped he might know more about soulbinders than he had said. But the porter had no answers either.

'I felt she was an evildoer, but how could I lift a curse?'

'What would you do if *you* were ill?' demanded Allyso.

Berneathy looked down at her, his fine brows drawn with worry. 'Healer Hilz has always been skilled enough for me.'

'Fine!' snapped Allyso. 'How lucky for you! I only wish he were skilled enough for Merrit!'

Gregory caught at Allyso's sleeve as she left Berneathy. 'Why not ask my mother?'

'Why? So she can tell me not to *worry* and say *go away*?'

'I am worried too,' said Gregory quietly. 'You know what Merrit has done for me, and how much I owe him. I can't help, but Gill knows something about curses. I remember her using kitchen charms when I was young, before we came to Torm.'

'Why didn't you say so long ago?'

Gregory shrugged. 'You know what Merrit is. He scolds enough about the birthchain Gill wears. He told her when we came she was not to use charms at Torm. I'm sure she remembers them, though, and she probably isn't the only one.'

'We should ask everyone here,' said Allyso. 'Someone must have some idea of how to deal with this, even if they were too afraid of annoying Merrit to speak up before.'

Gregory agreed, and the two of them began a round of questions, but the other castlers had their own concerns and gave short answers or none at all.

Hilz called for Gregory then, so Allyso went to visit Gill alone. Hilz had said to be quiet, of course, but Gill was the one who had nursed her as a babe.

'Gregory said you used to know kitchen charms,' she said. 'Isn't there something you can do for Merrit?'

Gill put her arm around Allyso. 'Hush!' she said shortly, then added in a whisper, 'You know I'd help you, Allyso, if only I could.'

'Gregory said you knew a lot.'

'I might ease a cough or nudge a cheese to ripen, but that is as much as I could ever do.'

'And that's more than anyone else will admit to!' said Allyso. 'All I can think of now is to find that soulbinder woman and force her to put things right. She did this to Merrit, so she must be able to undo it again.'

'What wild whim have you got in your head now?'

'Merrit's life is no whim, and besides, Gregory would come with me — or maybe Healer Hilz.'

'And it would do no good, whoever went with you,' said Gill. Her wise, loving face was set in stubborn lines, and she was twisting a sidelock of her greying hair. 'The wretch would never remove the hex from Merrit and likely she'd just curse you or Gregory as well. Don't put such notions in Gregory's head, I beg you, Allyso. He's just at the age for rushing off on some foolish quest, and you know he'd do anything for Merrit — or for you.'

'Then what *can* we do?' pleaded Allyso. 'Why won't anyone help us?'

'You don't understand.'

'I suppose you *do*?'

Gill's eyes went cool. 'I served for some years as a maid in an Ankoorian household, Allyso. I saw plenty of things I didn't understand, although my grandam was a notable kitchen crone. I have seen these dark ones before, these soulbinder women, and they never mean anything good.'

'Then why didn't you warn Merrit about this one? He wouldn't listen to Trader Mohr and Trader Dagg, but he would have listened to *you* ... You could have told him she was wicked.'

'Merrit listens to no-one,' said Gill. 'I've begged him time and time again to keep a Spellhound at Torm. A Spellhound sniffs out wickedness in a trice! But would he listen? No, he calls me nothing but a palm-mumbler for my efforts. So don't you talk to me about warning Merrit! As for charms, I have told you already. I may right a headache or a sneezing fit now and again when Merrit isn't near, but as well to pour a thimble of water on a marshfire as try a kitchen charm to nullify a curse.'

'But ...'

'And speaking of such things strengthens them,' said Gill. 'Even Merrit knows that. Why do you think he forbids it? In some ways he was right, and so I tell you, *hush*!'

Allyso hushed obediently. She would have hushed in any case, for her questions and the hostility they brought made her feel more alone than ever.

'They think the hex will infect them if they offer you help or comfort,' said Hilz. 'If some of them doubted the power of a curse, Merrit's illness gives proof they didn't want. No doubt many of them told

38

themselves a hex could cause nothing but a dose of colic or a twinge of joint-ill.'

'Are you afraid of curses, Healer Hilz? You say you have never studied them, but do they make you afraid?'

Hilz said nothing for a moment, but Allyso could see uncertainty in his light-coloured eyes.

'I do fear wickedness of all kinds,' he admitted, 'but not that I shall catch it like a fever. I am more afraid of its effect on the others here. Everyone seems suspicious and shamed, and I'd trust no-one far. Folk who have done wrong or let it be done may not care to try doing better.'

'I trust *you*, Healer Hilz,' said Allyso. 'I am sorry I was rude to you before.'

Hilz waved his hand. 'Merrit's distress is trouble for us all.'

'I trust Gregory,' said Allyso, 'and Berneathy and Gill. You all spoke plainly, and you all tried to explain. I know that none of you would ever do harm to Merrit, or to Torm.'

'I hope we may be worthy of that trust, Heir of Torm,' said Hilz. 'But take my advice and Mistra Gill's, and speak no more of curses. You will learn nothing useful and, at the very best, you will stir the mess that is here already.'

Hilz and Gregory spent most of their time at Merrit's bedside, and Allyso, when not there with them, roamed the castle, alone and frightened. Merrit had trusted the castlers, and Merrit had been wrong. He had welcomed folk who had not been welcomed elsewhere. It seemed the ones who had barred their gates and turned the strangers away had been much wiser.

What am I going to *do*? she asked herself dismally. Merrit has always said we are the blood and the spirit of Torm, but what can I do when everyone tells me to hush?

'If I were older,' she told Gregory, 'maybe they'd listen to my suggestions.'

'I listen, Allyso,' said Gregory. 'What do you want me to do?'

She wanted him to force a cure from the soulbinder, and knowing that was impossible, and remembering what Gill had said, she told him there was nothing he could do.

Gill was right. There was no help for Merrit in Allyso and Gregory being hexed as well.

Day by day, Merrit's body wasted and his spirit burned low and dim. As Torm's master dwindled, the castlers began to bicker fiercely among themselves, quarrelling over the goods that the soulbinder had left behind.

Travellers to Torm found a very poor welcome now, for Berneathy barred the gates against them all. And in its way, Berneathy's caution brought more disaster upon them, for angry travellers were forced to travel on without refreshment. Many of these headed northeast, where they sought shelter at the tall twin castles of Zimmerhanzel and Hasselsjo, and spread bad tidings of Torm.

'What of northern hospitality? Torm is closed to us!'

'A poor harvest they *said*, but could they not share a single meal? My Mistra was forced to walk without rest for another day, and our little one caught the weep-eye.'

'Merrit is ill, they say, but surely he has outer-castlers to offer a sup to strangers?'

'So,' said Lord Toombs of Zimmerhanzel when a traveller from Musson told an indignant tale of being turned away. 'Lord Merrit of Torm is ill? What does his healer say?'

The Mussonman shrugged. 'Who can say? The porter sent us off like so many strays from the gates. It may be a fever, for the place is shut up tighter than any siege.'

'But who has taken charge of his castle and lands?'

'Who knows? The only Blood left is a girl, and useless.'

Toombs smiled reprovingly. 'Why do you say that, Mussonman? Many a Mistra is just as able as a Master.'

'Not this one, Lord. She's not even fourteen, so they say, and looks more like eleven. Likely to take the fever from Merrit, if she hasn't done already.'

'What about the castlers, man? Can no-one stand as deputy?'

'There's no strength there. The stores are nearly gone, the porter said, but I'm sure I saw apples frosted and rotting on the trees. Looked to me as if Torm has been given up.'

Lord Toombs looked suitably shocked and grave but, behind his expressed concern, his active mind was pondering. How might this misfortune be turned to his own advantage? Like his neighbour, Lord Sheels of Hasselsjo, Toombs was a man of moderate means and high ambitions. He would never have coveted Torm in the ordinary way but, if Merrit had lost his grip, then Torm was ripe for picking. If not by Toombs of Zimmerhanzel, then surely by some other northern lord. Or even a foreigner from somewhere over the border. Most lords knew the value of a capable deputy, but a surprising number neglected to install one. Or perhaps it was not so surprising, thought Lord Toombs. Deputies had been known to overthrow their lords.

For the picking of Torm, he needed, not a deputy, but a supporter, and for this he chose Lord Sheels. Toombs did not especially like the man, but he was able, land-hungry and shrewd and would be a rival if he were not an ally. The two of them together would silence other contenders for the Lordry of Torm.

Not that they would call it a conquest, for they would be saving Castle Torm and its folk from ruin. It would be almost a noble move, if looked at from a certain angle and in a certain light.

A low growl, almost beyond the range of hearing, made Lord Toombs start and rub nervously at his neck. For a moment there he could have sworn his braided hair had tried to stand on end.

'What's amiss?' asked the Mussonman.

'It is just a hound that sometimes troubles this castle,' said Toombs. 'Fey, it is, and foolish.' He rang a bell for his groom. 'Find that creature of my son's, Bajen, and turn it out,' he said. 'Tell Scholar if I hear its whining near my quarters again, I'll have its skin for gauntlets.'

The groom went out, and shortly Toombs heard the sound of a blow and a yelp. The hound was vanquished for now, so he turned to his guest. 'About Torm —' he began, but caught himself up with a start.

'My Lord?'

No, thought Toombs, and rubbed his neck again. He must have been mad to think of it for an instant. Invading a neighbour's castle? It really wouldn't do.

Merrit would soon recover, no doubt, and all Toombs need do was to send a formal offer of help which would be formally refused.

As he dismissed the Mussonman to bed and dinner, a whine bit into the air. High and shrill as the sound of a stinging insect, it set Toombs' teeth on edge.

That *damned* hound!

He was about to send for his groom again when a woman entered the courtyard. She was dressed in a mantle and hood, and she wore a ring that was set with a shimmering crystal. She moved as silently as a loonymoth, but was by no means as prepossessing.

Toombs wanted to scotch the hound, and then to have his dinner, but courtesy won out over his impatience. 'What do you ask of me, Dame? Alms for the homeless?'

She clasped her hands, folding and unfolding her fingers so the ring winked in and out of view in the failing light of sunfall. 'My Lord, I ask for a place to stay, a bed and bowl and cup.'

'Are you alone? Have you no-one to take you in?' Toombs wondered how he might send this woman packing without too much discourtesy. There was always room for new folk at Zimmerhanzel, but only if they were young and strong and loyal.

A stale crust, thought Toombs wisely, should never be put in a crock that contained new bread. The crust could not be freshened, and it could cause the bread to moulder.

'There are several in my party,' said the woman.

'Then, to my regret, I cannot offer you accommodation. We are not a great castle, and have only limited room for charity.'

'It would be no charity, Lord of Zimmerhanzel. We carry goods for trade and pay well for our lodging.'

'I see.' Toombs heard the dryness in his own voice and so, apparently, did the dame.

'Richly indeed, my Lord, for we offer to pay in the coin that you most desire.'

The crystal flashed again, and Lord Toombs blinked. 'What kind of coin? Ankoorian stargems?' His hand half rose to shield his eyes. 'What could you offer that I do not have already? A way to silence that cursed hound?'

'For now I offer the coin of information,' purred the woman. 'You have a son, my Lord, who needs a castle of his own. I can tell you how to get that castle.'

Toombs smiled grimly. 'I have two sons, Dame, and one of them detests me. You could have learned that anywhere, for I make no secret of it. How could I when he crosses me at every turn? And why, if you have a castle, do you not live there yourself instead of asking other folk for housing?'

'I have been living there,' said the dame. 'For many moonspans I and my followers dwelt within its walls. And I know this castle sorely needs a Master.'

'Speak more plainly,' said Toombs. 'Tell me the name and direction of this castle that you offer. If it is some bleak place in Ankoor, I will not be interested, although it might do well enough to contain my son.'

'The castle is Torm,' she said. 'It is not so far from here, in North McAnerin. It begs for a Master, but perhaps I shall offer it to Sheels of Hasselsjo instead. I would rather deal with you, however, since we are distant kin.'

Lord Toombs was certainly not keen to claim a connection. This dame, with her hints and offers, and that flashing crystal ring, had something bitter about her, some sourness that stank of rottenness within. 'I am no kin to you!' he said, perhaps a little too quickly for courtesy.

'Your first Mistra was Ankoorian, I think. Jessamin of Western Port.'

'Long ago. She has been gone for many years . . .'

'Still, she was Ankoorian and, for her sake, I offer this gift.'

'What you offer is empty. How should I believe you?'

Toombs waited for her answer, but it was a long time coming. In the meanwhile, he found himself gazing at the flash of the crystal ring. It was a fine one, and the dame must be wealthy to wear it. Perhaps she *could* back up her extraordinary offer.

Slowly his ambitions began to glow. He saw himself commanding an army, he saw respect and gratitude. He saw his bothersome son established in a fitting position, well away where Toombs would not have to see him. Scholar was too much like his mother, that brief mistake who had fled back to Ankoor before her child was born.

Toombs saw it all, but it still seemed very unreal. 'Exactly what do you offer, and exactly what do you want?'

The woman clasped her hands. 'I have watched and waited, and I know that Torm is ready to fall. I offer the details of its malady. In return, I and my party claim due respect and a permanent home at Torm. A home its current Master denied us.'

So, thought Toombs, the woman had a blade of spite to grind? That made more sense than some dusty claim of kinship. 'What have you done?' he asked.

'Torm has brought its troubles on itself. It is rotting from within and is now an empty shell. Cut off the route to the village, set the blight-wards at the corners and the castle will be yours in less than a moonspan.'

Toombs stared. 'There is blight at Torm? I'll have no dice with that!'

'No blight that need concern you, if only you keep your bargain,' said the dame. 'Its lord is fading, though. That much is true, and the tales will fly. Blight-ward markers will serve very well to keep curious folk away while you secure your prize.'

Toombs stroked his beard. The thought was very inviting. 'Are you sure of your facts?'

'Very sure,' said the dame. 'Torm is going to ruin if no-one takes it in hand. I tell you, I have seen such things before.'

'But what of an army? My garrison can defend Zimmerhanzel, but it is by no means large enough to mount a siege.'

The woman smiled. It was the first time she had done so, and the effect was most unsettling. 'I can provide an army, my Lord, an army for you to command.' She paused, and added softly, 'Have you not heard that the Tenth Castle is astir?'

'The Tenth Castle?' said Lord Toombs suspiciously. 'What nonsense is this? There are nine great Castles in Ankoor. Seamasters, jewelmasters, lacemasters, beastmasters . . .'

'And there is also the Tenth, which houses the masters of chaos.'

'And they will march with us?'

'They will march, if I give the word. To other folk

they will appear to be guards to enforce the quarantine of Torm and its burden of blight.'

Toombs nodded. 'Perhaps we may deal together.'

'I have your bond on this?' asked the dame, and put her strong cold hand on his. 'You will humble Torm and keep a welcome there for me and for my kind?'

'You have my bond,' said Toombs.

'See that you keep it,' said the dame. 'If not, you will live with regret while you live at all.'

Toombs thought hard about the venture. Even after the dame had gone to rest in her new quarters, daydreams of power stayed dancing in his head. After consideration, he decided to send for his neighbour Sheels and ask his co-operation. The dame had told him how to bring Torm down, but her promised soldiers sounded like an idle rabble, and would need trained local men to lead them. If he and Sheels worked together, they might win the day and, since the design was his, he would take the better part of the plunder. Not that Sheels would need to know that yet ... The bare bones of the project would be enough to begin with.

At sunlift, Toombs sent a message to the Lord of Hasselsjo. It was carefully worded to give no hint of his plans to anyone else, and it was sealed for secrecy.

Sheels arrived at the gates of Zimmerhanzel well before the appointed hour. He had come alone, as directed, and was inclined to be suspicious and doubtful at first. After Toombs had laid out the plan for Torm, and the dame had spoken her persuasions, he gave his support to his neighbour.

'Let's take the air while we work on the details of this,' he said. 'If we are closeted together, folk might wonder, but idle conversation during a stroll is nothing strange.'

'Well thought,' said Toombs, and he took his neighbour's arm. 'We'll be doing the castlers a favour,' he added as he walked the castle grounds with Sheels. He thought it better not to mention the dame's revengeful words just then.

'A favour, yes,' said Sheels.

'The folk of Torm need a strong hand to guide them. Merrit was good enough in his way, but he has certainly lost his grip. The word is that he is close to death, if not dead already.'

'Close to death? If he has the blight, the castle will be diseased. It may be some time before it is fit for entry.'

'It is not the blight Merrit has,' said Toombs, 'but if others think it is, they'll not interfere.'

Lord Sheels gave his partner a shrewd and slightly wary glance. 'And whose strong hand were you thinking of, Toombs, when the castle is won? You have Zimmerhanzel, and I have Hasselsjo to manage.'

'I believe my elder son, Scholar, will make an excellent Lord of Torm.'

'Aye, Scholar!' Sheels smiled. 'A clever lad, I hear, who reads in foreign tongues. But isn't he going back to some learned place in Ankoor? I am sure my daughter said something of that.'

'I think he had some such notion,' said Toombs with a shrug. 'But now that must be forgotten. Torm is for Scholar, and so he must give his attention to it alone.' He paused, wondering why he was suddenly so certain of that, but Sheels supplied an answer.

'Of course he'll attend to it! Connering is not to be compared with the chance to Master a castle at his age.'

Toombs sniffed. 'Exactly. It is well past time he was pried from his books — and away from that mewling hound of his.'

'Fairly put,' said Sheels, 'but what is that to me? Why should I help place *your* son in a castle, Toombs?'

'You have daughters at Hasselsjo. Have you considered their futures?'

Lord Sheels nodded, the idea taking root in his mind. 'Tegwen is of age ...' He tugged at his lip, considering his handsome but wayward daughter. 'Your conner son, my clever daughter — I see how well it will work. Two fine Bloods combined, and a castle in proper hands. And you and me to give advice if need be. Aye, it would work very well, for Torm as well as for ourselves.'

Lord Toombs said nothing more, but Sheels was quite won over to the idea. Tegwen's voice and opinions were deafening Hasselsjo. Let them ring in the ears of Torm instead, and let Torm be grateful.

The dame must have sent a message, for the promised soldiers soon arrived from Ankoor. As Toombs had suspected, they came not as a disciplined army, but in gaggling groups. Quarrelsome and quick to strike out at one another, they drank hard, fought hard and showed little discipline.

'A rabble!' Lord Sheels sounded dismal, but he fetched his own strong guards from Hasselsjo. Together with the Zimmerhanzel guard, they moulded the rabble into something approaching an army.

The only hitch, to Toombs, was the occasional feeling that something was not quite right. He woke every morning to a bright dream of the future, but sometimes this would blur. A flash of light on water or the spark of sun on metal would dazzle his eyes for a moment, and he would feel as if something important were just beyond his memory. He shook the thought away and talked tactics with Brown, his younger son. It was Scholar he should have been briefing, but Scholar was being stubborn.

'I want no part in this wickedness,' said Scholar stiffly when Toombs told him of the scheme. He soothed the hound that was cowering by his ankles. 'You forget, my Lord, I am going home to Ankoor.'

'Your home is *here*, and you are coming to Torm.'

'You said I could go back to Westaway when I had spent time here.'

'Westaway! What has that to offer?'

'It offers the best conners' hall in all of Ankoor, and you gave me your word I could go.'

'My word has changed,' said Toombs. 'Ankoor has come to you. The Tenth Castle has risen, and you must come and help us secure Torm.'

The hound whined, piercingly.

'You have no *right*,' flashed Scholar.

Toombs, angry beyond endurance, raised his fist.

'Hitting me will solve this?' demanded his son. 'Do you think you can use your fist to change my mind as well as my face?'

'No,' said Toombs from behind clenched teeth, 'but I could use it to change the state of that hound at your feet.'

'If you touch Tace, I'll —'

'Then you had best keep it out of my sight,' said Toombs. 'Once we have taken Torm, you may keep the creature in your bed for all I care. Until then I must see you acting as a proper son of Zimmerhanzel.'

'I am *no* son of Zimmerhanzel! I was born in the Seventh Castle of Ankoor.'

'Who sent you to me and swore you were my son. You talk like an Ankoorian, unfortunately, but you are of the Zimmerhanzel Blood. Now, get out of my sight.'

With Winterwane, the army was ready to tackle Torm.

They came in hard and fast by night, drove off the herds and flocks, set out blight-wards at the four corners and then besieged the castle.

Lord Sheels and Lord Toombs, shoulder to shoulder, advanced on the gates and ritually informed Lord Merrit that they had come to annex his lands and holdings.

'Merrit!' cried Sheels. 'Admit your day is done, and open your gates!'

'Admit this place needs a stronger hand to set things right!' added Toombs.

They waited expectantly, backed by their army, but nobody answered their challenge.

'Put yourselves into our hands!' boomed Toombs. 'You may trust that none shall be harmed.'

'We come to make things right for Torm and to bring it back to health and its rightful standing!' proclaimed Sheels.

Their voices rang out handsomely and their borrowed army cheered, but from the castle of Torm came only abuse and a clang as the yellow-haired porter slammed the outer gates.

'It doesn't matter if they resist,' said Toombs. 'All we need do is wait for the plum to fall.' And so they waited. And tried to keep the army under control.

CHAPTER SIX

SIEGE

AFTER MIDWINTER'S DAY — 10TH MOON OF

THE YEAR OF THE HOUND

THE castlers of Torm were taken by surprise. A few of the men tried to break away, but they were driven back to the castle with jeers and blows from the flats of hastily hammered swords.

'We'll have no blight set free on the land!' said the soldiers.

'There *is* no blight at Torm.'

'Where is Torm's Master then? Where is Merrit Tormblood?'

'He is ill!' said one of the men.

'And you say there is no blight! Stay inside those walls, or face the consequences.'

The siege was oddly quiet. The soldiers used no battering rams, for the sound of these would carry and would not agree with an apparent quarantine. Instead, they sent fire arrows and showers of rock fragments raining over the walls. The watchtower was no longer a safe place to be, and the wellyard was deserted. Not much damage was done, and soon the arrows ceased. The point had been made, and Toombs and Sheels had something more to say.

'Yield!' called Toombs.

'Yield, and we will harm no-one,' added Sheels. 'All will be just as it was before we came!'

'What good is that?' growled one of the castlers. 'It was no good before!'

'At least we were free,' said his wife.

'Free! We've not been free since Merrit let that woman into the castle. She is with this lot, you know. I saw her down in the mob.' He shook his fist from the top of the wall. 'Get away, you carrion birds! There's nothing for you here! We have been picked clean already.'

Two of his friends dragged him down from the walls. They were just in time, for the archers below were nocking their arrows.

'No!' cried Toombs, in a fine, carrying voice. 'Lay down your bows! People of Torm, take heart! Surrender yourselves and your chattels into our care and you will not be harmed.'

No-one from the castle believed a word of that, and silence came as the sunfall faded from the sky. Allyso tried to hope the invaders would go away, but she had heard enough tales to know it wouldn't happen. Some castles, it was said, held out for a year or more of siege, but Torm's food stores were almost gone, eaten by the soulbinder's crew and wasted by the castlers themselves.

'What are they *doing*?' she asked Gregory, as he returned from the watchtower.

'Lighting fires,' said Gregory. His fists were clenched, and his normally good-humoured face was stiff and unfamiliar.

'They won't burn Torm,' said Allyso. 'They won't burn solid rock.'

'They're roasting strawcap hens. The pride of my mother's flock.'

Allyso bit her lip. 'At least they didn't knock down the walls.'

'Why should they?' demanded Gregory. 'A ruined fort is no use to them.'

'Then we should be safe? When they understand we don't have blight?'

'We're safe enough all right. Safe to sit and starve.'

'Someone will help us.'

'No-one will dare! Not with the blight-wards out.' Furious tears ran suddenly down Gregory's cheeks, and he turned and rushed away. Allyso was aghast, for Gregory *never* cried ... But Merrit had never been ill before, and Hilz had never despaired.

This could *not* be happening. Not to Merrit and Torm. And not to Allyso.

Blindly she stared at the scene below, and her eyes picked out a familiar figure. Dark and shrouded in a mantle and hood, it could have been one of a thousand dames, but from the lump in her stomach and the sickness in her throat, Allyso had no doubts. And now she understood why the blight-wards were out. This was no mistake on the part of Lords Toombs and Sheels, but part of the soulbinder's revenge.

Twenty days into the siege, Allyso stood in the window alcove outside her turret room and stared at the foreign soldiers beyond the walls. They made an almost homely sight, playing dice games and cooking over their campfires. Those fires had burned slowly but constantly all through the days and nights since they had arrived, and by now, most of the local fuel was gone. Only the stonewood grove remained, off to one side of the walls. The soldiers camped around it, but after a few early attempts and much swearing, they had given up trying to cut it down. There was no point, since stonewood wouldn't burn.

Sometimes, parties of men went off with hand-carts and fetched in logs, which they stacked beside the fires. These men wore white shirts, dyed in a chequerboard pattern. They seemed to be foreign, but their commanders were McAnerinian. Allyso was puzzled. What did these two lords want with Torm, and how had they come in league with the soulbinder? Her curse had humbled Merrit and was humbling Torm, but were the lords her tools or were they really Merrit's enemies?

'What if Merrit had turned the soulbinder away when she came?' she asked Healer Hilz. 'Would she still have cursed him?'

'Who can say?' said Hilz. 'I am not a seer.'

'You should be able to say!' snapped Allyso. 'You are supposed to be clever! What if Merrit had let her stay? Would she have cursed him then?'

'What do *you* think?'

'I think we would still have starved, whether she did or not,' she said. 'It was such a bad season and there were so many of them! They were like whipsucks. They burrowed into Torm and sucked it dry. And no-one does anything to help us. We can't from in here, and anyone else who is outside will be too scared of catching the blight.'

'I wish we could be helped.' Hilz sighed, then went to answer Merrit's bell.

Allyso stared blindly, her mind in a whirl. She closed her eyes for a moment, then forced herself to concentrate. There were the soldiers, their smoky fires, their far-flung sentries ... and there, from the south, two Traders came, trundling their high-wheeled wagon behind a patient garnerbeast. Mohr and Dagg were coming, but had they heard of the siege?

Traders could never take on an army, but Mohr had a clever tongue, and Dagg knew all the laws. Other passers-by had been sent off by the soldiers — easily done with blight-wards mounted at every corner of Torm.

Surely Mohr and Dagg would not believe there was blight? They knew that Torm was a wholesome place, and they would guess that something was wrong. At the very least, they would insist on a shouted message from their friends in the castle.

Allyso strained to see the details of the cart. Was it packed with weapons? Were those bundles really stores for starving Torm? Her eyes were burning with effort, and she saw the Traders pause. The taller one took off his slanted cap, showing silvered hair, and Allyso realised her mistake. It wasn't Mohr and Dagg at all, but Walton and Templeton, two men who lived southeast of Torm in the twin-towered town called Scarlet.

Allyso's heart still hammered with hope. These two were of High Trader caste, and were longtime friends of the Blood and of Torm. Walton was a quiet man, a jewel-miller, and slender Templeton was a crafter of silver and bronze. Surely they would ignore the wards and see through any lying tales?

Hope brought a tangle of plans. When the High Traders reached the gates, or even the outer wall, she would try to send them a message ... She could shoot a line from her bentwood bow, or cast a rope from the turret after dark. She could —

But it seemed she could do nothing, for even while her plans were building, the soldiers were surging forward to surround the two High Traders with a bristling forest of spears. The metal twinkled merrily, the pennons of the invaders shimmered on the breeze. The cream roe-hart of Hasselsjo and the gold wineskin of Zimmerhanzel looked bright and innocent, but all the colourful promise was a lie.

Walton and Templeton stood their ground, seeming to dispute with those who had them surrounded. Templeton was shaking his head emphatically, and seemed to be making demands. Demands to see Merrit, perhaps? To speak with Healer Hilz?

Whatever he said had no effect on the soldiers. They laughed and seemed to be jeering at their captives. Templeton said something more, and abruptly the merriment ceased. Four soldiers forced the High Traders to their knees, then hustled them away. Others swooped on the high-wheeled cart, unharnessed the garnerbeast and led it away, then tore away the awning and scrabbled among the spoils.

Allyso's hands were clenched, and her nails dug into her palms. Hopelessly, she listened to the cries and hubbub that rose from below the walls. There must be *something* she could do, besides stand here watching the humiliation of two more of Merrit's friends. She should be able to stage some kind of rescue, for wasn't she the Blood of Torm?

Numbly, she turned from the window, then went to the buttery to find a little food to offer Merrit.

CHAPTER SEVEN

CHANCE

WINTERWANE — 10TH MOON OF THE YEAR

OF THE HOUND

AND so it was on that twentieth day of the siege, that Allyso fetched food from the buttery to her uncle, and he refused to eat. She hated to tell him the latest news, but Merrit had no use for lies or evasions. He insisted on knowing what went on at Torm.

'High Trader Walton and High Trader Templeton came,' she said at last. 'I hoped they might be able to help us, but the soldiers grabbed them, and they didn't have a chance. I didn't even get as far as writing them a message.'

'It would have done no good,' said Merrit. His voice was a wisp of sound and his face so thin that Allyso could see every angle of bone beneath the skin. 'How can a handful of travellers or a few village folk stand against two lords and their followers? It would take an army to help us, and any McAnerin soldiers would fear the blight-wards.

There is no point in hoping for rescue, Allyso. Torm is lost.'

'There must be something we can do!' pleaded Allyso. She was tired of being desperate, tired of the cold white feeling of fright that had been going on so long. 'If you would just get well, we could fight these wretches,' she said. 'Please, Merrit, eat just a little. If you could get up and come out on the watchtower, folk would *see* you haven't got the blight.'

Merrit opened his sunken eyes and tried to smile at her. 'It is too late, Allyso. Try not to blame me too much.'

Allyso was silent. She wanted to be generous, but the things that Merrit had and hadn't done had been churning in her mind for twenty days.

'I made grave mistakes,' said Merrit. 'I would do anything to mend them now.'

'You made a traveller welcome,' said Allyso fiercely. 'Why should you be blamed for that?'

'I welcomed a traveller, and I also welcomed wickedness.'

'How could you have known? She seemed like a shabby dame who needed shelter. How could you have known what she was and what she could do?'

'I knew what she was, Allyso but, in my arrogance, I thought I could keep her under control. I thought she would do less harm if she were under my eye.'

There was no good answer to that.

'We might send a messenger south ...' she offered. 'Gregory or Berneathy could slip out through the gates in the night and get away to Fielding. They could tell folk there that the blight-wards are a lie. The Fielding

Traders travel all the time. They could spread the word out all over McAnerin.'

Merrit's head moved wearily. 'Too late for that. Too late for anything, saving the gem of time.'

'The gem of time ...' Allyso cast about in her memory. 'Trader Mohr spoke of gems of power and one was the gem of time. He was going to tell me the story, but he left instead. And didn't you say that was only a hearthside tale?'

Merrit said nothing, but his sunken eyes looked directly into Allyso's.

'You always say such tales are superstition!'

'I say too much,' said Merrit, and closed his eyes.

Allyso took his hand to get his attention. 'Merrit, talk to me! What is this gem of time and how could it help us? And where is it, anyway?'

'Some say here, and some say there ...' His voice was wandering.

'A seer might know!' she cried. 'Trader Mohr would tell me where to go to find one. He always knows things like that, because the Traders go everywhere. I'll send him a message —'

Merrit smiled a little. It reminded Allyso of the dying flicker that sometimes licked from a night-banked hearth. 'Wish for a dragon as well, while you are about it.'

'So I shall! A dragon would be very good!'

'Too late now, Allyso. The curse is in my blood. Perhaps it is truly the curse of my arrogance.'

'But what about the gem of time? If that could save us, even now, I need to know where to find it.'

'The years swirl back for the gem,' said Merrit. 'They swirl like the ocean tides ...' His voice was drifting, but suddenly, his eyes came back into focus.

'Forget the gem. No doubt it is only a fancy. When Torm falls, Allyso, disguise yourself and escape. These Lordlings want the castle, not a child like you.'

He was trying to reassure her, but Allyso detected the doubt in his voice. 'Why do I need a disguise, then, if they're not after me?'

Merrit turned his face away, and Hilz came quietly forward to the couch. 'The girl has a right to know, Merrit.'

Merrit made a weary gesture. 'Tell her then, Hilz. Make her understand why she must escape.'

Allyso stared from one to the other. Her shrunken, fading uncle and the precise, neat-featured healer, gaunt and strained, his blue and silver mantle limp and fading. 'Tell me!' she ordered. 'Why am I in danger?'

'You had better do as your uncle says and get out as soon as you can,' said Hilz. 'You are Heir of Torm, and it would be very bad if you were taken.'

'Are you saying these lords would kill me?'

'I am saying they could not afford to let you go free,' said Hilz carefully. 'Local folk are loyal to the Heir.'

'You mean they are loyal to Merrit,' she corrected. 'At least, they used to be.'

'And when you are grown, they will be loyal to you as the Mistra of Torm, even if you are in exile.'

'So —' Her voice trembled, and she swallowed and tried again. 'They really would kill me.'

'Bloodshed would set folk against them, so more likely they would put you away,' said Hilz. 'Which means you must *not* be taken. Torm will fall, but when you are grown . . .'

'I can take Torm back again!' Just for a moment, the thought stirred Allyso to a fierce kind of pride. She saw herself as the Warrior Mistra of Torm, driving out the invaders, reclaiming Torm for the Blood.

And then the martial picture crumbled to dust. She was no warrior, but only a skinny girl.

'We must get you out of the castle before they search for you,' said Hilz. 'That will mean you need a good disguise.' He bent over Merrit. 'A pity she is too young to wear healers' blue and silver, but I will see what can be done to keep her safe. You have my word on that.'

Hilz left the chamber, and Allyso tried to control her trembling. She would have to pass under the noses of these lords to escape from Torm. But how was she to conceal the unmistakable bronze of her hair, the amber of her eyes? Her skin, being the gilden tan of her bloodline, would also give her away. The castlers were pale as milk, or dark as the western clans. Only a girl of the Blood would look like Allyso.

'I can't just walk out the gates,' she said. 'Not even in disguise. The soulbinder knows my face.'

'So,' said Merrit, 'you must escape by the well-way.'

'Merrit, I *can't*!'

The well-way . . .

The well-way was the secret of Torm, but it was not something she thought of very often. Merrit had told her about it years before:

'Today you are ten, Allyso.'

She had smiled at him, expecting a gift to mark the occasion.

'I have a trinket or two for you, but your real gift is something to store in here.' Teasingly, Merrit had tapped her forehead. 'It is a secret that is only for the Blood of

Torm, and you must swear to reveal it to no-one but your heir when you should have one. Do you swear?'

'I do!'

'Swear by — by my life,' said Merrit.

'Yes. I swear. Do go on.'

'Very well. The secret begins with a story.'

Allyso remembered clearly how she had grasped Merrit's arm and begged him to tell. It had been exciting — then.

'Long ago,' Merrit had said, 'there lived a Lord named Torm. He was a very small man, a halfling. His mother was a keyre, so they say. He was slight and finely made, and hardly bigger than a child of eleven or so.'

'That isn't much of a secret.'

'Ah, but because he was such a small man, folk often thought he was weak. He was not weak, and would not be called so. He built this castle to prove them wrong, and in it he hid the well-way.'

'What is that?'

Merrit had taken her by the hand, and strolled with her to the wellyard, where he picked up a pebble and dropped it into the well. 'The well-way lies through there,' he had said. 'It is a secret tunnel. The entrance is under the water, and it runs clear under the walls of Torm and comes to an end deep in the stonewood grove.'

Fruitlessly, Allyso had peered down the dark maw of the well. 'But what is it for?' she had asked. 'A secret tunnel is not much good if no-one uses it.'

'One tale goes that small Lord Torm used to take his enemies down the well to show them the secret passage.'

'Don't you mean he showed his friends? If I had a secret like that, I'd show Gregory.'

'I mean his enemies, Allyso. He'd lead them into the tunnel and there they would stick forever, while he escaped through the way of the stonewood grove.'

'Ugh!'

'Then there's the tale of his keyre friends, outcasts, many of them. He would let them come and go through the tunnel, while swearing to folk who sought them that they had never come though the gates.

'And then there's the tale that says small Lord Torm liked to go adventuring. His Mistra fussed and worried so that he built the well-way when he was raising Torm Castle, so he could come and go without her knowing his plans. That might be why he built it, but after my own adventure, I wonder if he used it often.'

'How could you go down there, Merrit? You wouldn't fit.'

'I could not fit now, but I went down on the day I learned the secret. My father saw me drop into the well, but he was far too big to follow me. I was nearly too big for the tunnel myself, although I was just eleven. A very tight squeeze it was. My father whipped me soundly when he caught me in the stonewood grove but, even without a beating, I had no wish to try the journey again.'

'You don't want me to go down there? That's not why you told me the secret?'

'Certainly not!' Merrit had pulled a face. 'I would be forced to be furious if you did. No, Allyso, I told you just for tradition's sake. My father told me, and his father told him and so right back to the little Lord Torm who told his first-born son. And when you are grown and have an heir, you must tell him the tale as *well. But warn him, as I am warning you, not to try the journey.'*

The tale had been exciting and curious when she was ten, but now, close to four years later, the excitement had gone, and only the horrors remained.

'So,' said Merrit, 'you must escape by the well-way.'

'Merrit, I *can't*,' she said. 'You know I can't do that!' She was stiff with terror at the bare idea, remembering the story. 'I *can't*,' she said again. 'I'm much more than eleven. I couldn't even begin.'

'You must, or take your chances with the Lordlings,' said Merrit. 'I am sorry, Allyso, but you *must* escape that way. You *must* survive for Torm.'

PART TWO — ESCAPE

CHAPTER EIGHT

WELL-WAY

WINTERWANE — 10TH MOON·OF THE YEAR

OF THE HOUND

'I *can't*!' Allyso left Merrit's chamber in a shamed and shameful rush.

In silence, she returned to her turret window and gazed out into the fading light. She knew she had let Merrit down, but why pretend she could do what she could not? And perhaps it would be all right. The Lords might take her prisoner, but she would promise to do whatever they said. She would bide her time and escape when she was older. Or maybe someone would rescue her? Hilz or Berneathy. Gregory or Mohr and Dagg. Even if they did not, it mightn't be *so* bad.

Movement caught her attention and she realised several folk, including a man in healers' robes, were approaching the walls of Torm. The sentries stopped them and, from the angry gestures of the newcomers, Allyso gathered they must have relatives among the castlers. Did the healer think he could cure the blight?

Or did he have the wit to doubt there was blight at the castle at all? She felt a faint stirring of hope, for the word of a healer was valued by everyone.

The villagers never reached the gates, for the soldiers moved swiftly in and barred their way. They seemed to be shouting and jostling, but the villagers would not turn back. Led by the healer, they demanded entry into Torm.

'By blood, by water, by herb, by fire!' they chanted. 'We claim the right to enter the wards.'

Allyso held her breath, for this was the first real sign that anyone cared to make an active effort to help them. If these folk went to fetch others, perhaps enough of them would arrive to drive away the lords and their foreign soldiers ...

It seemed the same idea had occurred to the soldiers, for their gestures turned suddenly to violence. The healer staggered, breaking the chant; spears flashed in the dusk, and a villager went down. A sword slashed and a pool of darkness began to spread like wine from a broken barrel. Allyso jammed both fists against her mouth so hard that she tasted her own blood.

The scuffle below was brief, and when the soldiers drew back, the healer and villagers lay still on the ground. A soldier thrust his spear violently into the ashes of a fire, perhaps to clean off the blood. Another turned aside, fell to his knees and vomited. He had red hair, braided in the local fashion. He was no foreign soldier, then, but a man of McAnerin.

Allyso found herself gulping, trying to sob. From her vantage she could not tell if she knew the murdered men, but they were someone's fathers, someone's uncles or brothers. And they had come to help!

The redhead was wiping his face, his companions seemed to be laughing ... and there, to the side, a woman stood watching, muffled in her mantle.

Allyso felt cold and sick. It was short of supper time, but there was nothing to eat, nor had she the stomach for food. Back in her chamber she tumbled into bed. Slow tears coursed down her cheeks and wet the feather pillow.

She had tried to hope that something would set things right, that Merrit would recover, that rescue would come, that the lords would not be so bad ...

Now that hope was gone.

'So here we sit,' said Allyso. It was hours later, her tears had dried, and she was so cold that she sat up and bunched her knees inside the circle of her arms. Her stomach ached with emptiness, and she could feel that her bones were sharper beneath her skin. 'Here we sit, starving and miserable, and all because Merrit was kind to a homeless stranger! And nothing can help us, unless it's the gem of time ...'

The gem of time. If Merrit had sent for that when the soulbinder came, the siege need never have happened. But why would Merrit do such a thing when the problem seemed so small? And how could he admit that he really believed, after scoffing so much about foolish superstition? Allyso groaned as her mind ran back in its circle. If she were brave, she would go down the well-way, not to escape, but to tackle the soulbinder face to face! And then what? Another curse, especially for the heir? To confront the soulbinder would be simply to court disaster, so instead she would have to escape and find the gem of time. But how long would that take, and how long did Torm have left?

Allyso groaned, and mentally traced the steps she would need to take.

Escape from Torm. Find her way to Fielding. Search out Trader Mohr and ask about the gem ...

And that was just the beginning of the story.

Impossible! It *was* too much, too hard for her to do. She couldn't even face the first step. Escape from Castle Torm? No. She must ask Gregory or Berneathy to do it, or even Healer Hilz ... Yet, how would they manage the well-way? They were all much bigger than she.

The thought of the future made her ill, but when Merrit died, then Torm would fall and she would be forced to run, in any case.

Face the dark of the well-way, or face those brutes outside?

Find herself trapped in the dark? Or stabbed and slashed by steel like the villagers?

She could not face the well-way, but neither could she face those swords and spears. And especially not the soulbinder, who would watch and gloat while they did whatever they would do to her.

If she had to run, she might as well run now.

Allyso sat counting breaths and watching her shadow on the wall. Hilz would get her a disguise, but she knew it would never work. He was a healer, after all, and not a masquer, with skill at making costumes.

She pushed back the quilt and slid down from the high narrow bed. She was wearing her oldest tunic already, so she added leggings and a blue hooded mantle of Ankoorian reinbeast weave, then sashed a short, sturdy knife that Gregory had given her. She used it sometimes for carving honeywood favours; now it might have other functions. She wondered if she could use it to stab a soldier. Perhaps she could, if he tried to stab her first.

She wanted to farewell Merrit, but she feared she would lose her courage. Hilz might be there. Or Gregory. If Gregory knew what she was planning, he would offer to go instead. He was not quite grown, but he was certainly much bigger than Allyso.

Gill's words came back to her. *'Don't put such notions in Gregory's head, I beg you, Allyso. He's just at the age for rushing off on some foolish quest, and you know he'd do anything for Merrit — or for you.'*

And besides, she had sworn to Merrit that she would never reveal the secret of Torm to anyone but her heir.

I am the Blood of Torm, she thought. That means I must be strong. I am the one who must rescue us all or die trying.

Brave words, like the words from some stirring tale of Mohr's, but they would bring no comfort if and when she faced that death.

She crept out to the wellyard. There was still some rubble about, and a few scorched marks from the early days of the siege. Her soft boots made no sound on the paving, but crunched a little on the grit and debris as she neared the well. It didn't really matter. If the castlers heard her, they would suppose she needed a drink. She thought they might wish her well if they knew what she intended. Help from the gem of time would save them, too.

The years swirl back like the ocean tides. So Merrit had said.

If the gem could really turn back time, the soulbinder's visit could be undone, and the castlers would never dice for her miserable goods. Merrit would live and Torm would thrive, and all would be the way it should have been ... The gem of time could put things *right*.

Reaching the well shaft, she hitched up her mantle and perched on the stone coping. Even through her leggings she felt the chill that rose from the well. The water was pure and cold, bubbling from some hidden place, deep underground. It must force its way through clefts in the rock, but she had never known how it happened or whether the wellspring had been found or designed.

Allyso shivered. The water would get no warmer for waiting, and she would get no braver.

But she knew she couldn't do it after all. Sitting there, breathing the wet stone smell, she suddenly knew it was impossible. She had been daydreaming, wishing, hoping she might be brave enough to try.

She couldn't do it, but neither could she face the thought of spears and swords. Of letting the soulbinder gloat at her winnings.

With a surge of desperation, the Heir of Torm slid into the depths of the well.

The chill took her breath, and it was some seconds before she could gulp enough air to steady her lungs and force herself to duck beneath the surface. Her mantle tugged at her shoulders, and a flurry of bubbles tore past as she felt desperately around the shaft of the well. Merrit had drawn her a sketch when she was ten, but she hadn't been able to keep it in case it was found and someone studied it. In any case, he had drawn from his own long-ago memory, so it might not have been very accurate. He had said the well-way led from the eastern wall of the shaft.

She concentrated her efforts on that side, but the lining stones felt solid and complete. Three times she had to rise to catch her breath against the hammering cold, then dive again and continue her search. At last her numb fingertips found the tunnel's entrance. So — it really was there!

The mouth of the well-way was narrow and low and a snug fit even for Allyso. She gusted a sigh of mingled relief and dismay, marked the place as well as she could, and rose to gulp one last breath of castle air. She forced herself to wait until the frantic thudding of her heart had eased before she made her final dive. By now she was racked with cold, but she never considered climbing out to warm herself and rest. Once out, dripping in the familiar wellyard, how would she ever get back in the water? She would know, all over again, that this was impossible.

She counted ten three times over, then dived again, dragged herself painfully through the gap and squirmed into the underwater passage.

The fit was unpleasantly tight, and Allyso knew her breath wouldn't last for long. Here at Torm there was little opportunity for swimming, and she had never practised much even in Highsummer. She could not turn back, for the tunnel held her close on every side. She might have been rolled in a blanket of stone.

She clawed her way through the drowning darkness and came to what seemed to be a solid wall. Her lungs began to ache and a fizz of black and red spots rose before her eyes, but her groping fingers found a ledge.

It was high above her head. She reared and dragged herself over the lip, to tumble, gasping, scraped and bruised, onto the damp slick surface of another tunnel.

The relief of drawing breath was enough for that moment, but the chill was gnawing at her bones, and who knew what else the well-way had in store?

Bones, perhaps, from the ill-fated enemies of the first Lord Torm? Nonsense. If he had been so very small, his enemies would have been much too big to make it this far.

Allyso sucked her numb, bruised fingers for a moment. Now she was out of the water, at least she could crawl. Choking on a sob, pretending it was nothing but an extra-big breath, she felt around for her bearings and set off again.

The tunnel was a nightmare that went on and on. She had no idea how long she had been in the darkness, nor how far she might have travelled. She could see nothing at all, could hear nothing but the faint fizz of water in her ears and the drip of moisture from the roof of the tunnel. She thought she might crawl forever and never find the end. Would the enemy lords be satisfied then? They would never find her body, and so they would have to wonder forever if she might turn up again.

It would serve them very right, but her death would be too much of a price to pay for their discomfort.

At last, when she had all but given up any idea of success, she came to a dead end in the tunnel. She felt all around her. Her hands were so cold she could feel nothing that she touched, but every contact made a jarring up her arms. She could hear a very faint rasp of her skin on stone and realised, after a while, that the thing in front of her was a rocky slab. To the side was a ridge of something that might have been stone but, despite her numbness, she had the impression it was warmer and more alive. She traced her fingers down it, wondering, and realised with a jolt that it must be the root of a stonewood tree. Merrit had told her the well-way led to the midst of the stonewood grove, but if it ended under the roots of the trees, she would never break free.

She scrabbled with broken fingernails, growing a little less numb with her efforts. The roots were hard as rock, but the earth around them was only earth. And there must be a way out, for Merrit had come this way when he was eleven. How long ago was that? Thirty years, perhaps? Long enough for criss-cross roots to grow around the exit. But nothing grazed beneath a stonewood tree, and so the ground should not be too compacted. Belatedly, she reached for her knife. Its blade was stronger than her nails, and desperation helped to give her a grip. She rolled painfully onto her back and began to hack at the mass of soil above her.

It took a very long time, and debris rained into her face. She closed her eyes against the dust for, as far as seeing was concerned, it made no difference whether or not they were open. It was so dark that coloured discs of light seemed to dance against the blackness.

Because she could not see, and because her arm was so leaden, it took some seconds to notice when her knife broke free of the soil. When she felt the lack of resistance, she hardly dared to hope, so she used her wet sleeve to wipe her eyes, then cautiously opened them. Although the light was very dim, to Allyso it dazzled like the breaking of day.

Numb with relief, she began to widen the chink that had opened above her. She wanted to work at top speed, but exhaustion held her back and so did fear of discovery. She had reached the stonewood grove, yet where would she emerge? If she rose from the ground at the edge of the trees, she would be in plain sight of the soldiers. And so she worked slowly, carefully, pausing often to listen.

She was, she soon discovered, well inside the grove. Even when she had opened out a burrow above her, the light remained quite dim. Could it be early morning? Surely she had been in the well-way for longer than that!

She peered about and realised she was almost entirely enclosed in a forest of gnarled grey trunks. The stonewood grove must be as old as Torm, and folk would never push through the rigid branches when they could just as easily walk around. Stonewood trees were eternal as the rocks and as unforgiving.

Shivering with tension as well as cold, Allyso hauled herself out of her burrow and kicked the earth back into the cavity she had made. It was obvious that it had been disturbed but, unless her quest was successful, no-one else would ever need the well-way. The knowledge of its existence might die with her.

Had it ever been used for more than a prank before? She thought of the young boy Merrit and wished that it had been he, and not she, on whom Torm's fate could rest. He had come this way for *adventure*! She remembered the relish in his voice when he had described his journey. And what about small Lord Torm? Had he made this route for sport, for murder or for escape?

She worked her way through the stonewood, pulling her mantle closely about her sides. Though the reinbeast cloth was sodden, it gave some protection from the twigs and branches. Gill always said it was the toughest and most durable cloth to be had in any land. Still stonewood was not to be trifled with. Its twigs were as harsh as pinnacles of rock and as sharp as crystals.

The light grew brighter as she approached the edge of the trees, and she saw, in dismay, that the grove was surrounded by tents. She could not emerge from the shelter wringing wet and filthy, so she retreated a little. At first, she thought she might wait until the soldiers went elsewhere but, after a time, she realised they were unlikely to move. The business of the siege was for them to stay where they were. She must get dry, and try to look like a village child who had come to see the sights.

SCHOLAR

WINTERWANE — 10TH MOON OF THE YEAR

OF THE HOUND

DRYING herself in the depths of the grove would take too long, so Allyso turned her attention upwards. She knew, from games of seek-me when she was younger, that most folk didn't look up without good reason. With this in mind, she set herself to climb into the stonewood canopy.

It was not like climbing other trees, for the branches would neither bend nor snap. Reaching the first one was quite a problem. She could spring and leap, but she was afraid of the noise it would make. She finally discovered a jutting spur just a little above her, scrambled up to stand on it, then step by step she worked her way aloft.

Once she had gained the canopy, she settled into a nest of branches. The leathery leaves were sparse enough to allow the weak Winterwane sunlight to fall on her arms and back. She removed her hood and peered down to the outer edge of the grove. From her vantage point she could see the chequered-shirt army, disturbingly close, but unaware of her. She could hear them too: the hiss of stone on metal, the harsh scrubbing sound as they polished blades and spears.

She tried to pick out Lords Sheels and Toombs, but it seemed they were not in her vicinity. The dead villagemen must have been taken away, and as for High Traders Walton and Templeton, she had no idea what had happened to them. She could only hope they were still alive. She could never rescue them; it would be hard enough to save herself.

If she found the gem of time, of course, it would rescue the captured traders, too. And save the villagemen from death?

She glanced at the sky and decided the sun had been up no more than an hour or two. The cookfires were flickering, and savoury smells were taunting her. To take her mind from her hunger, Allyso peeled off her mantle and spread it to dry, then rubbed her face as clean as she could without a looking glass.

She peered down again, and saw a soldier remove his cap to reveal a long red braid. He had a book in his hand, and a small hound was crouched at his side. The hound moved restlessly, and whined, making the man look up. His eyes narrowed as if against the dazzle of sunlight, then he soothed the hound and began to read again. She thought the redhead was the soldier whose stomach had rebelled when the villagemen were killed, but she wasn't sure and of course it didn't matter, anyway.

Time plodded on. The Winterwane sun shone like a faded lantern. Her tunic and leggings slowly dried on her body. The tunic felt stiff and crumpled, but at least she was warmer now. The soldiers below her went about their business. Allyso strained to hear what they said, but most of it seemed to consist of grumbling. It appeared that some of these mercenaries were tired of the situation and wanted to batter the castle until it surrendered.

'The Lords didn't complain when we slit those yokels,' said one. 'Why should they care for a pile of rocks and mortar?'

'They want the walls still standing,' said another. 'Villagers are two to a coin, but a castle takes years to rebuild. Who wants to live in a ruin if he can have good walls?'

Another soldier yawned. 'They promised us action, where's the action now?'

'There was action enough for those poor souls that got skewered,' said the redhead. 'Go and grumble somewhere else. Your gabble sickens me.'

A possible ally? It was tempting to hope, but also dangerous. After all, he was helping besiege her home. Sick he might have been at the sight of slaughter, and perhaps he liked to read and was fond of his hound, but he was *here*, and so he could mean no good.

At last, as the sun began to dip, the soldiers settled to rest. And they were eating again! Baskets of food were handed about, with hard dark bread, onions and a sharp yellow cheese so strong the smell was carried to Allyso on the quiet air. Her mouth watered and she could almost feel the hard rough texture of the bread and the waxy flavour of cheese. She swallowed several times, then closed her eyes to shut out the sight as the men tore at the food, and tossed unwanted lumps of it into the fire. One tried to feed the hound with a rind of cheese, but it turned its head aside and went back to its master's side.

If only Merrit had refused to admit the soulbinder! If only the castlers had never bought her wicked wares! If only —

'Stop that!' whispered Allyson. That well-worn circle of thought would do no good at all.

Her mantle was dry, so she put it on, lifting the hood to screen her neck from the growing chill of the breeze. The men below had finished their meal and now they sprawled about, complaining of boredom and lack of activity. Some had edged closer to the fire and gone to sleep.

Allyso dozed a little, then woke with a gasp. Her limbs were cramped, and she knew if she waited much longer, she would simply fall out of the tree and make the invaders a gift of herself. It was coming on to sunfall, and she had wasted most of a day already. If she had only thought to try the well-way at nightfall instead of close to dawn, she could have been long gone from here by now. She could have crept past the soldiers while they slept; they would have guards set, but they wouldn't expect anyone to emerge from the stonewood grove.

Regrets had not helped Merrit and would not help Allyso, either. She would stop these might-have-beens, make her choices and trust that they were good.

She began to clamber down the stonewood tree, wincing at the soreness of her hands and legs. A sharp pain under her ribs made her stop and twist about, thinking a stonewood spur had caught her through her tunic.

'Keep still, brat.'

The words were delivered in a low voice that held none of the hiss of a whisper. There was nothing particularly frightening in the tone, yet a swift glance sideways showed she was in trouble. It was not a stonewood spur that pained her, but a spear.

Instinctively, she tried to twist away. The spear-point jabbed at her again.

'Be quiet, brat, and come down,' came the order.

She nodded, once, and the pressure was removed so she could scramble the rest of the way down. Her feet had barely touched the ground when the spear-man seized her by the collar. 'Answer, and keep it quiet. If you scream, it will go worse for you than for me.'

The accent was foreign, but a low, continuous whine from beside her feet gave her a clue to her captor's identity. 'I'll be quiet,' she said.

'All right, brat. What were you doing in the tree for so long?'

'I wasn't there long. I was only —'

'Don't lie. I've been watching you, and so has Tace.'

'Tar-chay?'

He jerked his head towards the little hound. 'Her name is Tace. But tell me, what were you doing?'

She swallowed, keeping her head low, hoping the hood still covered all her hair. 'T-trying to see over the castle wall.'

'What for? Didn't you see the blight-wards?'

'I have friends in the castle,' she pleaded. 'I know one of the serving men and Mistra Gill. I wanted to see they're all right.'

Abruptly, the spear-man turned her to face him and used his free hand to force up her chin. She bit her tongue, and her eyes welled with tears. Through them, she had no trouble recognising the redhead with the braid and the little hound. Now she saw him up close, she noted that he had parti-coloured eyes, one blue, one green. She would usually have found this intriguing, but now was not the time for noting the colour of someone's eyes. She had no idea if he recognised her for Torm Blood. They had never met, but the soulbinder might have given him and the other soldiers a clear description.

'Quiet, Tace,' he said, apparently to the hound. 'It's only a harmless brat, so drop your hackles.' Then he added to Allyso, 'Where did you come from, brat?'

She shook her head.

'I should hand you over to my father,' said the redhead. 'He'd get a few straight answers out of you, but right now he's with that filthy dame. You know the one I mean.'

Allyso winced, but managed a questioning sound. 'A dame? What dame is that, soldier?'

'Dark and ugly, and wears a ring that squirts light and puts her face to shame. She's bewitched my father, and Tace here hates her even more than she hates him.' His hand left her collar and closed over her shoulder. 'You're all starved to bones,' he said. 'You came from the castle, didn't you?'

Allyso tried to deny it, but the hound was whining again, rearing up to press a cold muzzle into her hand. 'There is no blight at Torm!' she managed. 'There is only one person ill, and that is from a curse.'

'I know that. But you still can't help them,' he said bleakly. 'The place will fall, and they'll fall with it. The sooner the better, for them.'

'No.'

'Take my advice, brat, and get away from here. *I* would, if I could. If I had my way, I'd be headed for Ankoor by now, along with Tace. Here.' He took a piece of cheese from a fold in his mantle and gave it to her. 'Start eating and —'

His words broke off abruptly, as someone spoke, much too close behind them.

'Scholar? Where have you got to?'

'Here!'

Allyso was aghast at this betrayal, but she had no time to protest or try to run away. He shoved her up against the stonewood tree and put his arms around her, leaning close and trapping her against the rock-hard bark. 'Ssh!' he whispered, and she felt his cheek come down on the top of her head. 'Push your face into my shoulder . . .'

Allyso, nearly smothered by the coarse stuff of his mantle, did as she was told. She could feel the young man's heart thumping hard against her, and it came to her that he was frightened, too.

'Scholar?'

'We're here,' he said irritably as someone pushed in towards them. 'And for the stars' sake, keep your voice down. You want *everyone* to hear?'

'What? What have you got in here?'

'Nothing. No-one. Just a friend.'

Allyso's ear was burning with mingled outrage and unease, and the sudden snort of laughter from the newcomer made her stiffen.

'Some friend, Scholar! Let me see —'

Allyso shrank back against the tree, keeping her head low as Scholar moved away.

'She's no-one special,' he said. 'Just a houndmaid — she's taking Tace back home to Ankoor to be bred.'

'That's likely,' said the other soldier, but he sounded amused. 'Better come out, we've drawn the sunfall watch.'

'You go on, Kell,' said Scholar. 'I'll just tell Tace goodbye.'

'You do that, and I'll forget I saw your houndmaid *friend* — or should I be telling Sheels you've played the Mistra Tegwen false already?'

Scholar snarled at him, and the other man laughed and departed.

'Much Kell knows, or Sheels either,' muttered Scholar. 'I'll take no Hasselsjo Mistra, whatever they say.' He turned his attention back to Allyso. 'Go,' he said abruptly. 'Do what I said you'd come to do. Take Tace through the other side of the grove and get away from here.'

'I can't take a hound to Ankoor! I have to —'

'Take her,' he said. 'That's the only reason I'm letting you go, to make sure she's safe. She likes you.'

'But —'

He picked up the little hound and cradled her in his arms, then thrust her at Allyso. 'Go on, take her. Somewhere. Anywhere, so long as it's far from here. I will find you when I can.'

Allyso received the warm little body and stared at the young man. He sounded foreign but looked McAnerinian, and it seemed that his father was an important member of the invading force. He seemed used to having his own way, but he certainly had no social manner. Could he be the son of one of the Lords, fostered, perhaps, in a distant place?

She didn't ask him, for too much curiosity might make him curious in turn. 'Won't your hound be better off with you?' she asked instead.

'No!' Scholar's voice cracked. 'She and that dame hate one another, and I'm afraid I'll find her cursed or poisoned some day. Take her with you!'

He picked up his spear from the tree where he had leaned it.

Allyso stood numbly, clutching the hound, so he turned her with one hand on her shoulder. 'Get going, brat. If anyone stops you, just say you're a houndmaid and a friend of Master Scholar. Say you're taking Tace home to be bred.' He touched the hound's head with gentle fingers. 'Go with the brat, Tace,' he said, and left abruptly.

Allyso made her way through to the other side of the grove. It was getting dark, and she had lost a day, but she walked away unchallenged.

She was free and out of the castle, but she realised that she had never really expected to get this far. And now that she had, she couldn't congratulate herself on a task completed, for this was only one more step of the way to the gem of time . . .

There was another challenge to face, another journey, and many other problems. Any of these steps might be as hard as the one she had just completed. Tears of exhaustion ran down her cheeks, and she didn't even notice until the little hound whined in her arms and reached up to lick her cheek.

'And what *am* I to do with you, Tace?' she asked. 'How will I feed you and keep you from running back to your master? And what if this is all a plot so he can accuse me of stealing you?'

It was all too much to worry about, so she shook her head and walked towards the distant trees marking the high road that led down to the south of McAnerin and on to Fielding Village.

The next thing to do was to search out Trader Mohr.

PART THREE — CANDLE IRON

CHAPTER TEN

TACE

WINTERWANE — 10TH MOON TO 11TH MOON

OF THE YEAR OF THE HOUND

ALLYSO knew it would take some days to reach Fielding Village. She hoped she would be able to find the way, but she was afraid to ask directions from passers-by. What if one of them knew her face? If they thought she carried blight, she would be in even worse trouble than she was now. And what if they recognised the little hound?

She looked at it doubtfully, but she couldn't see much in the gloaming. It seemed a sweet-natured thing, looking up at her face as if they had not been strangers.

She thought it might rather walk than have her carry it, but what if it ran away? She would wait for sunlift and then contrive some kind of harness.

Her mind darted to and fro, faster than her feet could tramp, trying to settle on the safest thing to do. It would be a terrible waste if she went to Fielding and could not find Mohr and Dagg. It had been six moonspans since she had seen them last, and who knew where they might have gone by now? She didn't know their routine, but of course all Traders spent a lot of time in travel. On the other hand, who else did she dare to approach?

'If you go on like this, Allyso Tormblood, you might as well give up and cry like a baby,' she said aloud. Then she glanced over her shoulder to make sure no-one had overheard.

She was trudging into the night by now, for the last green glow of sunfall had left the skies. Her feet ached and her eyes blurred with exhaustion, but she refused to let herself rest. The farther she managed to travel that night, the less likely she would be to meet someone who would know her for the Blood of Torm. She had seldom travelled before, and never without Merrit.

As the light faded, she stepped off the trodden way, for even strangers would have thought it odd if they met someone of her apparent age walking alone at night.

'If I'd been bigger,' said Allyso regretfully, 'they would have taken me for an apprentice or a page. But then, if I *had* been bigger, I would never have got through the well-way. And if I had been older, perhaps I could have made Merrit listen to Trader Mohr and Trader Dagg.'

Her voice sounded steady, but talking to herself was a sign of weakness. All right then, in future she would talk to Tace.

'The trouble is,' she said to the hound, 'I have never really been alone. There's always been *someone* to give me advice, even if it were only Gregory or that strange master of yours. I suppose *you* can't tell me what to do?'

Tace sighed, then tucked her muzzle under Allyso's mantle. It was getting colder, and Allyso could feel the hound's occasional shivers.

The green smell of the McAnerin grasslands seemed stronger in the dark, and Allyso stopped to pick some waist-high stalks of bitterstem. The juice was sour enough to pucker her mouth, but it staved off thirst and helped to keep her alert. She watched the sky as she plodded on, seeing the wheel of stars above and about her. The stars were always there. They wouldn't care who held the reins of Torm, nor what happened to the last of the Blood.

She stumbled again, and lost her balance, twisting to avoid the hound. The bitterstem cushioned her fall, but her legs felt tired and weak.

'I can't walk any more tonight,' she said to Tace. 'I hope you're not too thirsty. If you are, you'll have to chew some bitterstem, like me.' The hound nosed at the mantle, burrowing her muzzle through the fastening.

'I see,' said Allyso. 'You might as well. At least it will keep you near me.' She opened her mantle and the hound crept down inside where she snuggled against Allyso's ribs with a sigh, making a welcome patch of warmth.

Holding Tace in the crook of her arm, Allyso wondered if she would ever see Merrit again. She tried to hope this was all a bad dream. Then she slipped into a bottomless pit of sleep.

She woke to the slow drip of water on her face. For a hazy moment she thought it was Gregory, trying to wake her for some venture beyond the walls. Then she realised she was somewhere on the road to Fielding. The drops were nothing but dew, sliding down the tall bitterstem plants. She half sat up, dislodging the sleeping Tace, and ran her fingers down the blade-like stalks. She collected liquid in her palm and licked it up while she considered her situation. The morning was already well advanced, and the upper side of her mantle was dry. She opened the fastening and drew out the hound, seeing her clearly for the first time. Tace was a brindle, with flecks of chestnut colour liberally spattering her black and white coat. Slanted brown eyes gleamed from under her smooth brow, and her ears, set wide apart, were still relaxed from sleep.

'Hello, Tace.' Allyso rubbed the silky ears and then tugged free the lower thong-fastening of her mantle. 'If we're going to be travelling all day you'll have to walk at least some of the way.' She looped the thong and slipped it over the hound's head.

Tace accepted it well enough, and turned to lick at the bitterstems, lapping up the moisture. Occasionally she would raise her head and sniff the air.

Allyso washed her face with dew. Her muscles creaked and whimpered with pain from all the unaccustomed exercise of yesterday, but she had no time to think about that. 'We'll feel better when we get warm,' she said to Tace, and began to cast about to locate the road she had left in the dark.

The flat McAnerin plain was low on landmarks and she was not adept at telling direction by the sun. She thought she would chance the main way, rather than risk getting lost and taking too long to reach Fielding. It was such a clear morning that she was sure she would hear or see any other travellers in time to avoid being recognised. And perhaps, if she saw some High Traders, she might ask their help for Templeton and Walton.

And perhaps, whispered temptation, they would help her as well. They might even take her straight to the gem of time. But perhaps they would bundle her back to Torm instead!

She stumbled onto the road before she expected to and set off at a good pace towards the south. Her stomach felt hollow, and she wondered how far she would be able to walk without food. Trader Mohr had tales of adventurers who travelled for many days without complaining of hunger. They seemed to eat berries and roots, but there were no berries on these plains at this season, and as for roots — Allyso turned aside to pull up a bitterstem plant. She eyed the fine scarlet threads that had held it in the soil and decided they looked even less satisfactory than the leaves.

'Are you hungry enough to eat that, Tace?' She held it down for inspection.

The hound sniffed and sneezed, then began to investigate the ground. Allyso replanted the bitterstem, then watched as Tace snuffled her way in a circle. She seemed particularly interested in a small depression a few paces off the road, sniffing loudly and scraping the soil with her paw.

Allyso loosened the leash, and the hound began to dig with both forepaws, pausing now and again to sniff and whine.

'What is it?' Allyso was both alarmed and curious. Gruesome thoughts of death-burials came to mind, and she tried to pull Tace away. The hound proved unexpectedly stubborn, dragging steadily towards her task until Allyso gave up and let her be.

The busy paws scraped up turf and clods of earth, then a shower of fine, friable soil. The hole grew rapidly deeper, and Allyso had time to wish she had had Tace to help when she dug her way out of the well-way tunnel. Could hounds swim under water? She felt in her sash for her knife with the idea of assisting the hound, but her fingers closed on an empty fold of cloth.

'No!' She looked wildly about, crouching to pat the grasses with her palms. Leaving Tace to continue with her digging, she made her way back to the place where they had spent the night. There was the flattened bitterstem, the half-moon depression made by her body but, though she searched about, she did not find the knife.

'It could be anywhere,' she said aloud. 'Anywhere at all between here and Torm!'

She hurried back to Tace and found the hound had dug herself almost out of sight. All that Allyso could see were two neat hind paws spread wide apart to gain good purchase and a pert tail that quivered with the effort of digging.

'*Stop* that!' She was sharper than she meant to be, and tugged quite hard at the thong. Surprisingly, Tace stopped digging and scrabbled her way back up to level ground, waving her whip of a tail and panting with triumph.

Allyso peered into the hole. At first, she didn't recognise the cluster of cream-coloured globes at the bottom, but then a waft of their fragrance drifted up.

'Sweetloaves!' She fell to her knees, scooping out the firm, egg-shaped spheres. Their texture was cheese-like, their perfume that of new-baked bread. 'How clever of you!' she added. She set down the fungi and hugged Tace before scraping away at the bottom of the pit to collect the rest of the booty.

But no — she must leave one. She remembered Merrit telling her that one sweetloaf must always be left to provide the parent for a new crop. Odd that she should remember that, for she had never seen these delicacies anywhere else but served on a kitchen platter.

Crouching on her heels, she selected one and bit into it. The skin was a little gritty, and the flesh inside mealy and satisfying. It seemed a long time since she had eaten the scrap of cheese Scholar had given her, and longer still since the meagre bowl of gruel she'd had in Torm.

She became aware that Tace was watching with gleaming eyes, licking her lips and giving the occasional soft whimper.

Allyso almost choked at her own ingratitude. Tace had made the discovery and done the work, and of course she was hungry, too. She selected another sweetloaf, brushed away the clinging soil and offered it to the hound. Tace took it delicately and set it between her paws, then began to gnaw with evident enjoyment.

Allyso ate her fill, then picked a few of the peppery cresses that grew amongst the grasses. Gill used those as a garnish for dishes of fowl and game, but they went well enough with sweetloaves.

She bundled the remainder of the fungi into the

front fold of her mantle, hoping they'd keep for at least the rest of the day. 'We'd better move on,' she said.

She filled in the delve and smoothed the soil, then dusted off her hands, looped the thong over her wrist and stepped back onto the road.

The weather was fine and cool and, with food in her belly, she felt better than she had the day before. She stepped out, and Tace trotted beside her, just as she might have trotted with her master.

The hours wore away. Without the urgent fears of the day before, Allyso found it difficult to keep up her pace. Torm's plight was sour in her mind, but the road was so quiet she found herself wondering if the matter could be quite as terrible as it had seemed. Surely a siege at the castle should have brought folk hurrying to its aid? Surely they couldn't *all* have heard and believed the blight-story?

As sunfall came on, her feet were uncertain with exhaustion. Her heels were sore and her mantle seemed heavy on her shoulders. She was wondering if she should stop for the night when Tace made the decision for her by stopping and sniffing the air.

'More sweetloaves?' Allyso had meant to save some for the next day, but walking was a hungry business and she had days of lean meals to make up. She had shared them all with Tace, hoping the hound would be able to find something more.

Tace was on the move again, veering off over the grasslands. A fine whisper of smoke met Allyso's nostrils, and she followed the tang of it to a trodden clearing where the remains of a way-fire smouldered. A few unburned peats remained and, weary almost beyond thought, she dropped down and coaxed the fire back into flames. By its low, clear light, she saw that some of the peats were not peats at all, but a cluster of dragonpods.

Peeling the fruits without a knife was a painful and difficult business, but Allyso knew better than to try to bite through the horny skins. She found a fire-split stone and, after a few attempts, managed to find a grip that would cut the dragonpod but not her skin. The pod was just as tough as it looked, and took several blows before it split raggedly across. The pulp was stringy but juicy, and Allyso shared it with Tace, laughing a little at the hound's distasteful expression. It was nearly dark, so she rolled them both into her mantle and went to sleep.

They were off again as soon as it was light, with Allyso carrying three of the dragonpods looped in the front of her mantle. She would have taken more, if they had not been so heavy and hard to hold. She sashed the sharp stone blade, and wished she had thought to fetch a firepot from Torm. A flask would have been useful, and so would extra boots . . .

'Why not wish for a brace of reinbeast and a carriage, or a sturdy garnerbeast to carry us!' she said to Tace. 'We might as well.' She replaced the thong in her mantle. It seemed obvious that Tace did not need a leash.

Again the road was quiet. So quiet that Allyso was startled when she saw three chattering marketgirls ahead. They were striking across from one of the eastern sidetracks, and hailed her cheerfully as their pathways intersected.

'Have you heard the news?' asked one.

'Of Torm? I —'

'No, no, the trouble in Ankoor!'

'The what?' She knew she sounded foolish, but it had been so many hours since she had spoken to anyone other than Tace.

'The Tenth Castle is rising!'

'Or so they say,' said one of the others.

'We hoped you might know more.'

'How could she know *more*, Gawenna? You can see well enough she is foreign. She must know less than we do.'

'She might be a foreigner who has travelled from Ankoor ...'

'Not with that hair. More likely from the Rargonian clans ...'

The girls began a laughing argument about Allyso's origin, but none of it touched on anything like the truth.

'Wait!' said Allyso. 'Have you heard nothing about Torm? Nothing at all?'

'Is that a village?' asked one girl, frowning a little.

'No, I mean Castle Torm.' She paused, and added cautiously, 'They say Merrit, the Lord, is very ill, and two other Lords are trying to take it over. They are pretending there is a blight.'

The second girl shrugged. 'Lord of the Manor, Lord of the Castle ... makes no difference to us.'

'We'll stay clear if there's a blight ...'

'There isn't really a blight, that's just a ruse ...' But Allyso could see they were not at all concerned. It seemed odd and wrong that a matter of life and death to the Blood of Torm could mean so little to eastern marketfolk. 'What is this Tenth Castle you mentioned?' she asked.

'A rabble,' said one girl, but the second shook her head.

'No, no, it is folk who are outcasts among the Nine Castles of Ankoor. They have bound themselves into a pact to take what no-one will give them.'

'Oh!' said Allyso. 'What is that?'

'A place to live and prosper,' said the third girl. 'Good luck to them, I say.'

A place to live and prosper. Allyso felt cold. The soulbinder had used those words when Merrit had asked her to leave.

She stepped aside and watched the marketgirls pass off to the west.

'They didn't care at all,' she said to Tace. 'If it had been their village taken over, I would have cared.'

But how would she have heard if something had befallen their village? Time was, when Torm had heard all the important news of McAnerin, and much from beyond but, since that fateful Highsummer, the flow of information had slowed to a sluggish trickle and then dried completely. How long since she had spoken to someone unconnected with Torm? Over six moonspans! No wonder she had put up such an ill showing with Scholar and now with the eastern marketgirls.

'I must do better when I find Trader Mohr and Trader Dagg,' she said to Tace. 'At least they will understand how horrible it is. I'll explain exactly what has happened, and I'm sure they'll be able to help.'

CHAPTER ELEVEN

CASTLE-FALL

WINTERWANE — 11TH MOON OF THE YEAR

OF THE HOUND

THE soulbinder was eager for the end.

'This siege is too drawn out,' she told Lord Toombs. The gem on her finger winked in the morning light.

Toombs frowned. He wanted to say something cutting, to put the shabby dame in her place, but he tried to sound reasonable instead. 'Matters of conquest must move at their own pace, Dame. How long have we been here, after all?'

'Too long. I tell you Torm is rotten and ready to fall. It should be in our hands by now.'

'It will be.'

'But when? Move fast, Lord Toombs, or this prize might slip away.'

'And how could that happen? No-one can go in, or out, and we have your word there is little food inside.'

'The High Traders you took could bring you down.'

'Two men?' Toombs let his eyebrows rise. 'Two men against an army?'

'Two High Traders,' corrected the dame. 'Making for Western Port Fair. What if they are missed by others going there?'

'They will be thought to be delayed along the way. As for Torm, these things must and shall take time.'

'Give me these High Traders. I shall send them safely on their way.'

'Mercy from *you*, Dame? I thought you did not know that word.'

The woman spat at his feet. 'Take care how you insult me, Toombs, or your name may become your dwelling.'

She left abruptly, and Toombs winced as a drop of sweat rolled into his eye. Savagely, he blotted his face with his arm.

For days he had been having spells of wishing he had never listened to the soulbinder and never begun this siege. It had seemed a just and simple matter in the beginning, but the High Traders did present a dilemma. He could not kill men who had offered no resistance, but neither could he let them go to tell their tales. Whatever he did, they were trouble.

And then there were the foreign mercenaries. They were violent, yet lazy and arrogant too. If they had not reacted so swiftly, he could have settled the matter of Walton and Templeton himself. He could have spun them a tale they would have believed.

And as for Scholar!

Toombs' frown became more personal. His son was a sorry specimen who showed no interest in these arrangements for his own future. He looked pale and sickly enough at the best of times, but when those interfering villagers had been cut down, he had turned faint. He also showed a weakness for that meek and puling hound he had brought with him out of Ankoor when his mother's people had sent him south into McAnerin. Toombs' foot itched suddenly to kick the creature. It cringed and whined enough already, raising its hackles whenever he came near. Why not give it a reason to cringe and whine?

'You there, Kell!' he said abruptly to a lounging soldier. It was one of his own men, a McAnerinian, and one that he could trust.

'My Lord?'

'Fetch me that creature of Scholar's.'

The soldier stared at him.

'Don't stand there like a stonewit!' said Toombs irritably. 'It won't bite you.'

Nor would it bite anyone else, he thought. Nor whine for very much longer.

'My Lord, the hound has gone.'

'So someone tired of the bleating thing and skewered it.' Toombs felt cheated. He should have had Bajen kill it back at Zimmerhanzel.

'No, my Lord. The houndmaid fetched it away to be bred.'

'The *houndmaid*?' Had he had less on his mind, Toombs might have pursued the matter, but it was hardly of interest now. The hound had gone and, with luck, it would not reappear. If only his other troubles could melt away so simply.

While Lord Toombs considered his problems, the soulbinder was moving through the camp like a pillar of smoke. She made her way to a makeshift palisade where the two High Traders slumped, shackled to their own wheeled cart.

'You are friends of Torm, High Traders?'

'We would not be here, otherwise,' said the older man. His voice was hoarse and his thin face was very swollen.

The soulbinder produced a pot of salve and removed the lid. 'Use this.'

The other man stirred. 'Templeton has more sense than to take anything from a dark-hearted dame like you.'

The soulbinder raised her hand and let the gem on her finger wink. 'I mean you no harm, High Trader,' she said softly.

'No? We have met your kind in Ankoor, Dame. You stink of the Tenth Castle.'

The soulbinder's eyes flashed at the insult, but she simply scooped some salve into her palm and rubbed it into her own face. 'See? It does no harm, and will bring down the swelling.'

'Why should you care?'

'There is a task that needs good men like yourselves, and needs them in proper health.' She moved her hand, playing the light of the gem across their faces.

There was a silence, and then the second man spoke again. 'What has *your* sort to do with good men, Soulbinder?'

'Little enough, High Trader, but the day of Torm is done. You must see that. Whether the folk in there live or die is of no interest to me, but *good* men might wish to save them from the blight.'

'This is some kind of trick,' said Templeton.

'It is a plan,' she corrected, 'to end this pain and speed my own ambitions. You are known at the castle, and so they will let you in. If you add this draught to their well, the blight will no longer trouble them.'

'If that is a cure, you should have sent it long ago,' said Templeton. 'It seems more likely you are sending them poison.'

The soulbinder held up the bottle of liquid. 'It is a herbal mixture, no more,' she said. 'It staves off blight and other ills. Now, try the salve and you will see my skill is good ...'

Cautiously, Templeton rubbed some salve on his bruises. The crystal ring flashed as it caught the light and his head ached. He closed his eyes against the glare, but could still feel the play of light across his eyelids. After a little while, his pained expression smoothed itself away, and he opened his eyes. 'You speak the truth this time, Soulbinder,' he said. 'It does feel better.'

'It looks much the same to me,' said Walton shortly.

'Rest,' said the soulbinder. 'Leave your pain and uncertainty. Rest a while, and when you wake, you will go to Torm and give my gift to the folk inside ... I give you my word the blight-wards will soon be down, and the problems of Torm will be done.'

The two High Traders never quite recalled what happened that day. They had a blurred impression of dosing the well for the castlers and then, somehow, they were headed for Ankoor again, perplexed to find themselves running late for their arrival at Western Port Fair.

The Castle of Torm fell that night.

'Your prize lies bare, my Lord,' said the soulbinder. 'You may take it now.'

'I may take it, yes,' said Toombs uneasily, 'but will I manage to keep it?'

'That,' said the soulbinder, 'depends on you.'

'It depends on my son,' said Toombs.

'Then maybe I should take the lad in hand ...' She twisted her ring, stroking the clawed setting. 'I shall be living here, and you may be sure I will be his advisor.'

Lord Sheels was even more mystified at the sudden collapse of Torm. He did, however, remember the rules of conquest. 'If Merrit is dead,' he said to Toombs, 'we must secure the girl.'

'Of course,' said Toombs, 'but remember this: she is *not* to be harmed.'

'She must swear loyalty to us before witnesses,' said Sheels. 'The High Traders are of a suitable rank to record her oath, and it will be good if they hear her swear to us of her own free will.'

Toombs nodded, noting that Sheels must share his unease about the High Traders. Unfortunately, Walton and Templeton had left the camp some hours before, and Toombs did not care to publish the fact just now. 'We must give the Heir her chance to abandon any small claim she may have,' he agreed. 'After that, we must find her a suitable role.'

'Perhaps,' said Lord Sheels, 'she might serve my daughter Tegwen when she is Mistra of Torm? She must know a good deal about the ways of the castle, and she would be grateful to be allowed to stay in her old home.'

Toombs made no direct answer. He had never actually lied to Sheels. He had never *said* young Tegwen would be chosen as Scholar's Mistra.

'We must find the Heir,' he said, 'and take her oath at the best opportunity. It must be done formally and publicly, so there is no doubt. But first, we must occupy the castle.'

Once again, he and his partner prepared to formally annex Torm. This time, no porter rushed to bar the gate, and no-one yelled abuse. There was no reply to the formal challenge at all.

Disgruntled, Toombs ordered the soldiers to collect the castlers at a single point. 'I want every soul, living or not, brought to the wellyard and kept there for inspection.'

He beckoned to his reluctant son, noting with sour pleasure that it was true: the hound was not at the boy's heels. 'Come, Scholar,' he said, 'you and I will examine these sorry folk.'

'What are you going to do with them?' Scholar sounded bored, and his oddly hued eyes, which always angered Toombs, were sullen.

'Whatever has to be done.'

'Then you'd better call for my brother. He never minds wringing necks or slitting the throats of game.'

'*You* will come with me,' said Toombs. 'This is to be your home and your command. You must seem to assist in decisions.'

'I see.' Scholar regarded his own feet for a moment. 'And if I do not?'

'Then perhaps,' said Toombs from between clenched jaws, 'you will catch a blight, and Brown will become my heir. You are not my only son.'

Scholar brushed his braid away behind his shoulder. 'In that case I'd better come. I'll make an ill kind of Lord, but not as bad as Brown. By the way, who dies in the shackles and who gets slit today? I need to know whose face I should bother to remember.'

Toombs jerked his head for his son to follow. 'They'll be your serfs, so let them live, as far as I care. The only problem is Merrit, and he's probably dead already. As for his heir, the Blood of Torm . . .'

'I suppose she dies today?' said Scholar bleakly.

'Not at all,' said Toombs. 'I have plans for the Blood of Torm, and I need her alive and healthy. Find her and bring her to me.'

Scholar shrugged. 'There may be plenty of brats. How am I to know which one to fetch?'

'You will know her by her peculiar gilden skin, the mark of all the Tormbloods.' Toombs gave his son a sharp look. 'Brazen skin, mismatched eyes — together you'll have ugly children, but what can one expect?'

Scholar's eyes narrowed until they were nothing but jewel-bright slits in his pale face. 'So *that's* the plan. You want her as breeding stock, to make it look as if the Blood is still helming Torm. What about Tegwen Hasselsjo?'

'Nothing was promised to the Mistra Tegwen *or* to her father. Find the Blood of Torm and leave Hasselsjo to me.'

Scholar had loathed this mad campaign from the beginning, but now, for the first time, he was afraid for himself. So the brat who had taken Tace had been the Heir of Torm! His father would be furious when he found that the heir had fled and, if he ever discovered Scholar's part in her escape, he would have no mercy.

With apparent diligence, he set about searching the castle, appalled by what he found in every hall and corner. The castlers were half-starved, thinner even than the brat of the Blood had been. Their skin was dull and stretched too tightly on their bones. He had expected this, but he hadn't expected to find them deathly ill. Surely the blight-wards had been nothing but a ruse to keep passers-by away? It seemed the lie had come true, and blight had really settled in the castle.

Some of the folk he found had died already, while others were staggering about in delirium. Scholar stared in silent horror at the fair-haired porter, whose breathing came in fits and starts and then trailed into silence.

Above the sound of the search and the moans of the dying, he heard his father's voice, raised in disgust. 'What ails these people? Are they so weak that a moonspan of siege will have them dying in their droves?'

Scholar could not believe that, and besides, the brat had not been ill. And hadn't she said that only Torm's Lord was stricken? There was wickedness here, above his father's callous move to take over the castle. Had this mysterious blight anything to do with the empty cups that were scattered about?

He crouched beside a youth of around his own age, who was wearing the garb of a servingman. The coat was much too big, or rather, the lad had lost substance since it had been made. Scholar propped him up and spoke urgently. 'What happened here? How did this illness begin?'

The lad rolled his head to one side. He had fair skin, and his hair was done in the McAnerin manner. 'Merrit — is dead,' he gasped.

'I supposed he was,' said Scholar. 'But what is wrong with *you*, Master Server? Is there a healer who can help?'

'Hilz says ... the water must be ...' The boy's eyes widened, and he died.

Poison! Scholar was sickened. He doubted if his father or Lord Sheels had ordered this mass murder. Why should they? Indeed, how could they? Torm had been closed against them until a few hours ago. This had the soulbinder's touch about it.

And now Lord Toombs was storming up from the wellyard to grip Scholar painfully by the arm. 'Find that Heir! Dead, alive, whole, or in pieces! Find me that Heir and bring her to me — if you want to live.'

And so it was time to go. Scholar told himself he had known this would happen sometime. He had no wish to be Lord of Torm, and he certainly did not wish to find Torm's heir for Toombs. If his father learned he had let the heir go free ...

He hadn't known, then, that the brat from the castle was Allyso of Torm, but that would make no difference to Toombs.

Scholar sighed. He must find that brat and give her fair warning when he recovered Tace.

He slipped out of Torm, then set off for Zimmerhanzel, where he had left some cherished possessions. He never reached that castle, however, for the blight-wards were out in all their baleful scarlet.

The wineskin standard was gone from the gates and sentries stood on the walls. Above the tower there fluttered a white flag dyed with a familiar chequerboard pattern.

Scholar stared. His mouth went dry as things began to come clear. While his father and the garrison of Zimmerhanzel had been besieging Torm, someone else had come in and calmly taken over Zimmerhanzel. And from the look of that standard, the invaders were of the same blood as the army his father had led to Torm.

'The Tenth Castle!' said Scholar aloud. His stomach clenched with a fear that was wider and deeper than indignation at the annexation of his father's property. How many of these Tenth Castle folk were there, and how long had the second wave waited before taking over Zimmerhanzel?

Scholar walked smartly away, his neck prickling in expectation of an arrow. Tace would have howled a warning, but he did not need her counsel to know what would happen if the invaders caught him now. Scholar Ankooria, the new Lord of Torm! That was a joke. His life was worth nothing at all.

And so, what now? He really had two choices. He could turn his back and leave Zimmerhanzel to its fate. Or else he could hasten back to Torm to warn his father of this treacherous double-cross. But perhaps he should go to Hasselsjo first, to warn the castlers there to watch for similar trouble.

He tramped through the heavy meadowlands that separated the two castles. If the foreign soldiers had taken over Hasselsjo as well, he would *have* to return to Torm and warn his father and Sheels.

Scholar stared blindly at the rough, heathery ground. Warn his father and Sheels that they had been taken for stonewits by a flock of sleightmasters? Warn them that their greed had cost them their own holdings and probably the lives of their households? Warn them that the Tenth Castle seemed set to take over McAnerin bite by bite?

No. Scholar knew what happened to messengers who brought *that* kind of news to castle Lords. The kindest thing he could expect would be a broken jaw. No. It was done now, and his father and Sheels would find out soon enough. The best thing *he* could do was to tell the folk at Hasselsjo to raise its defences and send for its lord. And while it did so, he would slip away to find the elusive Heir of Torm.

CHAPTER TWELVE

TRADERS

WINTERWANE — 11TH MOON OF THE YEAR

OF THE HOUND

SIX days after her flight from Torm, Allyso limped into the outskirts of Fielding.

Gardeners were tending the plots inside the walls, and they took little notice of her approach. Fielding was a Trader village, so comings and goings were only to be expected.

'Where shall I find Trader Mohr?' she asked in what she hoped was a confident tone.

'Go along as you have been, lad,' said one of the gardeners. 'Mohr's house is the last before the well. And watch that hound of yours around his cat!'

Trader Mohr's house was rather like Mohr himself, tall and carelessly elegant. The windows were hung with fine flaxcloth and the door had a metal knocker in the shape of an arched cat. A faint plume of smoke wisped from the chimney, suggesting that Mohr was at home. Allyso rapped on the door, which was opened almost immediately. She had built so much on this encounter that she was shocked to discover that Mohr apparently failed to recognise her. He looked down rather distantly, and made a shooing movement with his hand.

'Trader Mohr, please —' Allyso found herself stammering, her knees shaking.

'No, thank you, my lad, I do not require an assistant.' Mohr's voice was not unkind, but it was very dismissive. He seemed surprised that she didn't leave at once.

'Trader Mohr!' she said again. 'Please don't send me away. I need your help!' She turned back the rim of her hood, letting the slanting Winterwane sunlight touch her face and hair.

Mohr stared, transfixed. '*Allyso?* Allyso of Torm?'

'Yes, but please, may I come in?'

Mohr glanced behind her. 'I never expected this. Is Lord Merrit with you?'

Tears rose behind Allyso's eyes, and she pressed her knuckles to her mouth, trying not to wail like a child.

Mohr's gaze sharpened. 'Where is Merrit?' he prompted.

'He is d-dying,' said Allyso. 'The s-soulbinder —' She swallowed and brought her voice back under control. 'That soulbinder brought down a curse. I am sorry to trouble you, Trader Mohr, but you and Trader Dagg are the only folk I can trust to believe what I have to say. And you *did* say you were at my service.'

'So I did.' Mohr sounded less than happy. 'Come through to the kitchen, Allyso. And bring the Spellhound, too. It seems a well-conducted creature.'

Allyso followed him into the house, sat down on one of the bluecloth couches he indicated, and rubbed her hands wearily over her cheeks. Then she realised what Trader Mohr had said. '*Spellhound*?'

Mohr contemplated Tace. 'That is an Ankoorian Spellhound. Didn't you know?'

She shook her head, bewildered. 'I had no idea. She belongs to one of the soldiers. He let me go and asked me to take her with me.' She looked down at Tace. 'But Gill says Spellhounds are copper-coloured.'

'Most of them are,' said Mohr. 'This one is a brindle outcross. That might make her less or more valuable, depending on whom you asked.' He stretched out his hand to Tace and smiled a little when the hound sniffed politely at his fingers. 'Soldiers, though? Where did you meet a soldier?'

Allyso's tears overflowed. 'I'm s-sorry —'

'You must be hungry if you have come alone from Torm,' said Mohr quickly. 'It is a long way.'

Allyso sniffed. 'We found sweetloaves and d-dragonpods.'

'You look half-starved, so you should eat before you tell me what's going on.' Mohr tore a piece from a loaf, then dipped broth from a cauldron that simmered by the fire and poured it into two bowls. 'There's a pump just out the back if you want to wash while it cools. I won't be long.'

'Where are you going? I need to ask you things … You won't tell anyone I'm here … ?'

'*Tell* anyone?'

'The s-soldiers. The Lords of Zimmerhanzel and Hasselsjo —'

'What have they to say to anything?' Mohr sounded perplexed. 'I'm going to fetch Dagg.'

'All right, but please don't tell anyone else I'm here.'

'Trust me, I won't.' Mohr slung on a mantle and departed, stopping only to dip one shoulder for his cat.

Allyso tried not to think about betrayal after Mohr had gone. Mohr was Merrit's friend and had often enjoyed the hospitality of Torm. Yes, but the soulbinder, too, had enjoyed that hospitality ...

She bit a dark-rimmed fingernail, then looked down at her grimy hands. She was very hungry, but the Heir of Torm must show some dignity. Arriving in such a bedraggled state and begging the Traders for help was bad enough; the least she could do was to clean herself up and try to make a sensible tale of it.

'What do you think?' she asked Tace. 'If you are really a Spellhound, you should be able to warn me if Trader Mohr means harm. You seem to like him, so I suppose he really *is* a friend.'

In the walled courtyard, Allyso tossed aside her mantle, and sluiced herself and Tace under the pump. She used a piece of hard soap to wash her hair and clothing, then peeled off the wet tunic and leggings and bundled her shivering self back into the mantle. It felt good to be clean again, but she couldn't help thinking wistfully of the hot herbal tubs she used to enjoy at Torm.

She hung the garments over a clothbush, then went to shake out her hair before the fire. Drops of water hissed on the hearthstone, and she took a cloth from the chest beside the door. Trader Mohr had *said* he was at her service.

She bundled her hair in the cloth and fastened the mantle firmly across her chest. It was much too loose since she had lost so much weight in the siege.

The broth was cool, so she set one bowl down for Tace, dipped a crust into the second and ate hungrily.

Mohr was troubled as he made his way to Dagg's cottage. This news of Merrit's illness was shocking, for the Lord of Torm was a good friend to the Traders of Fielding. Mohr did wish, however, that Merrit's heir had not decided to come to *him*. It did his reputation no good to have distressed girl-children seeking him out.

'Stars save us!' he said to his clinging cat. 'Whatever possessed me to offer my service to a child? And how does she imagine *I* can help to lift a curse? She'd have done better to apply to Mistra Gill in the castle, or to that Healer Hilz. And what were they about to let her come alone?'

He rapped on Dagg's door and quickly, softly, stated his business.

'Mistra Allyso of Torm?' Dagg's voice went up in surprise. 'Are you sure?'

'Sure as I stand before you,' said Mohr glumly. 'I doubted my eyes until she put back her hood.'

'That gilden skin is unmistakable,' agreed Dagg. 'I never saw it in anyone except the Blood of Torm. But what does she want? Where is Lord Merrit?'

'She says he's dying of a curse, and begs our help,' said Mohr.

'*Dying of a curse!*'

'I trust she exaggerates. You know how children make the worst of things. But there's certainly *something* amiss. She looks half-starved.'

Dagg's wife came in and nodded a wary greeting.

'Good day to you, Mistra Bay . . .'

'Master Mohr.' She inclined her head.

'Come on, Dagg,' said Mohr hurriedly. 'The sample I told you about is at my house, and the sooner you come to see it, the sooner you'll be back for your supper.'

'Dying of a curse!' said Dagg again as the door closed behind them.

'I do trust not,' said Mohr. 'But matters must be bad, or Merrit would never have let her come. Unless the foolish child has run away on a whim?'

'Surely not . . .'

'Who knows what a child might do?'

When they reached Mohr's house, the Heir to Torm was huddled in her mantle before the fire. Her hair was steaming damply, and her face and hands were clean. Her eyes were reddened, her face was drawn and she looked very, very young. The Spellhound lay beside her, a well-polished bowl between its paws.

A good thing it had eaten his offering, thought Mohr. If the Spellhound had been unfriendly, there might have been ill-luck in this meeting.

'Mistra Allyso!' Dagg held out his hands to the girl in formal greeting. 'Mohr tells me it goes ill with Lord Merrit.'

'It does, Trader Dagg. It could not be w-worse.'

'Tell us from the beginning,' said Mohr. 'And then we will see what, if anything, we can do to help.' He sat on the other side of the hearth, and his cat slithered down his shoulder, like a furry waterfall, to settle in his lap.

The tale the girl told was brief and unhappy and her situation much worse than he had hoped. The soulbinder's curse was bad enough, but how had this siege come about? And why had the news not travelled south by now? And what, if anything, had it to do with the Tenth Castle of Ankoor?

'The soldier tried to tell me there was blight in the castle,' she said. 'That was before he knew I'd come from there. They've put the blight-wards out.'

'Then that explains why few folk ventured near,' said Dagg.

'I knew that dame meant trouble,' said Mohr when the tale was done. 'I tried to warn Merrit not to let her stay — I *did* —' He glanced at Dagg for support.

'I know you did, Trader Mohr,' said the girl. 'You *did* warn Merrit, but he would not be warned. And now he is paying the p-price. And so is Torm. It's too much. *None* of us deserved this!'

She rubbed the back of her hand over her eyes, and Mohr thanked the stars he and Dagg had left the doomed castle so quickly. If a strong man like Merrit of Torm could be struck by a spellbinder's curse, what chance had two young traders?

'Perhaps it is not as grave as it seems,' said Dagg. 'Lord Merrit is not easily struck down. Besides, this dame wishes to teach him a lesson, and how can a man learn lessons if he is dead?'

'There was no lesson to be learned, except that he should not have been so generous,' snapped Allyso. 'It was nothing but spite and wickedness that made her turn on him. He gave her shelter, but she wanted more and more and she turned the castlers against one another. She is a destroyer.'

Mohr sighed. 'She may be right,' he said to Dagg.

'And even if he *doesn't* die, the Lords of Zimmerhanzel and Hasselsjo have stolen Torm by now,' said Allyso miserably. 'We were starving when I left — Merrit said the castle was sure to fall. So did Scholar, the soldier who gave me Tace.'

'You accepted a gift from a *soldier*?' said Dagg. 'Is he not one of those besieging Torm?'

'He wanted Tace away from that soulbinder. He would have handed me over to Lord Toombs if I'd refused.' She sighed. 'If she really is a Spellhound, she would have hated that dame.'

'This hound is his ears and eyes — she hears and sees whatever you do.'

'Nonsense!' said the girl and, for a moment, she looked a lot like Merrit. 'Tace is my friend. I keep her safe, and she has found food for both of us. And how can a hound be a spy? She cannot speak, so she cannot carry tales. That Scholar did me a very good turn, whether he meant it or not.'

Mohr cleared his throat. 'Perhaps Merrit will win back Torm when he recovers. There are many fine tales of folk who have fought and won against great evils, and someone will be suspicious if the blight-wards stand too long.'

'Fine tales are no good in a disaster like this,' said Dagg. 'Mistra Allyso needs shelter, not tales. My Mistra and I will take her in until her kin can be found.'

'I have no kin,' said the girl. 'No-one at all but Merrit. We are the Blood of Torm, all that is left.' She stared bleakly into the fire, and Mohr saw the flames reflected in her strange, amber eyes before she looked up again. 'Have you really heard nothing about the siege from anyone else? Or even a rumour about the blight? That is hard to believe.'

'Not a whisper,' said Dagg, 'though now I think of it, there *have* been fewer folk coming down from the North.'

'Fewer? I'd say there has been none at all,' said Mohr. 'If I had bothered to think, I would have said that Winterwane was keeping folk at home.' He wished he could still think that. 'There was no reason for us to know,' he added. 'Apart from our trading forays, Northern McAnerin is little to do with us.'

'The soldiers captured the High Traders, Walton and Templeton,' said the girl coldly. 'Is *that* little to do with you? It might have been you, Trader Mohr.'

'So it might, if we had not the sense to leave Torm when that dame was let in.'

Mohr thought, but did not say, that there was an obvious reason that there had been no general outcry. Since the Blood of Torm was brought so low it could make little difference to the local folk if Torm passed into other hands. They might even be glad. No-one could depend on a castle guided by a dying lord or a child.

Dagg was leaning forward to interrupt, so Mohr forestalled him. 'It is nothing directly to do with us, but we will help. I said I was at your service, and I will stand by that.'

'So will I!' said Dagg.

'We will certainly do what we can for *you*,' continued Mohr, 'but there is nothing we can do for Merrit *or* for our brother Traders. It would take an army to overthrow these lords, and Traders are never warriors.'

'We are not soldiers,' agreed Dagg, 'but we shall spread the word of Torm's peril wherever we go. We will tell them the blight is a lie.'

'What good will that do?' asked Allyso. 'Will folk from the villages rally to help us? The soldiers are mostly foreign, but Lords Toombs and Sheels are both McAnerinian.'

'No,' admitted Dagg, 'they won't rally. But if all Traders shun Torm, the army will lack supplies. They will have to leave before they starve.'

'The castlers will starve first! There is nothing left, I tell you.' She twisted her hands in the front of her mantle, and Mohr noticed how thin they were. 'Torm must have fallen by now,' she added. 'I came as quickly as I could, but we have been days on the road.'

'We cannot help them,' said Dagg with obvious regret. 'We can help you, though, Mistra Allyso. We will be honoured if you make your home in Fielding. It is a good village, and the folk will welcome you.'

Mohr could not bring himself to echo Dagg's words. Allyso of Torm was no orphan wench to be adopted into a kindly home. She was an Heir of the Blood, and too many folk would recognise her and wonder why she had come to Fielding. He could not imagine why she had not been captured along the way.

'How, exactly, did you escape the castle?' he asked. 'You didn't tell us that.'

'I — I just slipped out, Trader Mohr. I am small and no-one noticed me.'

'You slipped out?' he said suspiciously. 'Through the gate? Over the wall?'

She shook her head, and her gaze flickered back to the fire.

'Is there a passage, perhaps?' prompted Mohr, stroking his cat. 'If so, we might take food into the castle by night.'

'There is no hope of that,' she said firmly. 'It was kind of you both to offer me a home, but what I came for is information.'

He could not imagine what she wanted of them, but he nodded anyway.

The girl leaned forward, her bright hair gleaming in the firelight. 'I need to find the gem of time.'

Mohr felt his mouth drop open. 'You might as well ask for a shooting star!'

'You promised to tell me the tale of the gems of power.'

'So I did,' said Mohr. 'It is one of my most popular tales — and one of the most elusive. The gems of power are jewels as old as McAnerin, brought to this land from the mists of the beginning.' He saw the girl make an impatient movement and hurried on, paraphrasing the bardic language of the tale. 'They were put in the care of a keeper but, from time to time, one of them is found. If its nature is recognised, it will perform marvels, but the gems are elusive and dangerous.'

'And one is the gem of time,' said the girl.

'The gem of time is that which gives mastery over the years that were and are to come,' said Mohr, falling back into the well-known pattern, 'while the gem of truth is that which is always held by a seer who is the strongest in the land. The gem of portals is that which leads to unexpected places, and the gem of dreams is that which points the mind towards what one desires. The gem of ways is that which will sketch the way, and the gem of mist is that which is housed in the hilt of a weapon.

'There are also gems of lesser virtue that enhance the lustre of the one who finds and wears them.'

'Where can I find the gem of time?' asked the girl.

'That I cannot say,' said Mohr regretfully. 'We are Traders, Dagg and I, not conners or seers.' He stroked Greyson, and the cat purred. 'You might ask Wootton for information. He is the Seer of Conners' Hall.'

'I have never heard of that.'

'Why should you?' put in Dagg. 'Conners' Hall has been empty since my father's father's time. It was a great seat of learning, but too many of the conners took up wicked ways and so the place was disbanded. It is said they conjured a wraith, which was forbidden.'

'Then what is the use of telling me about this seer if he isn't there now?'

'Wootton will be there,' said Mohr. 'He is always there.'

'How shall I find him?'

Mohr hesitated. Although he had passed the way to Conners' Hall at times, he had never consulted the seer himself. Few folk did, most preferring to live in ignorance of what might be in store rather than pay the price for Wootton's information. The greater the request, the higher the price, and some of the tales of those prices made Mohr shudder. What would he ask for the gem of time?

'Wootton might have the information,' he said slowly, 'but he is a dangerous man.'

'Better if you stay here, Mistra Allyso,' put in Dagg. 'Mohr is right. It isn't safe for you to be ranging around McAnerin alone, and you cannot visit the seer without protection.'

Mohr caught his friend's anxious gaze and gave his head a slight, warning shake. 'Neither is it safe for the Heir of Torm to stay in Fielding,' he said pointedly.

The girl was staring at him with unblinking amber eyes. With the Spellhound at her feet and her gilded skin glowing in the firelight, she looked unchancy enough. Small and slight, but not so childlike any more. And she wasn't a child in the strict sense. It had been some time since that last meeting at Torm, and she must be around fourteen.

'I cannot stay,' she said. 'I promised Merrit I'd do my best to find the gem of time. It's better if you set me on my way and ask other Traders to stay away from Torm.'

'What of your father's folk?' put in Dagg. 'Can they not help you?'

She shrugged. 'I have no idea who my father is, or even if he's still alive. Merrit says he doesn't know, and my mother never told. But look at me! I'm Torm Blood, through and through, no matter who my father might have been.'

'And it seems you share Torm's destiny.' Mohr made up his mind. 'I can direct you to Seer Wootton.'

'Is it far?'

'Not far. Two days to the stonewood forest, by the most direct route. You might also take the longer way and overnight in Musson to break the journey.'

'I need the quickest way.'

'Then you will need strong legs and lungs,' said Mohr, 'and after you reach the forest, you will need to find Wootton's cave.'

'The seer lives in a *cave*?' She sounded startled.

'It is easier to live in a cave than to build a house of stonewood,' observed Mohr. Using charcoal, he drew a sketch on the hearthstone. 'We follow the road from Fielding, until we reach the Conners' Wayside

Fountain. We could take the main way to Musson, and walk around the hills, or strike off from the fountain, go over the plain to the Singing Tor, and then to the forest by way of the Conners' Pass. It was a well-trodden route once, but not these days.' He paused, wondering how much more he should say.

'Those hills ...' began Dagg, but Mohr held up his hand.

'You should see the stonewood forest from the top of the hills.'

'We shall, of course, escort you there,' said Dagg. 'It is no place for a young Mistra to be alone.'

The girl was staring at the sketch. 'Thank you, Traders, you have been very kind,' she said, then yawned abruptly. 'I am very tired now. I've been keeping time with the sun.'

'I have spare blankets and an extra bolster to make you a bed,' said Mohr, 'or would you prefer to go to Dagg's house? His Mistra is at home and she will make you welcome.'

'I will stay here if you don't mind,' she said, and yawned again.

Mohr fetched the spare bedding, then left his guest to settle while he walked home with Dagg.

'It is cruel to take her to Wootton,' said Dagg reproachfully. 'If he helps her at all, he'll ask a terrible price.'

'I *know* that!' snapped Mohr. 'But she's paying a price already, poor child. The price of Merrit's arrogance.'

'We should shelter her.'

'And bring down these lords on our own heads? They'll be searching for her soon — if not already. If she looked like a Fielding girl, we could pass her off as a foundling or apprentice, but she is *Torm*. Torm Blood through and through, as she pointed out herself.'

'She is a *child*!' said Dagg.

'She will have to grow up very quickly if she is going to survive.' Mohr sighed. 'She has made up her own mind, anyway. She knows she cannot stay with us, for any of our sakes. And besides, she has the Spellhound with her. If there is any great danger from Wootton, the hound will warn her away.'

CHAPTER THIRTEEN

LEONARD

⧗

WINTERWANE — 11TH MOON OF THE YEAR

OF THE HOIUND

ALLYSO knew that Mohr was reluctant, and she saw she was putting the Traders in a difficult position. Merrit had brought down Torm with a piece of misjudgement. His heir did not want to risk doing the same thing to Fielding.

'I'll explain to Trader Mohr,' she said to Tace. The blanket and bolster seemed luxurious after her nights on the trail. 'He will understand. Trader Dagg is too gentle-hearted to listen.'

Mohr came in some time later, walked soft-footed to the fire and turved it over for the night. He set down a bundle that Allyso recognised dimly as her tunic and leggings, which he must have fetched from the clothbush. Then he set some food on the table before moving off to his own sleeping chamber.

Allyso would have thanked him again, but was too weary to form the words.

She woke, as she had on the road, at sunlift. The first fingers of light were gilding the roofs of Fielding, and the peace was immense. Tace stirred and yawned widely. Mohr's cat purred from his hassock by the fire, and Allyso got up. She pushed her hair away from her face, then crept out to the pump, followed by the hound. There was still no sound from Mohr, so she put on her tunic and leggings and ate some bread from the crock.

There were two journey-packs on the table. Obviously, Mohr was planning to escort her to the seer today. That was kind of him, but Allyso thought it better to leave right now. She knew the route, and she had Tace for company. If Mohr came with her he would be in charge, and she felt in her bones that this quest must be her own.

She looked around the kitchen in the growing light. It was tempting to stay, but time was moving on.

She put on her mantle, then crouched to check the route Mohr had sketched on the hearthstone. He had left a tinderflint and a tablet and stylus by the packs, so she copied the route and slipped it into one of the packs before cleaning the hearth with a cloth. She left no message for the Traders. It seemed doubtful that anyone would look for her here but, if they did, they would find no trace of her intentions and nothing to suggest the Traders had sheltered her. Taking the pack, she tugged on her boots and stepped out into the morning.

Fielding was still asleep as Allyso and Tace walked back along the street to the gardens inside the walls. The porter did not object to her departure. 'Go through the small postern, lad,' he called softly. 'It is too early to open the main entrance.'

Allyso lifted her hand in acknowledgement and passed through the lower gate.

The road was straight at first, and several travellers passed her by, but as the South McAnerin Downs began to rise, the way became confused. Routes split off to the west and northeast, carrying travellers with them, but Allyso kept on the main way. Two days to the stonewood forest, and she was not to turn off until she came to the wayside fountain ...

'We should have asked what it looked like,' she said to Tace but, when they reached it just after sunhigh, she had no doubt it was the one she needed.

The fountain was made of soft, pitted stone. Deep grooves were worn in the rim, but the water trickled sweetly out and ran away in a narrow stream. The base of the fountain was carved all over with lines of prose and scraps of verse. Some were so weathered she could barely see them, some had others carved on top, crisscrossing in a chaotic fashion. Allyso tried to read them, but most were in foreign languages.

'The Conners' Fountain,' she read. That writing was older than most of the rest, but it had been carved by a master's hand. She drank from the fountain and filled her flask, hoping it would bring her luck. Then she watched as Tace lapped from the flowing stream. All seemed peaceful, but suddenly Tace lifted her head. To Allyso's astonishment, the hound's muzzle wrinkled and she snarled.

'Tace, what is it? Is someone coming?'

Allyso looked about, knowing the hound could not answer and might not even understand. Tace was snuffing the air, lifting her hackles and growling all the while.

'What is it?' asked Allyso again, but there was nothing and no-one. 'We'd better strike off across the plain,' she decided. She swung on her heels, squinting through the dazzling morning light. 'The Singing Tor must be *that* way.'

She shouldered her pack, and set off briskly, accompanied by Tace. It occurred to her that she might be taking the hound into danger, but the thought of being alone was too dreadful. While the Spellhound kept pace, she felt comforted, even though Tace still grumbled in her throat.

'If something is following, we'd better hurry,' said Allyso.

The plain seemed endless but, before the day was over, she was climbing a rough path into the foothills. She glanced at the sky, at the slanted evening light.

'Nearly sunfall, Tace, so we must find some place to sleep.'

She felt weary and grubby, as if the comfortable night spent at Trader Mohr's had been nothing but a wayfaring dream. Too tired to climb any more, she spent the last light in finding a fold in the hills that sheltered a few low bushes. She patted the ground, removing stones and pieces of twig. Then she shared some food with Tace, rolled them in her mantle and went to sleep.

Both of them had nightmares. Allyso woke too often, shivering, to find the Spellhound yelping in her sleep. Oddly, she did not dream of the siege, nor of Merrit's illness. Instead, she was confused by a babble of talk, of criss-crossing conversation, voices raised and stilled. The very hill seemed to murmur when she pillowed her head on the turf, and she could find no way to settle. Before sunlift smeared the sky, she had given up and was setting off again.

'We might reach the top by the time it's light,' she told Tace hopefully.

The Spellhound seemed uneasy, stopping now and again to peer back the way they had come.

The hills were still murmuring as they climbed, and their peculiar structure of dimpled hollows and shallow grooves and folds became more evident. At first the darkness made it difficult to see where hollow began and shadow ended and, even as the sun began to lift, the mist came down.

Allyso climbed on through the weird blindness of mist. She hoped they were on the right trail. Mohr had drawn the route, but it looked different in reality.

The mist was cold on her cheeks, and she heard Tace lapping at the wet vegetation when they paused. It was too high for bitterstem, but there were dense curled cresses here and there. Allyso picked some and chewed them as she climbed. Their hot taste gave her something to think about besides her fear and her frozen feet.

There was no dramatic moment when the mist lifted or the top of the hills was reached, but soon she realised she was on a faintly-marked path.

'I suppose the conners came this way,' she said to Tace. 'I wonder what wraith they summoned, and why they would do such a thing? I should have asked Trader Dagg.'

She thought the Conners, whatever they had done, could not have been worse than Lord Toombs and Lord Sheels, and nothing so wicked as the soulbinder.

'*They* should have been disbanded,' she said, then wondered who could have made the decision to disband an army and a malevolent dame. Who, for that matter, had decided to disband the conners? She had known a great deal about how Torm was to be run, but what of the rest of McAnerin?

The way began to tilt downwards, and Allyso stopped and peered through the remaining scarves of mist. There were dark shapes clustered below, right at the hillfoot; could that be the start of the stonewood forest?

'It doesn't look very big,' she said but, a thousand paces on, she discovered that the height of the hills had deceived her. What had looked like squat green bushes was really masses of foliage supported on tall, stout pillar-like trunks. The trees were stonewoods all right, much more plentiful and more massive than those in the grove outside the walls of Torm. This forest was so thick that, as Allyso and Tace trudged down the slope and into its outskirts, night seemed to fall all over again.

Allyso sighed. Mohr had not said how she could find the seer, only that he lived in a cave. And where, for that matter, lay the ruins of Conners' Hall?

'Trader Mohr might have explained better if he'd known we were coming alone, but then he would have made sure we didn't get the chance,' she said to Tace. 'Can *you* find a hidden entrance? You sniffed out those sweetloaves.'

She was sure the seer's cave would be well-concealed; otherwise, he'd be constantly disturbed. She was still musing on this when Tace stopped, stiffened and gave an urgent yelp.

'Tace?' The Spellhound flicked an ear. Hackles rose from her shoulders, and Allyso's own neck prickled in response. 'Hello?' Her voice sounded reedy, and she licked her lips and tried again. 'Master Wootton?'

Swift as a spider, a figure stepped out of the shadows. It was tall and thin, muffled in a hood and a cloak.

'Who are you? Why do you want Wootton?' The voice was husky, the accent harsh and strange.

'M-master Wootton?'

'Wootton is busy. Who are you and where have you come from?'

Allyso glanced at Tace. The Spellhound was still alert, but her hackles had smoothed away. Did that mean this person offered no immediate threat? She had not come so far to walk straight into a trap. 'I have to consult the seer,' she said. 'I came over the Conners' Pass.'

'I told you, Wootton is busy.'

Allyso was recovering her nerve. No matter how eerie this person looked, the manner reminded her of Berneathy's when he was feeling obstructive.

'I don't mean any harm,' she said. 'I am looking for something important and Trader — and some acquaintances said I should consult the seer.'

'They give dangerous advice, these acquaintances of yours.' A slight shift of the cloak's outline suggested that whoever was inside it had folded its arms, tilted its chin and was waiting for her response.

Allyso gathered her dignity. She had watched Merrit do it often enough, though she had never before had to do it herself. 'I do not have time for this! I need to find the seer, and quickly!'

'Not,' said the figure triumphantly, 'until you give your name and tell me what you want.'

Allyso thrust back her hood. 'Who do you *think* I am?'

Silence. But the figure seemed to be staring.

'What?' demanded Allyso.

'Your skin — it's *gold*.'

'So?'

'I never saw that before.'

And he never would again, if she couldn't make this work. 'Never mind my face,' she said. 'It has nothing to do with you.'

'But you're just a kid — a child.'

She sighed. 'I am nearly fourteen, Master Hood. Show me your face. It's only fair. You've stared enough at me.'

'No-one sees the face of the Hooded One.'

'Then take me to the seer.'

'Who are you? *What* are you?'

Exasperation was boiling up in her, but she tried to sound calm. It would not be clever to let him know how desperate she was. 'I am a girl. Allyso.'

'Allyso of where?'

'Allyso of Nowhere,' she said with bitter truth. She didn't belong to Torm any more and never would again, unless she could complete this quest. 'What's *your* name?' she added, 'and where are you from?'

'Leonard. And I live — lived at Connishall. Now I live here with Wootton.'

'Nonsense,' she said. 'Conners' Hall is in ruins.'

'Suit yourself.'

'You know who I am and what I need, so take me to the seer!'

'No,' said Leonard. 'It can't be that important.'

'Stars that be!' Anger warmed her face. 'How would you know?'

'I know enough to say that things you think are important now won't matter a damn tomorrow. Save your breath for something that *does*.'

'This matters,' she said. 'I am trying to make sure my friends and I *have* a tomorrow.'

'That bad?'

She lifted her chin, expecting more argument, but Leonard seemed convinced.

'Come on.' He jerked his head to indicate that she should follow, and Allyso stared at him for a heartbeat of confusion. 'Never say you weren't warned,' he added. 'And leave the dog here.'

'The *dog?*'

'The hound,' he said impatiently.

'I can't leave Tace. She isn't an ordinary hound —'

'She's a Spellhound, right? Spellhounds warn of danger and she was sent to keep you safe. I can see that much, Allyso of Nowhere.'

'Then she comes with me.'

'No she doesn't. The point is, she *can't* keep you safe. Not here. Are you going to take notice of her warning and go back the way you came?'

'I can't.'

'Then don't let her come any farther.'

'I can't leave Tace.'

'Then go back over the Conners' Pass.' He sounded angry now. 'I mean it, Allyso of Nowhere. I like dogs — hounds — and I don't like seeing them upset for no reason. It isn't fair to them.'

'Stars that be!' exclaimed Allyso, exasperated. 'What happens if I leave her?'

'She'll be safe enough.' Leonard stretched black-sheathed hands to Tace. 'There now,' he said, in a softer voice. 'You are a good hound. A pity your owner isn't so sensible.' He moved his hands above the Spellhound's head, the long sleeves of the garment whirling in a complicated pattern. His voice dropped still more to a sibilant whisper, and he suddenly clapped his hands.

Tace whined, seemed to strain against invisible forces, then collapsed and slept.

'You cursed her!'

'I did not. It was a mazing charm, that's all. And I did it to keep her safe and contented while you were gone. Take off your coat.'

Allyso stared.

'I mean your mantle, you stupid girl! If you cover the hound with your mantle, she'll think you're with her and have good dreams.'

Allyso did as he said. 'Now what?'

'Now I'll take you to the seer and hope you don't regret it.'

CHAPTER FOURTEEN

SEER

WINTERWANE — 11TH MOON OF THE YEAR

OF THE HOUND

LEONARD was not a comforting guide. He moved in a brisk, angry fashion among the trees. Allyso found herself panting as she tried to keep up. Questions swarmed. How had he known she was coming? Why did he not show his face? Would Tace wake up when she returned or had Leonard lied?

All these questions buzzed in her mind, but she knew they wouldn't be answered. And they were nothing beside the others.

Why was it such a terrible thing to visit this seer? What would he do to her? Dagg had said she should have protection; she had thought that was Dagg's usual caution, but perhaps he had meant magical protection. If Leonard could maze a Spellhound so easily, what might his master do?

She closed her mind to speculations and tried, instead, to avoid tripping over the roots of the stonewood trees.

'You move too fast. I can't keep up.'

'Then go back,' returned Leonard.

'How did *you* come to be here?'

There was a pause, and she thought he wouldn't answer, but then he said flatly, 'I was living at Connishall. I opened a door that had been bricked up and ended up here. I couldn't find my way back, so Wootton took me in.'

'That was kind of him,' said Allyso.

'Wootton is never kind,' said Leonard. 'Don't make that mistake. He never helps anyone without a good reason. His good reason, not theirs. Are you quite certain you want to see him?'

'I *must* see him,' said Allyso. 'And why are you trying to scare me away?'

'I am trying to warn you. If you have any other options, use them! Wootton won't go easy on you just because you're a kid.'

Allyso felt her heart trying to jump into her throat. She remembered Tace's warning. But there were other things to remember, beyond her own fears and her own skin. There was Merrit, and there was Torm. There were her friends: Gregory and Gill, Berneathy and even Healer Hilz. How could she let them down?

'I *must* talk to the seer,' she said again.

'Right.' Leonard pointed at a cleft in the rock. 'Go down the steps. There's a lamp at the foot; light it with the tinderthing. Take a tunic out of the coffer. Take off all your own things, and I mean *everything*. Every stitch, boots and all, hair ribbon, anklet, chains or beads or whatever you've got on. Put on a tunic, take the lamp and then start walking.'

'But where do I find the seer?'

'He'll find you.'

With a last doubtful glance at his dark-cowled figure, Allyso turned to the cleft. Its darkness was not encouraging, but at least it wasn't underwater. After her nightmare journey through the well-way, this should be a morning stroll.

It was cold inside the cleft. The steps felt like rock, but were so irregular that Allyso suspected they were really stonewood roots. Cautiously, she felt her way down. It was slow, but she could not risk falling.

At the foot of the stair she found the lamp on a knee-high shelf, its tinderflint beside it. Her hands were shaking, but she struck the flint, watched the flame climb the lamp's wick and settle to a steady glow.

And then she looked around her.

She had expected a low, dark cavern, perhaps with an earthy floor or dripping walls. Instead, she saw no walls at all, but just the vastness of a twilit place broken by irregular pillars of stone.

It took a few breaths to realise what she was seeing. The cleft had led her under the stonewood forest, and here, by some freak, the trees grew up through air and rock, then plunged through the crust above.

The trunks were closely but unevenly spaced, giving the effect of winding avenues. Allyso gazed in silent wonder for a while, then remembered she was supposed to be looking for a coffer. She was used to the tall coffers of Torm, so it took her a while to realise that the low bench was also a storage chest, packed with folded tunics. She took one out, pulling a face at the limpness of the stuff. Gill would have boiled it in grainstarch to cure that.

She shook out another, but they were all much the

same. Some bigger, some small, all white and limp and probably unbecoming.

The chill of the caverns raised gooseflesh on her arms. She wondered if she could put the tunic on top of her own, but she supposed Leonard's instructions had had a purpose. She wanted a favour from the seer, and it wouldn't do to begin by flouting his orders.

She chose the most likely tunic and peeled off her own, laying it carefully in the coffer. Shivering, she put on the new one and tugged it into place, lifting her hair free of the collar. The skimpy garment left her arms bare to the shoulder and barely reached her knees. She removed her boots and leggings, then felt for a sash or belt, but there was nothing.

The ground felt cool to her bare feet, slightly soapy like candlestone, but she couldn't stand there forever. She was supposed to start walking.

'The seer will find you,' Leonard had said. Did that mean the seer was looking for her, or was she expected to signal?

She took a few steps in a random direction, frowned and shook her head. There was a strange humming in her ears, a singing just beyond the comfortable range of hearing. She backed away, but the sound was moving with her.

'What *is* that?' She was so in the habit of speaking to Tace that she didn't expect an answer, but she got one of sorts as the ringing grew louder and focused in front of her.

The lamp? Allyso put it down, then hesitated, staring at the glowing thing at her feet. She certainly needed light if she were to prowl through this labyrinth of stonewood.

Merrit had scoffed so often at the idea of spells and charms. 'They make some folk feel safe, and put fear into others,' he had told Allyso. 'The strong and the certain have no need of them, and the foolish would be better off to trust in something real.'

Merrit was wrong. What was a curse but a spell or a charm gone bad? The soulbinder's curse had opened Allyso's eyes to the truth, and Leonard's mazing of Tace had proved again that charms were as real as knives. This lamp seemed to be charmed in some way, but was it for good or evil?

'Danger,' Leonard had warned, and so had Dagg and Mohr. Tace had tried to persuade her away from this place.

To stay here was impossible, to go back was to swallow defeat. Allyso sighed and picked up the humming lamp.

Her footfalls were silent; there seemed no stirring in the air. The stonewood pillars dwarfed her, and she had to make so many detours she lost her sense of direction.

'Leonard?' The waves of her voice set the lamp to ringing louder, and she fancied she could see a rim of sound to echo the rim of light.

There was water running somewhere, and she was thirsty. The lamp seemed light on oil. What if it went out? And it was *so* cold. She should have listened to Leonard, to Tace, to Dagg and Mohr. She was as bad as Merrit. She never *listened* to sensible advice!

Allyso felt her courage fading to rashness, and then to the miserable feeling that she was served quite right. How could a skinny girl of her years complete a difficult, dangerous quest? It was probably nothing but starshine, dangerous dreaming lies ... The gem of time was only a hearthside tale.

The lamp went out, the singing died away. The silence pressed against her ears and the dark against her eyes.

And then she saw a glimmer in the distance. She made her way towards it and found another humming lamp. This one rested on a stone outcrop higher than her head. She would never be able to reach it but, far away beyond, she could see the pinpoint gleam of another.

Stumbling, almost sobbing with fear that the lights would go out before she reached them, she hurried from lamp to lamp, each a single link in a fragile chain of light. If one went out, she would see only one other, which might be far ahead or far behind, so she ran until her feet ached and her knees were bruised from falling.

And then, so far ahead that she thought her eyes deceived her, someone struck a light from a tinderflint. It was not Leonard, but a taller person, wearing grey. She increased her speed, trusting her feet to follow the safest path. She thought the kindler would move on before she reached him, but he must have heard her panting breath, even above the hum of the lamp he was tending. He turned to watch her approach.

'There you are, Allyso.'

It might have been Merrit welcoming her home from a foray to the village, or Gill explaining that supper was almost ready when she visited the kitchen. Except that Merrit and Gill would never have worn a cloak and cowl of grey.

'Please — are you Seer Wootton?'

'My name is Wootton, yes.'

'I need the gem of time.'

She knew, as she blurted it out, that she should have asked politely, but she was panting and shivering from running in the chill. Sweat ran down her sides, unimpeded by any belt, and she was feeling most unwell.

The seer adjusted the wick of the lamp. 'That is a large request, Allyso of Nowhere.'

If he had addressed her by her real title, she would not have been surprised. Instead, he had used the name she had given Leonard. And *that* meant Leonard had made a report on her. Which made her very angry.

'I *need* it,' she said, and almost stamped her foot.

He began to walk away, apparently to light the next in the series of lamps. 'You need to save your tomorrow, Allyso?'

'Yes!' She followed anxiously, keeping her gaze on the gleam of his grey robe. 'The gem could put things back the way they are meant to be.'

'And what way is that?'

'Merrit should be well, and he should be Lord of Torm! He's a good lord, the best, and it isn't *right* that we should lose everything because of one mistake!'

Wootton lit another lamp, then tucked the tinderflint away in his pouch. 'Come to the candle iron chamber,' he said. 'That is the proper place to deal with you.'

'Isn't this your cavern?' She glanced around at the vastness of the chamber.

'This is the Conners' Hall — all that is left of it. I live in a warmer place.'

Allyso's feet were numb and her teeth were

chattering now. A warmer place sounded good. She followed Wootton to an unobtrusive door, and through to a small cave, hewn from the same soft rock that formed the Singing Tor.

She screwed up her eyes against the blaze of light. A hundred stars seemed to beam at her but, as her eyes adjusted, she realised it was rank upon rank of stumpy candles, and, rising above them, in the centre of the chamber, a single candle iron.

Water splashed from a cranny into a stone basin, then ran down through a hole in the floor; a brazier glowed and the smell of roasting sweetloaves blessed the air. A lanky youth stood by the brazier, flipping the fungi over with the point of a dagger.

'Nearly done,' said the youth, without turning.

'Leonard!' Allyso was bewildered at the homely scene, but she was also angry enough for her toes to itch for the satisfaction of kicking her erstwhile guide.

Leonard arranged the sweetloaves on a platter, which he put on a low table, before setting a kettle to heat and turning unhurriedly to look at Allyso with a pair of warm brown eyes.

'You really do have gold skin! Half your luck. Or no — on second thoughts, I really don't want to be in your boots, even if you were wearing them.'

Allyso stared back, seeing a cluster of short reddish curls and oddly delicate features framed by the open collar of the cloak. A silver ring hung in Leonard's ear, flashing in the shine of the candlelight.

'You said no-one ever saw your face!' she said accusingly.

'I said no-one sees the face of the Hooded One.'

'But that *is* you.'

'The Hooded One is a role I play. The punters expect it. I'm really Leonard Gates.'

'You talk nonsense,' said Allyso flatly. 'And you're not even a lad.'

Leonard gave her an odd smile. 'I know. Does it matter?'

'It matters that you're a liar, Mistra Leonard,' said Allyso. She bit her lip. In other circumstances she thought she might have liked this girl.

'I haven't told you a single lie,' said Leonard. 'I never said I was a boy — lad. You just assumed it.'

'You told me there was danger here.'

'There is.'

'You told me Seer Wootton was never kind.'

'He isn't.'

'You —'

'You'd better have a mushroom,' interrupted Leonard. 'You're going to need your strength, and you look half-starved. Are you *really* thirteen? You look about eleven.'

'Yes.' Allyso gave her an unfriendly look. After her confusing experience in the deserted Conners' Hall, she had been keyed up to face whatever ordeal the seer might decree, and now she felt a sense of letdown. She had not come so far to share a meal with a girl who pretended to be something she wasn't.

She looked across at the seer, but Wootton's face was still in deep shadow. He seemed grey all over, with the exception of the blood-dark stone in the ring he wore on one hand.

Leonard stabbed a sweetloaf on her dagger and offered it to Allyso. 'Go on,' she said. 'It's quite safe to eat. You won't be turned into a toad or anything —

supposing you have toads in this place. And do sit down.'

Cautiously, Allyso took the fungus. Its creamy globe was puffed up crisp and golden, and she hesitated only a moment before sitting down cross-legged and biting into it. She might not have come for a meal, but she was hungry, and roasted sweetloaves were even better than the raw ones. She must remember to take some back to Tace.

She was wondering how she could get the conversation back to her quest when Wootton did it for her.

'Why do you seek the gem of time, Allyso?'

'We need to turn back time to make things right, Master Wootton.'

'So you said.' Wootton removed the kettle from the brazier and added a fistful of meadowbright. The homely scent, so familiar from Gill's kitchen at Torm, brought tears to Allyso's eyes.

'You must learn to think more clearly when you come to ask for favours,' said Wootton. He poured the brew into beakers and handed one to Allyso. 'To save tomorrow, you must first look hard at yesterday.'

'I have looked and looked at yesterday,' said Allyso. 'I have thought of every turn of every day.'

'And now you think the gem of time will undo all your mistakes.'

'It could lift the siege, and give us another chance. Or better still, it could make it so the siege has never happened. Then, if we went back to the time just before the siege began, I could make sure Merrit listened.'

'I suppose you know what you mean,' said Leonard.

'Of course I do!' said Allyso, stung. 'But I don't have time to tell you everything. I have to find the gem of time before things get even worse.'

'It is not only the gem you need, but also its master,' said Wootton. 'One is no use without the other, and you will find the master of time only when or if the time is right.'

'Will you tell me where to look for the gem and its master? If not, I've wasted my time in coming here.'

'Your time has not been wasted,' said Wootton, 'but this quest has dangers you can never even imagine. Tell me exactly where you think this problem began, and then I will give you my answer.'

'It began with the soulbinder,' said Allyso. 'And when Merrit wouldn't listen to Berneathy and to Trader Mohr . . .'

CHAPTER FIFTEEN

CANDLE IRON

'I see quite clearly why you believe you need the gem of time,' said Wootton, when Allyso's story was done.

Allyso looked up hopefully. 'So now you will tell me where to find it?'

During Allyso's tale, Leonard had been quietly packing up the cooking implements. Now she doused the brazier and took it and the low table away through a narrow door. A draught hissed in from the aperture, and the flames of the candles flickered so much that some of them went out. Only the candle iron glowed with a steady white light.

'The time-gem holds great power,' said Wootton. 'The gem is the power, but it needs its master to focus that power. Do you understand?'

Allyso's eyes were watering from the smoke of the guttering candles. 'I think so,' she said, trying to focus on the concept. 'The master of time uses the gem. It won't work properly without him.'

Wootton seemed to be waiting, so she stumbled on. 'That means he won't be able to give me the gem. He'll have to come with me to Torm and use it himself.'

'The master must will the gem to work,' said Wootton. 'The master must see the need and the way to do it and must never use the power on a whim.'

'I'll explain,' pleaded Allyso. 'I'll make him see how important it is.' Her throat was dry, so she sipped the brew in her beaker. 'Please, just tell me where to go.'

'I cannot tell you exactly,' said Wootton. 'I am a seer, but my vision of the gems is limited. The best I can offer is three pieces of information. If they are not enough, then all the words in the world would not be enough.'

Allyso clasped her hands around the beaker. The meadowbright vapour rose and mixed with the smoke from the candles. 'Tell me, please! I don't have time to waste.'

'First,' said Wootton, 'you must walk the Cloudway.'

'Where is that?'

'It is the old name given to the pass in the south of McAnerin, beginning at the Cleave,' said Wootton. 'It leads right into the Shrouded Mountains past McDaniel Waters, and few folk travel that way, or know it is there to be travelled. At one time it went clear to Makersland, but that route is now extinguished. You must climb the upper branch of the path, the one that leads to Cloudway End.'

'I see,' said Allyso, although she scarcely did. 'What then?'

'Then you must search in the Crystalium Caverns beyond the Dragon's Gate.'

'And I'll find the gem of time in there?'

'I believe you may.'

'Then it's just a matter of finding my way through the pass and then to the Crystalium Caverns.'

'That is what you must do,' said Wootton.

He sounded grave and Allyso waited, knowing it must be more difficult than that. 'What will happen to me?' she asked abruptly, shaking her head to try to sharpen her brain.

'I have told you all I can,' said Wootton.

'The Cloudway which begins at the Cleave, and then the Crystalium Caverns beyond the Dragon's Gate,' said Allyso. The very names held the ring of legend. 'They don't sound real,' she ventured. 'They sound like hearthside tales.'

'Tales are often true,' said Wootton. 'These places are there, but few folk hear of them, fewer seek them out and fewer still will find them.'

'I see,' she said. 'It sounds more real if I say I need to go south, then, down towards the pass.' She looked up and found the air in the cave was thick with smoke as more of the candles went out. There was no draught this time, so they must be burning very low. She blinked, peering through the vapour. 'What is the third piece of information you said you could give me?'

Wootton stood up, his grey robes blending with the smoke. 'The third is that you will not remember the first two if you leave as you arrived.'

'But I *have* to remember. Otherwise, what was the point of telling me at all?'

'Perhaps there is no point,' said Wootton. 'What you ask is not a simple thing. If the way to the gem of time were made easy, we should have folk turning time about on a whim as they turn their mantles.'

'But this is important! I didn't come here on a whim!'

'Everyone who comes here tells me that *this is important*. Sometimes, I even believe them. Can you imagine the trouble it would bring if all who come achieved their *important* desires? What if two lads came to me and each asked to win the same wager?'

'This is no *wager*. This is life or death for Torm!'

'All the more dangerous for that.'

'Then why did you let me waste my time? Why did you let me in?'

'Didn't Leonard warn you? Did *nobody* think to warn you how hard I could be?'

'Yes, but ...' Allyso put down her beaker and stumbled to her feet.

'Yes, but you chose not to listen to them,' said Wootton bleakly. 'And now you have chosen to listen to me, and yet you will not remember. A bitter irony, isn't it? And really, just like life? Curse me if you want to, but you really should go now because the lamps that light your way will be going out. Your route lies through *there*. And Allyso, if you reach the Cloudway, I think you may meet the Divided One beside McDaniel Waters.'

He took her beaker and his own, and pointed to the door by which they had entered. Then he left by the exit Leonard had used. Allyso found herself alone in the light of the few remaining candles and the glow of a single candle iron.

It stood before her, lily-petalled, white hot, burning with a steady glow the guttering wax candles could never match.

'All this way,' she said, 'and for what? I know I must find and walk the Cloudway, and look in the Crystalium Caverns through Dragon's Gate. But what is the point of knowing if I have to forget it again?'

She had no doubt that Seer Wootton had meant what he said, nor that he could take away her memory of the instructions. She had seen Leonard send a Spellhound to sleep, and Leonard was not much older than herself. Wootton's apprentice? Wootton's prisoner? Whatever she was to Wootton, Leonard's powers were already impressive, so Wootton must be very powerful indeed.

Allyso frowned. Leonard was not her problem. Her predicament *was*. She had no idea how Wootton would take her memory, but there must be a way of fighting back.

Think, she commanded herself. There must be a way of holding onto what she had learned, even if it were somehow rinsed from her mind. A way of holding on ... she must write a record of the meeting. She must write what Wootton had told her. It would not take long, for just a few lines would do. She could tuck it in her pack or under her sash and take it out when she reached the open air.

There was just one problem with this plan. Her pack and her sash were put away in a coffer, and so were the writing tablet and stylus she had brought from Trader Mohr's.

She squinted about the cave, but there was not even a piece of charcoal where the brazier had been. Perhaps Leonard would give her some ink? She could write the information on her arm. She crossed the cave to the door through which Leonard and Wootton had left, but though she could see its outline, she could find no catch or handle. She pushed, then slapped it hard with her palms; the sound was swallowed in stone.

'Leonard?' she called. 'Seer Wootton?' Even her voice sounded muffled, and she realised there was a humming in her ears.

Three more candles guttered into darkness, adding their curls of smoke to the pall in the cave.

And that was another warning, she supposed. Well then! She must hold the memory in her mind until she reached the coffer where she had left her own clothing. She would take out the stylus and write the information before she left the ruin of Conners' Hall. But could she hold the memory until then? The route through the pillars of stonewood was long and difficult, and she would have to give her attention to searching out the lamps. And when would she lose her memory of the route to the gem of time? As she left this chamber, or sometime later?

As Allyso stood there frowning, the last of the candles failed. That probably meant the lamps would begin to die.

She knew that she must hurry now, or be lost in the ruins of Conners' Hall.

The candle iron glowed. Its iron petals alone now lit the chamber and Allyso thought she must have been duped. This could not be the seer's living quarters after all. Apart from the splashing water and dead candles, there was no sign of habitation. No chairs, no beds, no books or implements.

Only the candle iron stood out.

So burning hot, like a brand.

Allyso stared at the candle iron. If she could take it with her, she could light her own way out. And carrying that, she would remember her time with the seer. She must remember, for where else could she have come by such a thing in a stonewood forest?

She would take the candle iron as far as the coffer where her belongings lay. Then she could write her message to herself and leave the unwieldy thing behind for Leonard to fetch.

She tugged at the stem of the candle iron, but it was set in solid rock. She stared at it blankly, as a new idea came stealing into her mind.

If she could not take the candle iron, she could surely take its image ...

Allyso raised her arm and stared at the pale underside. If there had been a knife in this place, she could have written her reminder message in blood. As it was, she must use the only other way there was. Or else give up, go back and return to Fielding. Dagg and Mohr would find her a place to live ...

Allyso clenched her fist and reached over the candle iron. She closed her eyes, recalling the terrible pause on the lip of the well of Torm. Faced with an impossible choice, she had chosen to go forward. Forward she would go again, because there was really no other way to go.

With a rush, she brought her arm down hard on the glowing metal.

The pain was worse than anything she had ever imagined. Worse than a beating, worse than the slash of a dagger. The hiss of singeing flesh was as sickening as the smell.

She might have screamed, but the breath was driven from her lungs with the shock, and her throat seemed to be closing.

Gritting her teeth, sick with pain, she lifted her arm from the candle iron and stared at the livid white lily-shaped sear-mark on the flesh of her arm. Already the skin was crinkled white, the crimson showing through.

'Now, take my memory if you can!' she whispered.

The candle iron burned cold and merciless, and Allyso turned for the exit. She half expected to find it barred against her, but it opened easily. She left in a rush, heading straight for the distant glow of a lamp.

It was, she recalled through her haze of pain, the last one Wootton had lit. The fact that it was still burning said nothing about those that had been lit before it. The stone was chill under her feet and all around in the dark loomed the ruins of Conners' Hall. Chambers and anterooms, storage and passages, all disused and housing nothing but stonewood and emptiness and the cold of the rock itself.

'Cleave and Cloudway,' she said aloud, to the rhythm of her footfalls. 'Crystalium Caverns beyond the Dragon's Gate. Cleave and Cloudway ...' She faltered, for the lamp ahead was looking dim. The notion of Conners' Hall seemed far away. This place was a series of caverns; how could it ever have housed a bunch of rowdy Conners? It was not a place of learning, but of loss.

'Cleave and Cloudway.' She began again, running faster to reach the next lamp. She found she could not see it, but if she stopped and listened hard, she could hear its beckoning hum. Run to the light, listen for the hum, run on, with cold air rasping her lungs and sickening pain making her shake and sweat.

'Cleave and Cloudway, Crystalium Caverns ...'

The light ahead was so feeble it was nothing but a loonymoth a long way off. And there was another beyond, but others swarmed off to the left.

She ran and ran, with no breath left to whisper her reminders, no peace to hold the pictures in her mind. The hum of the lamps was fading under the beat of blood and the constant gasp for breath. She must ... remember ... she ...

Leonard's fists were clenched, and a single angry tear ran down her freckled cheek. 'Have I told you lately how much I hate what you do and how you do it?' she said to Wootton.

'No doubt you have, and no doubt you will tell me again,' he said calmly.

She could have kicked him, but she knew from experience he would merely shift away. 'How can you be so cruel?' she demanded instead. 'You tell her mumbo jumbo, then lay a post-hypnotic direction on her to make her forget.'

'You used a mazing spell yourself today. How is that so different?'

'I had to use it to save that poor little dog.'

'And I had to use mine to save the girl of Torm from the consequences of this quest.'

'To save her! She *burned* herself so she'd remember. Does that sound as if she wanted to be saved?'

Wootton lifted his hands. It might have been a gesture of helplessness or he might have been giving up on the discussion. Instead, he let one sleeve fall back to reveal a pale bare arm. He thrust it in front of Leonard and displayed the scar of a long-healed burn. The brand of a candle iron.

'She wanted to be saved as little as I did when my turn came,' he said as the sleeve fell back into place. 'You might call it a brand of courage, or the key to knowledge. What she asks is all but impossible, but having put herself through such pain, how can she ever turn back?'

'I never heard of anything so barbaric,' snapped Leonard.

'I expect you have,' said Wootton remotely. 'Even in your own world.'

Leonard winced away from the thought of her own world. It was far from perfect, and barbaric things happened all the time. Still it was, or had been, home, and she had no reason to believe she would ever see it again.

'Why didn't you give her a straight answer when she asked what would happen to her? You're supposed to be a seer, after all!'

Wootton's cowled face turned slowly towards her, and Leonard's nails bit into her palms. She had given up trying to understand Wootton, but she couldn't help asking questions, trying to needle him into showing some human emotion. 'Well?' she persisted.

'There are too many ways this might turn out and, at present, it is pointless to choose one over the others.'

'You said trouble was coming. You said that before she came here.'

'Trouble *is* coming,' said Wootton. He gazed at his blood-red ring. 'If she succeeds,' he murmured, 'we shall have two of the gems of power.'

'And I suppose,' said Leonard harshly, 'you think that will save your world ...'

Wootton said nothing.

'All she wants is to save her own home, and you couldn't even offer her the garnerbeast to ride.'

'No garner can walk the Cloudway, Leonard. Even for most people it is a difficult way to tread.'

'Well, at least I can give her some supplies. I suppose you won't object to that?' Without waiting for his answer, Leonard stamped angrily off to the store-caves and began to make a selection.

Allyso was shaking as she reached the foot of the stonewood stairs. Faint light gleamed down from the entrance above and showed her a single coffer. The lid was askew and she pushed it back to reveal the contents. For a moment, she stood bewildered, staring at the heap of clothing in the coffer. The tunic looked like hers, but when had she taken it off? And what was she doing here, anyway?

She was breathing hard, and the brief white tunic she wore was not her own. Her feet stung and smarted with cold and grazes and one arm was hurting badly.

She stared at the angry brand on her inner arm. It was stamped with the shape of a candle iron, so deeply burned into the flesh that she would carry the mark for life.

She was changed. That mark had not been there when she'd come to the caves.

And slowly the words returned.

First, you must walk the Cloudway ... South of McAnerin ... beginning at the Cleave ...

What came next? She couldn't quite recall, but there was a fair beginning.

CHAPTER SIXTEEN

PARTING

WINTERWANE — 11TH MOON OF THE YEAR

OF THE HOUND

TACE was sleeping where Allyso had left her. She whimpered a little as Allyso put a shaking hand on her head, and her muzzle curled in distaste at the smell of burned flesh.

'Tace?' Awkwardly, Allyso lifted the bundle of Spellhound and mantle with her good arm.

Tace stirred, whimpered again, and woke. She licked Allyso's wet cheeks, then struggled to get down.

Allyso put on her mantle, still warm from contact with the Spellhound's body, and looked up at the Singing Tor. She thought she might as well go back to the main way at Conners' Fountain and continue south, making the best pace she could. Her shoulders ached already from the weight of the pack, but she began to trudge uphill, out of the stonewood forest and onto the foothills of the Tor.

It was a long haul to the top and she paused to rest, gazing at the slanting sun. She could not have spent a whole day and night in the Conners' Hall, so this must be the same day she had entered the place.

'Let's go,' she said to Tace after a few moments but, for the first time in their association, the Spellhound turned stubborn. Allyso tugged at her ruff, but the only result was a tiny, warning growl.

'I suppose you're hungry,' said Allyso.

She slid the pack from her shoulders and opened it. There was the tablet with the information she had noted down; below was the cloth-wrapped bundle from Trader Mohr. That morning it had contained a few doughcakes and some crumbly cheese, but someone had added some loaves and a large bag of powdery substance that smelled of well-spiced broth. A scrap of paper pinned to the bag said simply: *mix with water — hot if you can.* Tucked beside it was a kerchief of fine linen. It was green and patterned all over with tiny coloured flowers. Allyso had never seen such clever embroidery. But *was* it embroidery? Although she traced the flowers with her fingers, she could not detect any stitches.

'Leonard!' said Allyso with gratitude. It must have been Leonard who had given her this gift; Wootton would never have done so. She tucked the kerchief in her sash.

After they had eaten, Tace consented to continue, but soon she was acting oddly again. 'What is it?' asked Allyso. 'Trouble?' She was too sore and shaken to run, so was very relieved when Tace whimpered with evident delight and snuffed the air to the north.

'No, Tace. We have to go south. That's *this* way ...'
But Tace insisted and, when Allyso shaded her eyes to
see what was attracting the hound, she saw a familiar
figure approaching from the north.

Scholar.

Allyso was frozen with fear, but Tace yelped and
streaked away to greet her master, running so fast her
body seemed flat to the ground.

'*This hound is his ears and eyes,*' said Dagg's voice
in Allyso's memory. '*She hears and sees whatever you
do.*'

She had denied that, but what if it were true? Had
Tace betrayed her to the Lords through Scholar? But
why would this soldier have let her go and then come
hunting her now?

No prizes for the answer to that one. He had let a
brat from the castle go free, just to save his hound but,
at some time since then, he must have learned the
brat's identity.

There was no point in running away in this open
place. Her best chance was to brazen it out. She forced
herself to raise a friendly-seeming hand, hissed at the
pain in her other arm and walked slowly on towards
the Conners' Fountain.

Scholar was seated on the coping when she arrived,
with Tace lying blissfully in his lap. Allyso felt a slight
but definite pang. She had become very fond of Tace,
but it was obvious that the Spellhound was ecstatic to
rejoin her master.

'I did keep her safe,' she said.

'So I see, Allyso.' The soldier's face was blanched
and, though he was hugging the hound, he looked ill
and somehow frozen.

Her heart sped up, but she managed a puzzled expression. 'Allyso? Who is that?'

'You should know the name,' he said. 'Since you live — lived — at Torm. Allyso is the Heir of Torm, Merrit Tormblood's niece.'

'Oh, yes. So she is.' Her tone sounded unconvincing, so she wasn't surprised when Scholar reached out and seized her by the elbow. The gesture pulled the cloth of her mantle against the raw burn, and she gasped with pain.

'*You* are Allyso Tormblood,' he said. 'Torm has fallen, and my father said my neck was on the knife if I failed to bring you back.'

Torm had fallen ... Allyso knew she should have expected this, but the confirmation was almost the worst thing yet.

'Are they all right? Is Merrit all right? Gregory? And Gill?'

He shrugged impatiently. 'Some lived, more died. They didn't tell me their names. I had little time to ask, because my father told me to find you.'

'I won't come with you. I have to —' On the verge of telling him about her quest, she closed her mouth on it, hard. 'I have to live, for Torm,' she said instead. 'Merrit told me so. If I go back, Lord Toombs and Lord Sheels will kill me.'

She expected an offer of amnesty, or some false promise of mercy, but Scholar said harshly, 'They won't do that. I think they want you as breeding stock. *You* are the Heir to Torm, so your children would be heirs after you. If a child of yours were Heir Elect, the transition would cause barely a ripple.'

Allyso felt sick. 'I won't come with you.'

'*Will* you stop saying that, you stupid brat!' Scholar scowled at her. 'I told you what my father told me to do, not what I mean to do.'

'Your father is one of those two lords?'

'Toombs of Zimmerhanzel. And by now he probably doesn't give a snap of his fingers whether you live, die or fly away. He'll be far too busy trying to win back Zimmerhanzel — if he isn't dead himself.'

'Dead?' This was too much, and Allyso felt her mind ballooning with shock. 'I don't understand … *he* was the invader. The castlers were too weak to fight back, so why should *he* be dead?'

'That foreign dame,' said Scholar coldly, 'the soulbinder. She tempted my father and Sheels by offering an army made up from a rabble that calls itself the Tenth Castle of Ankoor. While they were besieging little Torm, the rest of the Tenth Castle crew was taking over Zimmerhanzel and Hasselsjo. And I doubt that was the end of their ambition. Probably other castles are falling by now.'

He let her go, but Allyso simply gaped at him.

'This has gone beyond your own skin or my father's schemes,' said Scholar. 'The Tenth Castle is eating into McAnerin from the north, and the stars alone know where it's going to end.'

'Then what do you want with me?'

'I want Tace, not you,' said Scholar. 'I advise *you* to get as far from north McAnerin as you can. My father is bad enough, but he wouldn't have killed you. He told me quite plainly he wanted you alive and healthy. These other creatures are killers, though. Where are you heading, anyway?'

'To the Cleave ...' she murmured.

'*The Cleave*? Whatever for? It doesn't lead anywhere.'

'You know the way?' She could scarcely believe she was asking directions from an enemy, but his news showed a future even more desperate than she had thought. The rot was spreading well beyond Torm.

'You'd need to go south,' he said. 'Down to the wastes and then to the Shrouded Mountains. The Cleave is a cave where the rock wall splits in two ... but what do you want that for? It's only a curiosity.'

Allyso lifted her chin. 'I am going to walk the Cloudway to find the gem of time.'

Scholar laughed, but it wasn't a happy sound. 'So you're not going to tell me any of your plans. Fair enough. Do whatever you really mean to do, and good luck with it. Just *don't* go back to Torm.'

'Thank you,' she said, surprised. 'I just wish I knew more about travelling. I've only been out with Merrit and, since we have no garnerbeast, we don't go far.'

'I can give you a map of these parts. It's very old, so I wouldn't trust it very far, but it's better than nothing. I found it in the library at Zimmerhanzel.'

Scholar tugged a ledger out of his pack and turned the pages. Allyso had a confused impression of pictures and ornamental script. 'This is the one,' he said, tracing one of the maps with his fingers. 'See? This is supposed to show you the quickest way to get to the port for Rargon.'

'Is that the way you're going?'

'No,' he said curtly. 'I'm making for Ankoor.'

'*Ankoor*! Whatever for?'

'Why not? They call me Scholar Ankoorian. I was born there and lived there most of my life until I was sent to my father. My mother's kin are still there, and I have a mind to return to them with Tace.'

'The soulbinder is Ankoorian ... so Berneathy said.'

'Listen, brat, they're not all bad in Ankoor,' he said. He took a knife from his sash and carefully sliced the page away from the others. 'It's probably more fancy than fact,' he warned, and handed it over to her.

Allyso took it gratefully, but warily. 'I can't pay you.'

'Call it payment for keeping Tace for me,' said Scholar. 'And mind you head for the port. *Don't* go back to Torm or Zimmerhanzel. And don't go to Hasselsjo either. Not if you want to sleep at night.' His frown deepened, and he suddenly turned aside and retched.

'What's the matter?' she asked. 'I mean, what is *really* the matter? You were sick when your friends killed the villagemen.'

'They are *not* my friends.'

'*Who did they kill this time?*'

'Too many,' he said, wiping his face. 'Stars! They even k-killed Tegwen Hasselsjo ... They, they —' He choked, and stuffed the ledger back into his pack. 'You don't want to know that, brat. Just be on your way. Oh — and I picked this knife up back in the grove at Torm. You might find it useful.'

He handed her the knife he had used, then clicked his fingers to Tace. The Spellhound looked at him adoringly, glanced at Allyso and wagged her tail.

Allyso took the knife and thanked Scholar before bending to hug the hound. 'Goodbye, Tace. I won't forget you.'

She turned her face to the south before her welling tears could begin to fall, stumbling blindly along through a blur of pain and confusion. When she finally dared to stop to look back, Scholar Ankooria and his Spellhound had gone. She looked at the knife he had given her and recognised the one she had had in the first place from Gregory.

Some lived, more died, said Scholar's voice in her mind, but she stuffed the knife in her sash and trudged on.

CHAPTER SEVENTEEN

CLOUDWAY

WINTERWANE — 11TH MOON OF THE YEAR

OF THE HOUND

THE map was a wonder of decorative script and tiny, fanciful pictures. Scholar had said it shouldn't be trusted, but at least it gave Allyso a starting point. Not for the Rargon port as he had instructed, but south towards the Shrouded Mountains, the wastes and the Cleave.

She missed Tace terribly, not only for her company, but also for her ability to discover and unearth sweetloaves. She would have gone hungry if it had not been for Leonard. The loaves were soon gone, but a small scoop of the spicy powder made a sustaining pottage when mixed with water.

Although her boots were wearing thin, she had no money to pay for a mending, nor did she dare apply for charity. She padded them as well as she could, and coated the soles with resin from a wounded honeytree. Sometimes passers-by tossed her fruit or loaves; she always acknowledged these with a jaunty page's bow and tried not to gaze with envy at the lucky ones who were mounted on garnerbeast. The great creatures covered the ground at a stride that far outpaced a man, let alone a weary girl.

She walked the main way by daylight, and by night she followed byways past villages and towns. Some were on Scholar's map, others must have been established since it was made. The most southerly village marked was named McAnerin End; beyond that, the main way dissolved into a maze of tracks crisscrossing the heaths.

The map showed little detail of the wastes, but the blue distant line of mountains beckoned her on. The silence was unnerving and, by the third day, Allyso was talking to herself, just to hear the sound of a human voice.

'The Cleave,' she said. She took out the map for the third time that day and finally found the name, lettered in almost invisible sepia ink. The range loomed closer now, and she saw, with a gulp of apprehension, how the Shrouded Mountains had found their name. Their lower slopes were streaked in mist; their peaks swam out of sight in billows of cloud.

And where, in this long line of rocky ramparts, was the Cleave?

Allyso was exhausted and, in the back of her mind, was the fear that she was much too late. She had hoped to fetch help for Torm before it fell; now it was taken over, and Merrit was probably dead. Was there any point in finding the time gem now? It might roll back some days, but how many?

It was not hope that kept her going now, but just the lack of other options.

The Cleave, when she found it, was a dark crease in the wall of rock. From most angles it looked like nothing but a fault, but a careful inspection showed a narrow slanting passageway leading off at an acute angle.

'Another dark hole!' said Allyso. 'I've had enough of them.' It was getting late, but she trudged on into the Cleave. It was so dark inside it could scarcely matter if she travelled by day or by night.

Inside, the floor rose in a steep, uneven ramp. There was no handrail or guideline, but she plodded and scrambled upwards until she was dripping with sweat and shaking with exhaustion. The burn on her arm was itching, and she pressed it against her side, which made it hurt again with sudden jabs. If this were a tale of Trader Mohr's, she thought miserably, she would have found a magical portal or a guide by now. In a tale, she would have travelled from the Conners' Fountain to the Cleave within the space of a well-turned phrase.

After a while, she discovered, it was not completely dark. Colour was leached from everything, but shadows of grey were visible as her eyes adjusted to the gloom. Whenever she thought she could go no farther, she forced herself to take another pace. Five, and then a rest. Ten more, and then a sip from her flask. She lost count of the steps and pauses, and the sullen ache of legs and shoulders loomed larger than her quest.

The climb was so exhausting that she scarcely noticed the growing light. Cold grey light it was, clammy and luminous, and it fell across her sweating face in a sudden breath of chill. And abruptly, she emerged from the funnel of stone into a blanket of mist.

She put one hand on the lip of the rock, then took a cautious step. Her foot slipped and her heart seemed to lurch. She blinked, hard, but her eyes could not adjust to the muffling mist. Her legs ached, so she let herself down into a sitting position. Her heels slid along the rock in front of her, then suddenly her feet were in thin air.

It might have been a dip in the rock, but Allyso had no doubt she was perched on the edge of an abyss. Emptiness threatened in the smell of the air, in the faint cold dampness rising from below.

She drew up her legs and rolled carefully onto her hands and knees, then felt for the width of the ledge. Behind lay the exit of the Cleave; in front, the hidden void. To her left was solid rock, but to the right, the way seemed clear. She stretched like a serpent, fingertips exploring the cold, slippery surface before she brought up her knees and stretched forward again. She had progressed several times her own body-length before she accepted that the ledge was probably a path. It was too cold to sit in the fog, too dangerous to sleep on a cliff, so she made the only decision she could: she rose to her feet and began to edge along the wall.

'I suppose,' she said aloud, 'this is the Cloudway. And I suppose it didn't get that name for nothing.'

Darkness came as she crept along. The way had widened and the rock wall to her right was lower now. It had towered above her at first, but now it was barely as high as her waist. Soon she had to bend to keep in touch with it, so she perched on top and leaned over. Her sore fingertips met the rough, scrubby tops of heaths and slender clothwood bushes, and she realised the wall was no longer a barrier on the edge of the path, but the edge of a plateau that must be of reasonable size.

To continue or to camp for the night? The answer was obvious. If the wall grew lower still, it would be more of a hazard than a guide, and she might wander off the path.

Allyso paced well away from the edge, removed her pack, burrowed down among the heaths and settled to wait for sunlift and the morning which, she hoped, might blow away the fog.

She still missed Tace's company and she woke once, just before daylight, thinking she heard the Spellhound breathing nearby. Had Tace followed her? Had Scholar changed his mind about taking her with him to Ankoor?

'Tace?' she said softly, hopefully. There was no answer, but the feeling of presence persisted. 'Tace?'

The sun came up, dissolving the mist into long cobweb shawls.

'Tace?' she said a third time, and this time an answer came — not the whine of the Spellhound, but a strange, wordless cry as a dark, hunched figure rose out of the heaths. Allyso screamed, but the creature surged forward and grasped at her arms, forcing her to face it, staring into her eyes.

'*Tollerman*?'

The soulbinder's page was in a terrible state. His dark hair was draggled and greasy, his mantle hung in tatters, but the blue eyes were the same, and so was the dreadful silence. Allyso met that gaze for a heartbeat, seeing, rather than hearing, the scream from the page's mind.

She wrenched herself from his grasp and pushed him away, swept by a scorching tide of anger.

'You *carrion*!' she spat. 'You wicked, soulless *spy*!'

She scrubbed her hands together, disgusted that she had touched him.

He made an urgent gobbling noise, and she turned her head away. 'You were the one who took the message, *weren't you*? You ate at our board and slept under our roof, and then you went and told those other filthy creatures where to come!'

She swallowed, almost choking. 'And of course you know what happened after that! Your *friends* took everything from Torm. Food, friendship, trust — and now Torm is fallen and some of my friends are dead. And I have no home left, and here *you* are again. Get away from me! Get back to your Tenth Castle!'

The anger scalded her, but berating the page could give no satisfaction. If the soulbinder had appeared, she thought she might have tried to push the woman out into the void, but Tollerman was mute and had always seemed half daft. He'd been thin when they'd met before, but now he was positively gaunt. The garments he was wearing were outgrown and shredded with wear, and his boots, when she glanced at them, were even more ruined than her own.

'Have you been following me?'

A fresh suspicion surfaced. If the soulbinder knew where Allyso was going, she might have sent Tollerman to intercept her. This idea filled Allyso with mingled fear and hope. If the soulbinder wanted to prevent her journey, it should follow that the quest was not as hopeless as she feared. It could also mean she would die right here on the Cloudway.

'Well?' she said. 'Have you followed me? It will do you no good if you have. I am leaving McAnerin, so you might as well go back to your evil dame.'

Horror bloomed in Tollerman's face, and then his eyes were as blank as ever. He sank on his haunches in the heaths, wrapped his arms around his shanks and bowed his head. Broken sounds came from his mouth, and he began to rock slowly back and forth. He looked like pure misery, but was he desolate with some private despair, or with remorse for what he had done to Torm?

Allyso wished she still had Tace, who would have assessed this unwelcome fellow-traveller in a heartbeat. As it was, she must follow her own instincts. It was no use trying to talk to him at present, so she looked about instead, peering through the streaks of cloud that seemed to be a permanent part of the landscape.

She had thought she was on a plateau, but the stretch of heath was little more than a narrow strip. Away to the left, as she had suspected, lay the abyss, with cloudbeds screening whatever lay below. To the right, as far as she could see, water shone through the mists and reflected back as if from a new-minted coin. Here and there its surface glowed with cup-shaped blooms as blue as the Highsummer skies.

'McDaniel Waters!' she whispered. 'The seer said I might meet someone here.' But was this meeting good or bad? Wootton hadn't said, nor had she thought to query him.

She went to the edge of the lake, drank thirstily, then washed her face and dried it on her kerchief. The water was cold and smelled faintly of the flowers.

Tollerman was still locked in his own private horrors, so Allyso moved off into the mist. She took off her clothing and waded into the lake, washed all over and dressed again. When she returned, her teeth chattering with cold, Tollerman was exactly as she had left him. She wanted to move on along the Cloudway, but what was to prevent him from following? What to do? Once and for all, she could *not* give up, nor could she try to kill him. He was bigger and stronger, despite his starved condition, and besides, she felt it would be wrong. If she found the time-gem, and if it worked, she might meet the page again, and meeting a lad she had already killed would be unthinkable.

She drew fresh water from the lake, then struck a fire from the tinderflint in her pack. There was little to burn in this cloudy place, but she coaxed a pile of heath and clothwood into a sluggish, charring glow. It was enough to heat a panikin of water, and she made a scoop of Leonard's powder into broth.

She drank it, then turned to consider Tollerman. He was still hunched over his knees, but the rocking motion had ceased. His pack rested beside him, and she guessed, from its flaccid appearance, that it was empty.

'Are you hungry?' she asked.

His head came up slowly, and he studied her face as if he had never seen her before. Then he nodded.

Allyso dipped more water in the panikin and added more of the powder. She heated it and held it out. Tollerman took it in both hands and gulped it down as if he had not eaten in days.

'Where are you going?' she asked. 'To —' She searched her mind for a destination and remembered the one Scholar had recommended. 'To the port for Rargon?'

He shrugged.

'Then you need to go back to the Cleave,' she said. 'You're on the wrong track here. This is supposed to lead to a place called Makersland.'

She had no real hope that he would take her suggestion, and he did not. Instead, he fixed his blue gaze on her and waited.

'You go on,' she said. 'I need to rest a while.'

He shook his head, touched his chest and made walking motions with his fingers. Then he pointed to her with his other hand, and did the same.

'I suppose,' she said angrily, 'that means you think you're coming with me. What for?'

He shrugged.

'Did the soulbinder send you to find me?'

This question seemed to upset Tollerman, for he folded in on himself and began to rock again, whimpering so that Allyso's anger dissolved into a kind of appalled pity. 'All right,' she said. 'I suppose you can come with me. At least then I'll know what you're up to. But you really have to wash yourself first.' She reinforced this idea by pinching a fold of his mantle and screwing up her face.

Meekly, he took off the mantle, went to the edge of the lake, and waded into the mist. She heard the sound of splashing, so she supposed he was following her instructions. She would have run if she'd thought it would do any good, but she knew he would catch her up again all too soon. There was nowhere to hide on the Cloudway, and she could not afford to turn back. Therefore, she waited until he was ready and then set off again, with Tollerman walking behind.

It was strange to have another companion. She would have much preferred Tace, but she found herself talking to the page as she had talked to the Spellhound, expecting no answers but supposing he understood. He spent much of his time in a kind of daze, and sometimes the horror she had seen that first day screamed out of the blank wells of his eyes. At other times, he seemed calmer, walking along the endless shores of McDaniel Waters and sometimes taking his part in tending their wayside fires.

On the third day, after she had sighed over the small amount of broth-powder remaining, he waded into the lake and surprised her a little later with two silvery fish. She took them gratefully, cleaned them with the knife that Scholar had returned to her, then roasted them on hot rock surrounded by a smouldering heath-and-clothwood fire. It was the first solid meal either of them had had in days.

When they had eaten, she turned and gazed at Tollerman. His hair was damp with the ever-present mist, and she thought he looked a little less vague.

'Who are you, Tollerman?' she asked. 'Where do you come from, and how did you come to be with that foul dame?'

Who was he? He didn't quite know.

The girl called him 'Tollerman'. He supposed it was his name. She seemed angry with him sometimes and, at other times, she seemed merely impatient or rather sorry.

He wanted to answer her questions, but there was something wrong with his mouth. He tried to work out what it was, but could explore it only with his fingers. Something was missing, and he thought it might be his tongue.

He tried to ask the girl where they were going. He pointed left and right and sometimes, with a shudder, over the abyss. He hated looking down, for the depths were screened by a flotilla of clouds. This looked comforting, but who knew what might lurk underneath that barrier? It was the same with the lake. The surface sent his reflection dancing, the blue flowers were sweetly scented, but what was underneath that glossy shine?

And what, he wondered, lay under the clouds in his mind?

Might it be the self he sensed he should have been, or was it just more terror?

'Who are you, Tollerman?' the girl was asking again. 'How did you come to be with that foul dame?'

Pictures rose in Tollerman's mind. He half-saw a figure dressed in blue and silver, garments he knew could be trusted. He saw himself go to her willingly, heard her promise him what he most desired ... She had kept her word, and then the horror began. Blinding pain and misery, the pad of feet on endless journeys, pity or revulsion in faces until he learned never to look.

He recalled a struggle he'd had with himself: not wanting to do what she ordered, but doing it anyway. And then he had been cast adrift, wandering, waiting for someone to tell him what to do and where to go.

The darkness had seemed as good a place as any, the cloudy path had beckoned and then he had woken from the blankness of sleep to find this girl. The sight of her had brought the pictures back to his mind, unbearable pictures, but better than the void he had known before. He had cried out, surprising himself with the dreadful sound that came from his throat, and she had responded with a spurt of abuse.

And now she was reminding him, and asking who he was!

PART FOUR — DRAGON'S GATE

CHAPTER EIGHTEEN

KEEPER

WINTERWANE — 11TH MOON OF THE YEAR

OF THE HOUND

McDANIEL Waters seemed endless but, by the evening of that third day, the lake began to taper away until it was just a narrow slip of water that wisped off into a few paces of marsh and vanished. The plateau had narrowed, too, rising to form a high rock wall impossible to scale. The Cloudway clung to its edge, reverting to a narrow, rocky path. And then it wasn't even that.

Allyso stared at the cliffs ahead. The only way to travel now was to edge along with her heels to the wall and to slide each foot in turn. To make it worse, the wall bulged out, so she could not see how far, or even if, the ledge extended.

'Do you want to turn back?' she asked Tollerman. Her voice wavered and she longed again for Tace. The Spellhound's reaction to the Cloudway would have given her courage to go on or justification for retreat.

Tollerman looked doubtful.

'If the ledge runs out, we might not be able to get back after this,' said Allyso.

The page gave her a strange, bitter smile.

'I suppose we don't have much to go back *for*,' she said. 'Unless you want to find your mistress?'

His head came up, and he made a violent spitting gesture.

'I wouldn't, either,' agreed Allyso. She pondered for a moment, then said abruptly, 'Can you write, Tollerman?'

His eyes widened, but he nodded, as if the information surprised him.

'In that case, you can tell me what you were doing with that woman!' She reached for her pack, but the motion unbalanced her. She caught a dizzying glimpse of the cloudy abyss as it swayed in front of her before Tollerman grabbed her arm and pulled her back against the rock.

'Thanks!' Her voice was shaking but, after a while, she added, 'I suppose we might as well go on.'

She edged around the bulge, wondering at the page's lack of fear. She also wondered why he had steadied her. He had been a party to Torm's disaster, but he hadn't made any move against her during their time on the Cloudway. Was he waiting to see where she was going before he acted, or was he simply a tool for whatever hand held his reins?

She was trembling in every limb by now, but there was no opportunity to rest. The Cloudway branched suddenly into two paths, one of which narrowed almost to a hand's width and ended a few paces on in a broken jumble that looked as if a huge bite had been taken from the rocks. This one, she supposed and hoped, was the path that had once led to the place Seer Wootton called Makersland. The other path, the one she could still follow, began to climb the cliff-face, offering crude hollows or ledges in place of steps.

Allyso climbed; her hands were wet with fear as well as with the pervasive mist. She hardly dared to pause for breath, even to rub her hands on her kerchief, in case a ledge gave way or her fingers slipped. She could hear Tollerman climbing behind her, matching his pace to hers. He was taller and stronger, and she supposed she should have asked him to lead, since he would be the faster climber ... She dragged herself wearily up to another ledge, and another, until suddenly there was nothing left above her.

She leaned forward, resting her aching arms on the top of the cliff. The burn on her forearm stung and throbbed, but she was used to that by now and peered at the place where this upper branch of the Cloudway ceased to be.

Away to the left, the mountain ended in a bluntly rounded isthmus jutting out into thin air, while just ahead lay a frowning black rock, set, incongruously, with a rusting iron gate. It was a shock to see an object like this so far from the nearest village. Allyso stared at it for several heartbeats, then clambered onto the clifftop, followed by the page.

'This must be Cloudway's End,' she said. 'I suppose the path to the Makersland would have carried on around the other side of the bluff.'

She walked to the iron-jawed gate. It fitted snugly into the rock, two or three shades lighter in colour, but every bit as forbidding. The heavy lock was pitted. She reached up to touch it and found it rusted fast.

A light wind blew, bringing with it the waft of a bitter smell.

Tollerman came up beside her and, from the distaste on his face, she thought he must smell it, too: a heavy, sulphurous smell, such as might hang about an iron foundry or a sludge-pit.

At first, there seemed nothing to account for it, but then she began to notice greasy patches on the rock. She touched one with a fingertip; it came away covered with oily soot.

If the Cloudway had ended, this must be the Dragon's Gate. Beyond it, she thought, with a gulp of excitement, lay the Crystalium Caverns, where she must seek the gem of time.

Getting in was the problem. The lock was immovable, the gates so massive there would be no hope of breaking through. Knocking was no help; her puny fist would make no sound on a thing like this.

'There must be someone here to let me in,' she said to Tollerman. 'If not, I've wasted my time.'

She tried to imagine the porter of such a gate, but nothing made sense. Who would spend his time so far from other folk?

'Porter?' she called, but her voice sounded thin. She picked up a chunk of rock and slammed it hard against the gate. The *thock* of stone on iron was dull, but it set up singing echoes. Note after note poured out of the darkness beyond the gate, swelling as if a hundred beaters were striking a hundred gongs.

The rock fell from Allyso's fingers, and she cringed and covered her ears. The echo continued to strike at her through the soles of her worn-out boots. Just as she thought she could bear it no more, the torrent of sound began to fade.

Cautiously, she removed her hands from her ears, then gazed at the gate with dread. She had found a response of a kind, but not for worlds would she strike the gate again. She glanced at Tollerman and saw without surprise that he had dropped to a crouch and buried his face in his arms.

The silence continued a while, though echoes still rang in her ears and set her teeth on edge. Then out of that silence beyond the gate came a voice, harsh and grey as the voice of iron. It grated and jangled, and could have come from no human throat. It was as if the gate had spoken.

'Who calls the Keeper, and with what cause?'

Allyso licked her lips, for her mouth had gone as dry as a Rargonian desert. 'I am Allyso,' she faltered. 'I have come to fetch the gem of time.'

The silence resumed, then came a creaking, a grinding, as if rocks were being rolled together.

'Allyso,' mused the iron voice. 'That is no name for a hero.'

Allyso lifted her chin at that. 'I never said I was a hero, Keeper. I said I was Allyso.'

The grinding continued, and the Keeper bloomed out of the darkness. It was as if the rock itself had come alive, but it wasn't only the mode of arrival that made Allyso stare.

'You — you're a *dragon*!' she faltered. And so it was, the first she had ever seen. It blinked at her with heavy-lidded eyes, black as pools of ink, full of the thoughts of the ages.

'I am a gemdrake,' creaked the dragon, 'but why have you disturbed me, halfling?'

Allyso swallowed. 'I need the time-gem.'

The gemdrake roared, and the sound was borne on a gust of sulphurous breath that made Allyso cower away from the gate. She was aware, out of the corner of her eye, that Tollerman was crouched behind her. She put her hand back, almost absently, and touched his arm as she would have patted Tace. The tendons were straining under her hand; he must have clenched his fists.

'Why should you have a gem of power?' gusted the gemdrake. 'Give me a reason, halfling, and beware. If I judge you unworthy to seek such power, I will burn you to the bone before I return to my rest.'

'I need the gem,' pleaded Allyso. 'My home has fallen and so have other northern castles. If I have the gem and find its master, I could get him to roll back time and give my uncle warning. He will know what to do to keep the rest of it from happening.'

'He did not act wisely before. He will not act wisely again.'

'This time I will warn him! So please, Keeper, you see my reason is a good one.'

'Let *you* wander the marvels of my Caverns? Let *you* seek the gems of power? I think not, halfling,' said the gemdrake softly. 'You should turn and flee, while you still have flesh and muscle on your legs.'

Allyso bit her lip, hard, trying to keep it from trembling. 'I've come so far,' she insisted. 'I've faced so much already!'

'No doubt you've scratched your face and bruised your knees, so you whimper to me of hardship,' said the gemdrake indifferently. 'Go, before I lose patience, and burn you to your bones. Then, with the stench of your charring flesh in your nostrils, *then* you will know the meaning of pain and hardship. A pity the knowledge will come too late to be of any benefit.'

'I came through the well-way, and I have walked the Cloudway.'

'So you swam and you climbed and expect my commendation.' The gemdrake exhaled. Flames flickered from its nostrils, dancing purple and golden in the air. 'Go,' it said. 'Scratches and bruises and whimpers can't make you worthy.'

Allyso's anger burned as hot as any dragonfire. She had come so far, she would *not* be turned away. Not by a lazy old lizard who could not be bothered to open a rusty lock. She flung aside her mantle and thrust out her arm. Cold metal brushed the burn, and the pain rushed back. 'Scratches and bruises!' she cried. 'Do you call *this* scratches and bruises, Keeper?'

The gemdrake stared at the mark of the candle iron. 'How came you by that, halfling? Who has branded you?'

'I did it myself!' she snapped. 'I did it when the seer at Conners' Hall told me the way to come here, then said he'd take my memory away. I burned myself so that I *would* remember, and you can see that it worked.'

The gemdrake rumbled a laugh, and a jet of white-hot flame poured from its throat, danced about the gate for a moment, and melted the heart of the lock. 'Enter then, Allyso,' said the gemdrake. 'You bear the sign of fire, and so you may seek the gem of time.'

Just like that?

Allyso was caught off balance by the gemdrake's sudden change of mind. 'What about Tollerman?' she said nervously. 'I can't leave him alone.' No, indeed. He might be more devious than he seemed, and who knew what he might do while she was in the dragon's lair?

The gemdrake laughed again. 'That sorry scrut that hides behind you?'

'He isn't hiding. He climbed up after me.'

'He can't come in,' said the gemdrake. 'He'll wait. I'll see to that.'

Still she hesitated, knowing how easily mistakes could be made, and how hard it was to unmake them.

'Enter now, or never,' said the Keeper, so Allyso summoned her courage and stepped past, flinching back from the touch of the scaly hide. The creature's claws were iron-clad, and its tail made a rattle like chains upon the rock.

It was very dark beyond the gate, and the tunnel smelled of the dragon.

'Are you the master of time?' she asked. It seemed a reasonable question, since the gemdrake looked older than any other being she had met.

'I am not the master of time. I am the Gemdrake, the Keeper of the Gates.'

'Then where shall I find the master of time? Does he live in these caverns?'

'No-one lives here,' said the dragon.

'*You* do.'

'I live in the rock and I am of the rock. I come from the place beyond when the gate is calling. You have asked enough questions, halfling. I grow weary of you.' A flame flared up behind her, making her wince.

'Where do I begin?' she asked.

'You will need this orb,' said the dragon. 'How else will you find one gem among so many?'

The dragonflame gleamed on a small round object that lay on a ledge, painting it crimson, then letting it dull to black.

'Take this orb in your hand. It will light your way through the caverns.'

'I'm not such a fleewit!' said Allyso. 'I don't want to brand my hand as well as my arm.'

The gemdrake laughed. 'Fool or not, you'll not get far without it. Take the orb. It will give you dragonsight.'

CHAPTER NINETEEN

DRAGONSIGHT

🕑

WINTERWANE — 11TH MOON OF THE YEAR

OF THE HOUND

ALLYSO'S eyes were beginning to sting and water from the fumes of dragonbreath, but she reached for the coal-black orb. It was about the size of a strawcap's egg, cold and heavy as sin, but she cupped it easily into her palm. 'A lamp would be better,' she muttered. 'How does it work?'

'The orb remembers light from another day. It gives it up until that light is exhausted.'

Allyso coughed. 'How do I get to the Crystalium Caverns?'

'Through the tunnel,' said the dragon. 'Go. You have until sunfall.'

Sunfall! Allyso glanced behind her. The sun was already riding low. 'That is not enough time.'

'At sunfall, the gate will close.'

'You could open it again for me. The porter at Fielding did.'

'I am not the porter at Fielding. Nor is this gate the Fielding portal. I have opened it once and that is the only time.'

Such a little while to find the gem of time! It was somewhere in the Caverns, but how vast might they be?

'Are you coming with me?' asked Allyso.

'No,' said the dragon. 'I am Keeper of the Gate, so here I stay while the gate is open. Besides, did you not charge me to watch your mute disciple?'

The dragonflame was dimming and, when the gemdrake had retreated to the gate, the fire snuffed out, leaving Allyso alone in the smoky dark.

After the Cloudway, the air in this tunnel seemed unbearably close. This quest seemed to favour dark places, when it wasn't favouring heights. The dark of the well-way, of the Conners' Hall and of the Cleave. And now more darkness in the gemdrake's Crystalium Caverns.

But *was* it so dark? She could almost picture her surroundings. That peak of lighter rock a little ahead, the patch of yellowish rubble on the floor. The place where the tunnel opened into the cavern.

I'm remembering, she thought. I'm remembering what I saw in the light of the dragonflame.

That impression lasted for a few heartbeats but, as she edged on down the tunnel, she realised it was wrong. There was a vein of deep purple rock up high to her left, and a glitter of golden streaks as she rounded a bend. And far ahead was a scrap of blue, so intense that for a moment she thought she was seeing a bloom from McDaniel Waters. And another flash of thought exploded in her mind, bringing cold sweat to her palms and face. She was out of the tunnel and into the Crystalium Caverns, on the verge of success at last!

She pulled her kerchief from her sash and blotted her forehead but, as she tried to tuck it away again, a draught from the tunnel whisked the cloth from her hand. She bent to retrieve it, but it didn't seem to be there.

'Bother!' she said, for she knew she could not stop to search. She must find it on the way back. After she found the gem of time ...

As she passed deeper into the cavern, the impressions of streaks and clusters of colour became more frequent and more intense. Violet and gentian, the green of bitterstem, the cloudy white of snow. She saw blood-red crystal and then a chorus of colours, blending together like a piece of fantastic embroidery. The hues were enchanting, and the sounds of her steps were stirring the pattern of echoes. Colours and sound-notes blossomed about her, but Allyso could not admire them. Her time was running out, and the task was all but impossible, and the beauty worked against her. With all these jewels around, how would she know the time-gem if she saw it? It could be any colour, any shape, anywhere. She realised, too late, that she should have asked for a description. Seer Wootton might have known what it looked like; the gemdrake certainly would. Even Mohr or Merrit might have heard some rumour or remembered some tradition. Gold or green? Red or white or violet? Round or ragged, crystalline or shaped like a frozen tear?

She searched in frantic earnest, clutching the orb and running her free hand over the masses of gems. They were hard and smooth as ice, and almost as cold, and none of them seemed more significant than the rest. How could she have assumed that she could simply pick up the time-gem inside the caverns? As she searched, she began to panic. Time was racing on. She found herself counting breaths and heartbeats, trying to judge how long she had been in the cavern, but the echoes were disturbing her, and she could not keep the numbers straight in her mind.

'Where is it?' she whispered, and began to feel hollow with panic. The sun must be almost down, and she had not searched a tenth of the Caverns. With every turn of the labyrinth, another rank of crystals would appear. They glittered with a fire far deeper than the dragon's, beautiful and terrible together.

She must ask the gemdrake for help. She turned from a cluster of emerald teardrops and hurried back towards the Dragon's Gate, dodging around the outcrops and clambering over lavaflows of gems. She still had some distance to go when she heard a grinding clang.

And then there was nothing more.

The girl had vanished beyond the iron gate. Tollerman would have followed, but the gemdrake barred the way.

Not for you, Unwanted.

When the gemdrake had spoken to the girl, its voice had rasped like iron, but now the words were forming in Tollerman's head. He clapped his hands over his ears in protest, but the sound within would not be shut out.

There's nothing here for you, or anywhere, said the voice. *You have thrown away your destiny. You are nothing.*

Tollerman fell to his knees, for his head seemed stuffed with dragonfire, flickering through the contours of his skull. He screamed with pain, for he still had a voice, though not the tongue to shape the words he needed.

Why do you follow the girl? Why are you here?

His head would burst, he thought. The girl would find him broken when she returned.

You are broken already. You have let yourself be shattered like an egg.

The voice was beating relentlessly, but how could he deny its accusations?

What's left is no use to anyone. Not even to the hag who had you in thrall. You did your worst for her, and she turned you loose. You're not worth keeping and not worth killing, either.

No.

You have no self, nothing but your name.

This was unbearable, and he need not bear it. Tollerman lurched to his feet and reeled towards the end of the jutting spur. He slipped on greasy rock, jarred his palms and bloodied his knees, but dragged himself on towards the edge.

Look at you! jeered the voice in his head. *Not even worth a proper pair of leggings.*

Tollerman clawed his way to the cliff, stumbled to his feet. The cloudy wastes were calling, so he raised his arms and willed himself to fall.

You can't even jump. You expect the wind to throw you off the world.

I will jump! I *will*!

But when he tried, a jet of pure white fire shot out before him. It touched the rock, then lapped around to form a ghostly wall of flame.

'Back, you fool!' The gemdrake's voice clanged in the air as Tollerman staggered back. 'I said I would watch you,' it complained. 'How can I watch if you vanish into the clouds and fly to Makersland?'

Tollerman struggled for speech, but the sounds that came from his mouth were garbled and broken. The gemdrake dowsed the fire and jerked its massive head. 'Your dreams have turned on you and will drive you mad.'

The nightmare voice had gone from his mind, yet his head still ached with a roaring emptiness. He glanced at the lip of the spur.

'Tell me who you are,' said the gemdrake. 'I seem to know your blood.'

Tollerman's hands were smarting where he had fallen, and his knees were oozing drops of red. He stared at the gemdrake and pointed to his mouth.

'You've lost your tongue, so make me silent words.'

How ... ? Dully he remembered the girl had a writing tablet. Did dragons read? Did voiceless rubbish write?

He took the tablet and stylus from the pack, then sat cross-legged on the rock. His mind was clouded, but here and there were sharpened spurs of memory. Most of them made him wince with remembered pain. And there was something else below the clouds. Something he would never face. He would give this creature what it wanted, and then he could jump and be free.

'What is your name?' asked the gemdrake.

I am Tollerman of Musson. The stylus seemed to form the words without much help from him.

'Why do you want to die, Tollerman of Musson?'

I am nothing. She took my tongue when she took my father's talisman.

'The thing you call your father's talisman was a gem,' said the gemdrake. 'One of the gems of power.'

He wore a wooden talisman about his neck. It was no gem.

'I know my own,' said the gemdrake. 'Talisman or not, that gem is the gem of dreams.'

It hurt his head to think, but he remembered a shining thing before his eyes. It had dazzled him and brought him pain on the day that Zara —

'Your father left you the gem of dreams,' said the gemdrake. 'Where is it now?'

It is gone.

'The gem is lost,' rasped the gemdrake. 'You cast away your chance.'

Tollerman bowed his head, then put the tablet away. Writing had given him a voice of sorts, but it had made him tell his shame.

'Follow me,' said the gemdrake. 'The sun will soon be down.'

Tollerman glanced at the spur, but the gemdrake looked at him with knowing eyes. It could wall him with fire inside a heartbeat. He would have no chance to jump, and he could not face the fire. To fall through the cold cloudy air to crushing death below was tempting, to burn and scream for endless heartbeats was certainly not. The gemdrake must have known it had made its point, for now it returned to the gate, crouched against the rock, and stared at the sinking sun.

Tollerman sat down and clasped his knees. A phantom danced in his mind and touched his hand, and he cringed away. *Zara, no! Please don't make me remember.* The sun slid down among the clouds. Soon it would be dusk.

You are nothing. The voice was sly and cold.

I am Tollerman of Musson.

You are a fatherless whelp. You are nothing.

The rim of the sun gleamed for a moment, then vanished. A grinding clang made Tollerman jump, and the gemdrake stirred at last.

'The gate is closing now, and time is up.'

The rasping voice was fading, and the craggy shape of the gemdrake faded, too, moulding itself back into the rock out of which it had come.

It happened so quietly that Tollerman was scarcely shocked.

CHAPTER TWENTY

GEMSTORM

WINTERWANE — 11TH MOON OF THE YEAR

OF THE HOUND

ALLYSO ran. Her boots were worn so thin that she could feel the individual shapes of the gems. She ran through galleries and vaults of stone, past waterfalls of crystal and tumbling heaps of solid fire. Down this path and that she tore, but she never found the rusty Dragon's Gate.

'Keeper!' she cried, and set the echoes chattering around her.

After that, she tried to hunt in silence. The gate must be this way — or maybe not. She was not even sure how many chambers she had searched.

She ran and then she walked and then she stumbled, but everywhere she looked was the savage beauty of gems. Nowhere could she see the passage that led to the iron gate.

Allyso pushed down panic. She would not be trapped for long. Surely the gemdrake would let her out at sunlift. If not, it would have to let her out next time the gate was opened. But the lock had been rusted fast. How long since anyone else had summoned the dragon?

If she had just remembered to ask what the gem was like! Such a tiny mistake. An oversight. And now she would pay with the future she might have had. Just as Merrit had done.

'But I was trying to help!' she whispered. 'Why should invaders prosper while people like me lose out?'

Tears welled and ran down her face, making warm trails on the cold skin. She couldn't sob aloud amid those echoing crystals, so she stood there crying as silently as she could. She was trapped by her own mistake and lack of care. It was no use blaming the dragon, who had tried to warn her away. It was no use blaming anyone but herself.

She should have been better prepared. She should have asked what the gem would look like. She should have asked exactly where it might be found. If she had only asked the questions and had more time ...

Time!

Stars, but she *would* have time! It wasn't over, not at all! She could find the gem today or tomorrow, even a year from now. It didn't matter *when* she found it, for was it not the gem of time? With that gem of power in her hand, she might turn back time to the point before the gate was closed. And then she could escape.

She was dizzy and faint with relief, but it was quite a while before she realised she was also faint with hunger. It seemed a long time since she had eaten her share of those fish. Her mouth was dry, and she began to fear that thirst would overtake her before she could find the gem. Perhaps her boundless searching time was not so boundless after all. There was water on the mountain — McDaniel Waters was proof of that — but was there water here in the Crystalium Caverns?

Allyso went to search, heading instinctively for the lowest point of the caverns. Through the galleries she went, past lakes of glassy sparkle and chips of blue. Once she thought she had found a pool, but the glitter was only shattered pieces of crystal. She wondered how they had broken, and peered up to see if something might have fallen. Above her hung a host of crystal spears, delicate leaf-like blades, growing from the vault above.

'Ohhh!' sighed Allyso, and the crystals responded with the faint tremble of a harp.

'Keeper?' she called, and the music came again.

'Kee-per!' She risked a shout. The music rang high and hurt her ears, higher and higher still, while she pressed her hands to her temples.

Then there was silence as the sound rose and slid out of her range of hearing.

And then a crystal snapped, making no more noise than the icicle it resembled. It fell like a shooting star and dashed itself to pieces on the ground. The tinkle of that fall spun out in the echoes, and another spear fell in response. This one hit the ground near Allyso. She leapt away, and more rained down, hissing and pinging as they broke on the floor. Sharp chips of crystal rebounded, stinging her legs and arms, even through her mantle. A crystal splinter cut her brow, narrowly missing her eye. She tried to get out of range, but there was no guessing where the next gem would fall.

Instinctively, Allyso dropped into a crouch, shielding her head with her arms. The noise of the gemstorm was full of terror, its music worse than harsher sound would have been. It seemed to go on forever, and she crouched in a shaking heap. Blood was trickling down her brow and seeping into her mantle, but she dared not lift her head to wipe it away. If she were struck in the eye, she might be blinded.

At last the deadly rain of crystal eased. Allyso's battered ears began to pick out individual sounds, and her nerves felt stretched to the limit as she found herself waiting for the next round of cacophony. But the next one failed to come.

Stiffly, Allyso dropped her arms and stared at the ruined crystals piled around her. They weighted the skirts of her mantle and lodged in the folds of her sleeves. She stood up with a clatter of crystal, brushed some chips from her collar, then raised a doubtful hand to her stinging brow. The blood was blurring her sight, so she groped in her sash for her kerchief to stem the flow.

Her fingers met an empty sash and, slowly, memory returned. She had lost the kerchief somewhere in the caverns. When had that happened, exactly? When had she held it last? She had seen a patch of blue, and stopped to wipe her face before she began the search … She remembered the wisp of draught that had swirled it out of her hand.

Allyso staggered as the cavern whirled around her. The colours blurred and blued and, suddenly, the kerchief was soft between her fingers. A patch of blue ahead, and, as she turned, she saw a glitter of gold.

A sudden draught tugged at the kerchief, and it wisped away. She bent to retrieve it, but it didn't seem to be there.

'Bother!' she said, for she knew she could not stop to search. She must find it on the way back. After she found the gem of time ... For now she must blot the blood from her face with her sleeve. She pressed her fingers against the cut and, when the bleeding had abated, she began to pick her way out of the heaps of broken crystal ... but there was *no* broken crystal! The ground was clear, and she seemed to be standing in the mouth of a passage ... She winced. That blow to her brow — she must be losing her mind! She closed her eyes, swaying and dizzy, her left hand clenched around the orb that gave her dragonsight.

Something was *very* wrong.

She blinked and peered at her bare right hand. It was stained with blood, but *had* she held the kerchief? She tried to remember exactly how it had been. She had seen a patch of blue, and stopped to wipe her face before she began the search. She had tugged the kerchief from her sash.

A maddening flicker of light, and the kerchief was in her hand. Her fingers clenched with shock, and the sudden tug of a draught swirled her mantle around her legs. And Allyso was left with the kerchief in her hand, staring at the scatter of flowers that decorated the cloth.

Her first lucid thought was that the kerchief had been charmed. It had come from Leonard, who had some mazing power. Her second thought was that it couldn't be the kerchief. The piece of cloth was the same as it had been before. It was Allyso who had changed. *Had* she been hurt in the gemstorm, or had she bumped her head on the rocks and the other was nothing but a kind of dream?

Frowning, she thought back to the shattering sound, the bounce and strike of the crystal —

And it was happening again! Crystals speared from the ceiling, hissing and pinging as they broke on the floor. The chips were stinging her legs and arms; one sliced across her cheek. She dropped in a crouch, bringing her hands to her face, striking her chin on the dragonsight orb. That hurt, but she stayed in her crouch until she heard the gemstorm subside. And her right hand was empty, whereas her left ... Allyso stared at the dragonsight orb. It was black and small, and it gave no light, yet enabled her to see.

Nervously, she laid it down on a bed of shattered crystal. Her hand had been clutching it for so long that she had to remind her fingers to uncurl. She withdrew her hand and darkness fell like a curtain. Hurriedly, she reached for the gem again. There was no blaze of light, but the dragonsight returned. She had no idea what was going on, but she thought of the kerchief again. Thought of wiping her face with it, thought of the sudden draught ... and found herself holding the linen, holding it tightly so it couldn't be blown away.

Her back was to the tunnel, the Crystalium Caverns lay ahead but, if her suspicion was right, she had no need to search them for the gem of time. She stared again at the orb in her hand. The gemdrake had never told her exactly what it was ...

'I wonder!' she whispered, and she thought of the gate, just before it closed.

The gemdrake crouched against the rock and stared at the sinking sun. It appeared to be calm, but Tollerman knew how quickly it could move. He sat on the rock and clasped his knees and watched as the sun slid down among the clouds. Soon it would be dusk, and the gate would close. And what if the girl were still inside? What could *he* do but struggle with memories he didn't want?

Zara — but it hurt too much. He jerked his head against the rock, hoping that pain would distract him from the other.

You are nothing. The voice was sly and cold, nudging at his mind.

I am Tollerman of Musson, he thought.

You are a fatherless whelp whelp whelp. You are worth nothing nothing nothing.

Tollerman moved uneasily. Something was very strange ... The rim of the sun gleamed for a moment, and its final beams struck out across the rock and touched the gate. The iron hinges creaked as the portal began to close, and Tollerman started up. He had a wild idea of diving through to try to help the girl — but then he saw there was no need. She was stepping out of the shadows, with blood on her face and her hand held high.

'You should have told me what it was,' she said to the gemdrake. 'I could have died of thirst in there, looking for something I already had in my hand.'

Tollerman stared. She had been gone for just a while.

PART FIVE — BEGINNING

CHAPTER TWENTY-ONE

TIME-WAVE

WINTERWANE — 11TH MOON OF THE YEAR

OF THE HOUND

ALLYSO was deathly tired, but so keyed up she had lost the way to sleep. She paced about, trying to think of the questions she must ask.

There must be no more mistakes, no oversights! She thought and planned and asked her questions, but the gemdrake was little help.

'I have the gem,' she said, 'but what about the master of time?'

'It doesn't matter, halfling,' said the gemdrake.

'I've wasted enough time already!'

The gemdrake grated a laugh, snorting acrid smoke.

'So, time might not matter, but I *must* know what I have to do next.' She groaned. 'It's a long way back to Torm, and what if the master is south or west or east? Torm isn't the only problem, Scholar said. And what if I make even worse mistakes?'

'Don't,' said the gemdrake.

'What if I have more trouble?'

'Don't,' said the gemdrake.

'You had enough to say before,' said Allyso angrily. 'You kept on saying you'd *burn me to the bone*. Now all you say is *don't*. I *have* to finish this. Don't you see? I would never have done any of it if there had been any other choice.'

The gemdrake said nothing.

'*Well*?' said Allyso. She was so keyed up she thought she would fly to pieces if she didn't get sound advice. 'What am I meant to do next?'

Silence fell, and she realised the gemdrake had gone. She could see the hulk of its body but, when she went closer, she realised it was nothing but a shoulder of rock. She touched it, finding it cold and unresponsive.

It was almost dark, and a freezing wind was blowing over the spur. The Dragon's Gate seemed rusted fast again, and points of snow were whirling from the clouds.

Tollerman was crouched by the wall.

'There *was* a dragon here?' said Allyso uncertainly. 'A gemdrake? It was talking, right, and then it turned into stone?'

The page's arms tightened around his knees, and he began to rock. A whimpering sound came from his mouth and was plucked away by the wind.

'Don't do that,' snapped Allyso, as bitter snowflakes stung her cheeks. 'We have to get away from here. We'll freeze to death if we stay.' Her hood had slipped and her hair was blowing in eddies round her face. Her mantle strained against her and, as she pulled it closer, her journeypack began to slide across the greasy rock. She lunged for it, and scooped up Tollerman's as well. 'Come on,' she said. 'We'll have to go back the way we came. There's nothing for us here.'

She dropped the pack on Tollerman's knees, wondering what to do if he wouldn't come. She supposed he was no concern of hers, but he had helped her at the lake and on the ledge. She had thought he was feeling better, but now he seemed to have fallen back into his pit of misery.

'Come on, Tollerman.' She touched his shoulder. 'You can't stay here. I'm sure this isn't the way you're meant to be.'

He continued to rock, and she felt like shaking him. 'It would be better if you could tell me what you want to do,' she said. 'You must have been able to talk once!' She wondered how long it had been since he had spoken. A year or two? More or less? And had he made sense when he did?

She pictured him in clothes that fitted, groomed and able to speak ...

And the world went wild as a wave of darkness spun up from her hand and shattered over their heads.

CHAPTER TWENTY-TWO

THICKET

SUMMERCLIMB — 1ST MOON OF THE YEAR

OF THE HOUND

WHEN the world steadied, she was standing in a thicket of honeywood trees. The air was warm and damp, as if it might soon rain. Her head still spun, so she put out a hand to grasp the branch above her while she thought about what she had done.

The gem of time had brought her here. But where was *here*? And when?

She supposed she could go back by thinking of the place and time she had left, but what if she landed balanced on the ledge that had led to Makersland and now led nowhere? She could stagger and fall, and that would be the end. Breathing deeply, she clung to the branch as if it would anchor her, then let it go and began to make her way through the trees.

It was almost moonhigh when Allyso reached the edge of the thicket, and she paused in the shadows to catch her bearings. A few lights to the east seemed to come from a village, but she had no idea which one. It wasn't Torm, nor did she think it was large enough to be Fielding. She was wondering if she should go in that direction when she saw the youth and his hound. At first, she thought it was Scholar with Tace at his heels. It would be just like him to show up where he wasn't expected. He had said he was going to Ankoor, but she didn't know how far back she had come. Would he recognise her, or was this a time when the two of them had never met?

As they came closer, Allyso realised it wasn't Scholar after all. This boy had darker hair, and the hound was dancing behind him in a way that Tace would never have done. It looked to be brown, with white markings, and its ears were so fluffy they swung like flowing tresses as the animal leapt and twirled.

A dancing hound! Allyso was so entranced that it took her a few heartbeats to realise the dark-haired boy was Tollerman — a Tollerman dressed in a Highsummer cloak and leggings. She had thought about him just before the timewave had hit, and the gem of time had brought her to the subject of her thought.

She was wondering whether to call him, when she saw the healer step out of the thicket's edge.

Tollerman knew he must hurry. The moon had climbed, and he had been delayed in his escape from Musson Manor. He had had to swallow his usual draught, and spitting it up had taken longer than he had expected. At least no-one had heard him; he slept away from his cousins in an isolated wing of the manor.

'He's always moaning and screaming,' the cousins said, and glanced at him half in fear and half in amusement. 'He grinds his teeth and throws himself about.'

He couldn't remember doing that, but neither could he argue that he didn't. Why else would he wake in the mornings huddled and bruised on the floor beside his bed? Why else would his throat be aching and his jaw-muscles sore? And sometimes he bit his tongue and woke with it bloody.

'He's possessed,' said folk from the village, and most of them avoided him when they could.

His kinsman had done his best, giving the orphaned boy a home and letting him keep the litter-runt hound that had strayed onto the manor grounds. Zara was the best friend Tollerman had ever had, a dizzy dancing creature who could always make him smile. As a child, he had wondered whether he was evil, as the other children said, but Zara's friendship was proof that he wasn't bad. It was just as well he had her, for his trouble was getting worse. The dreams had always plagued him, but now they were coming every night, and casting their shadows over his days as well. His kinsman gave him a sleeping draught most nights, yet the dreams still hung in his mind.

But now he had found the answer in a healer's booth at a travelling fair. If all went well, he would pay the healer's price tonight and be rid of the misery forever.

He shivered as he ran, and a sudden chill swept over him. Hadn't he been this way before? He almost stopped to think it through, but he was afraid he would be too late. And there was no mystery really.

This was the way he had gone to see the fair. He had crept out of the manor on that occasion, too; his kinsman was none too pleased to have him roam around alone.

No mystery, but the feeling was growing stronger. A ghostly figure seemed to pace beside him. And suddenly Zara growled.

Tollerman slowed to a walk, for the healer had emerged from the path through the thicket.

'Greetings, Dame; I hope I am not too late?' His voice sounded odd to him, shocking and unfamiliar, as if he had not spoken in a while. He cleared his throat, but the strangeness persisted.

'You swore you would come alone.'

'So I did,' he said, puzzled, and cleared his throat again. 'I am alone, except for Zara.'

'Leave the creature here,' said the healer. 'Our dealing today is private.'

Tollerman frowned. 'She is just a Merryhound, Dame, quite harmless. She keeps me company.'

'Then you'll not want her to suffer.'

'Suffer? You are going to heal me!'

'When a malady is plucked from one, it may appear in another. For one to win, another one must lose.'

Tollerman bit his lip. He was almost tempted to call Zara and return to the manor, but what if he never had another chance to be cured? He was less than nothing to anyone but Zara but, if he were rid of the dreams, he might make himself a life.

'Zara can wait for me here,' he said. He signalled the Merryhound to sit, and she dropped obediently to the ground.

'You have brought my price?'

He lifted his hands to display it, but the woman grasped his wrist.

'Not here, you fool. The exchange must be done in the proper manner. Come!'

Tollerman followed the healer into the depths of the thicket. It seemed strange that they should do business in such an uncomfortable place, but he supposed she would use some kind of ritual to cure him. Some folk frowned on this as wicked magic. She had said she dared not do it at the fair.

They came to a small clearing. A brazier burned in the centre, glowing brightly. Did she plan to use forbidden smoking herbs? The healer bent and removed some objects from her pouch, then crouched beside the brazier for a moment.

'Now,' she said, rising to stand before him. 'Tell me again of your malady, Tollerman.'

'I have terrible dreams,' said Tollerman. 'They trouble me so that my kin think I am mad. They keep me in the manor, and I am of no use to anyone.'

'I can take your dreams, pluck them out of your head,' she said, 'but, as I told you at the fair, you must pay my price.'

Tollerman raised his hands again, and this time she did not prevent him as he removed the chain from around his neck. From it hung a marvellously carved timber-nut.

'This talisman belonged to the Blood of Musson?' she demanded. 'It is not as fine as I expected.'

'It is the best thing I have, apart from Zara. My father wore it around his neck as a luck-charm. He died before I was born, and so my kinsman kept it for me.'

'It seems to have brought *you* no luck,' she said. 'A curious bauble.'

'Is it enough?' asked Tollerman.

The healer took the timber-nut and held it in her hand. 'I believe it will suffice. Do you give your father's treasure to me willingly in exchange for your dreams?'

It hurt to part with it, but Tollerman had to believe his father would wish him health and happiness, and his kinsman had always said the bauble was of no great value. 'I give it to you willingly in exchange for my dreams,' he said.

The healer swung the timber-nut from its chain. 'A clever ruse of your father's. A pity for you his son was not so sharp. Shall I show you its true colours, now it is yours no longer?' She reached into the bag at her waist and drew out a pair of pincers, then gripped the timber-nut in the jaws and squeezed.

Tollerman cried out, but the pincers held firm and the timber-nut snapped in pieces. The healer stirred the fragments in her palm. 'And here we have the kernel,' she said. 'A most ingenious hiding place, a trinket that would be kept as an ornament, yet never tempt a thief.'

Tollerman stared at the crystal that had nestled in the heart of the bauble. All these years he had worn the talisman, and had never recognised its true form. And now it was too late.

'A dangerous thing to give a child,' said the healer. 'Your father cannot have valued you much.'

'He never knew me.'

'And yet he left you a trinket that would slowly drive you mad.' The healer turned the crystal so that it flashed in the moonlight. 'You never had the wit to see what it was, and now you have given it, willingly, to me.'

Tollerman blinked. His face felt frozen with shock, and the cruel words beat against his ears, but his body felt oddly heavy. 'You said ... you would ... take away the dreams,' he said thickly.

'I will take away the dreams, I will pluck them from your mind. And that is not all I pluck ...'

Tollerman staggered as something dashed itself against him, almost knocking him to the ground.

Zara! He would have warned her away, but his mouth was too numb to form the words. The Merryhound was licking his hand, then she bounced around and brushed against the healer. And the healer struck her down with her foreign knife.

The healer led this younger Tollerman into the thicket. It seemed an odd place to go, especially for a healer. Intensely curious, Allyso walked to the place where they had disappeared. The dancing hound was there, lying with chin on paws, but she leapt up merrily when she saw Allyso, and began to prance around her.

'Hush,' said Allyso, and cautiously patted the hound. It was nothing like Tace, but still she envied Tollerman for having such a charming companion. The thought brought her up sharply, for there was certainly no reason to envy the Tollerman *she* knew. She glanced at the high moon. It told her little, but the leaves on the honeywood trees and the balm in the air told her it was probably Summerclimb. And, since Tollerman looked around the same height that she remembered, it could not be more than a few moons before ...

The hound was pretending to worry her mantle, and Allyso detached it gently. 'I'm shabby enough now without you making it worse,' she said. She moved on into the thicket, curious to find what Tollerman was about. Was he voiceless yet? Did he hope the healer might cure him? The murmur of sound gave her direction, and a sudden cry brought her up short. Tollerman?

She peered through the screening branches and saw the page staring at the brilliant thing in the woman's hand. There was a flash as if a crystal caught the moonlight, and Allyso gasped.

The soulbinder! Dressed in a healer's robes, she was well disguised, but it *was* the same woman. And there was the crystal she had worn in her ring! It was not a ring now, but it flashed with just the same white glitter, and she spun it in the same confident way.

She was speaking to Tollerman, and he answered, but seemed unsteady on his feet. Allyso shuddered. She wanted to intervene, but what if she ended up cursed as Merrit had been? She willed Tollerman to move away, but the page was swaying as if he had drunk too much wine.

The dancing hound burst into the clearing. She might have followed Allyso, but it was Tollerman she had come to find. She flung herself at the boy in welcome, then whirled away. Her vigour must have startled the soulbinder, whose sudden movement brought her robe too close to the brazier. There was a stench of scorching cloth, and the soulbinder took revenge. The hound cried once and Allyso saw the knife, red with blood . . .

Tollerman screamed.

'Enough!' said the soulbinder, and the knife fell with a sizzle into the brazier.. The crystal flashed again and again as the woman kept murmuring, and she began a strange motion with her fingers, pulling the air as if she were drawing thread. Allyso's eyes blurred with horror, for she had seen just such a movement before.

Tollerman's expression was agonised, but slowly his eyes went blank while the soulbinder's face was dark with triumph.

'No more dreams,' said the soulbinder, 'and no more words.' She bent to the brazier and drew back the knife and Allyso saw that the blade was a sullen crimson. 'Open your mouth,' said the soulbinder. 'Here is your cure.'

Allyso almost screamed herself, but fear kept her standing rigid, eyes stretched wide, waves of faintness washing over her. To interfere would bring disaster, but how could she watch and do nothing while Tollerman was maimed? She clenched her hands around the gem of time.

There was no time to plan, no time even for hope. Frantically, she fastened her mind on Tollerman as she had seen him earlier, running over the grass with the dancing hound.

The world spun and she was back on the edge of the thicket.

It was almost moonhigh, and she saw the lights of the village. Her eyes were blurred with tears, and she was shaking, but there was no-one in sight. She peered in the direction from which the boy and hound had come before. There was no more light than the moon, and she wished in vain for dragonsight. The gem of time had not been here in daylight, so it seemed to have no remembered light to give.

She strained her ears, hearing nothing but the slight breeze in the thicket. And then she saw them again:

Tollerman and the hound, running through the grass. She opened her mouth to cry out a warning, but what if the soulbinder heard? It was certain the dame was here already, waiting in the thicket.

Allyso's flesh crept as she realised she might have met the soulbinder herself. If Tollerman hadn't come, it might have been *she* who suffered the spell and the knife. She could not cry out to warn Tollerman away, but she could leap out of the fringe of trees and wave her arms to attract his attention. But mightn't that attract the soulbinder, too?

He was coming fast, and she had to act *now*. She stepped out of the shadows and waved, but he didn't seem to notice. He was looking at the sky, possibly calculating the time from the angle of the moon.

'Tollerman! *Tollerman*!' she said urgently, but he was already past her. She heard herself whimper as she saw the soulbinder step out of the trees. And then it was too late, for the two had come together. In moments, they had gone on into the thicket. Allyso went to the hound, and picked it up, restraining it in her arms. It seemed to think this a game, and began to bark excitedly.

'Hush!' she whispered, and muzzled the hound with her hand. If she only had some weapon! An arrow might drop the soulbinder before she had time to react. A lance, or a spear would do, but she would need skill and strength, as well as a weapon, and she knew she had neither. She had only the gem of time, and she couldn't risk throwing that, even if it were large enough.

She heard a cry from Tollerman. The hound heard, too, and her playful struggles became serious. She thrashed like a landed fish in Allyso's arms, her claws catching the brand on the girl's forearm. Allyso choked back a cry of pain, and the hound was free, bounding into the thicket.

And then, horribly, Allyso heard a bubbling scream ...

She ran, blinded by tears and crushed with guilt. She could only imagine what Tollerman must be suffering, and surely, somehow, she should have been able to prevent it.

TWENTY-THREE

ZARA

SUMMERCLIMB — 1ST MOON OF THE YEAR

OF THE HOUND

MUCH later, Allyso slept in a huddle in the grass. She woke in the cold grey before the sun had lifted and found her memories worse than her nightmares. She put her face down on her arms and wept.

'There *must* be some way,' she whispered, when she had sobbed herself out. It seemed an echo of what she had said to Merrit.

'*There must be something we can do*!' she had pleaded, and Merrit had said it was too late for anything but the gem of time.

Now she had the time-gem in her hands, but already she knew it was not an easy answer. It had shown her its nature back in the Crystalium Caverns, but since then it had tossed her around in time and dumped her in a nightmare. If all it could do was to show her scenes of horror, what was the point of it? And if it couldn't change the fate of one boy and his hound, how could it ever undo the huge and terrible wrongs at Torm?

Allyso had been lying in the grass, but now she sat up and rubbed the dried tears from her cheeks. The crystal cuts on her face throbbed, and her eyes felt hot and puffy. She thought of Tace, then of the little dancing hound and how it had died.

Scholar had been right to fear for Tace if the soulbinder got hold of her. Allyso thought she had helped a little by taking Tace away to safety, but now she had undone that help by letting another hound rush to its death.

It wouldn't do. She wouldn't let it do. She closed her hands around the gem of time, then slowly relaxed. She must manage it properly this time! She opened her pack and drew out the writing tablet, meaning to list the things she must remember. And that was odd, for there was writing already on the tablet, a tight, small script that was nothing like her own. Could it be Trader Mohr's? No, for there was some of her own on the same page, the information she had had from Seer Wootton. The seer could not have written this extra script, nor could Leonard and, since leaving them, the only folk she had really been close to had been Scholar and Tollerman.

Allyso peered through swollen eyes at the script, which ran line by line down the page. In some places the words trailed off the edge of the tablet, as if they had been written in poor light.

I am Tollerman of Musson.

I am nothing. She took my tongue when she took my father's talism —

He wore a wooden talisman around his neck. It was not a ge —

It is gone.

She put the tablet away. After reading that, she no longer felt like writing anything herself. She must work to undo the harm that had come to Tollerman and his hound, for if she could not do that, the gem of time was useless.

It was no use trying to intercept Tollerman as she had done before. If she stepped out openly or called to him, the soulbinder would have them both. She would have to warn him away before he reached the thicket, well out of range of the soulbinder's hearing.

She would need to return to the thicket and then walk in the direction from which Tollerman had come. His tracks and the hound's should be still on the grass, for the dew had not yet lifted.

Allyso was not too sure how far she had fled after hearing that agonised scream, but she found she remembered the general direction of the thicket. She shuddered as she approached it, though common sense told her the soulbinder would have left by now. And Tollerman, too? He had certainly been with the soulbinder when she came to Torm, but how could he travel when that terrible thing had been done to him? Surely he would be bleeding.

With a sickly feeling she recalled that the knife had been glowing red-hot. She had once seen Healer Hilz cauterise a wound with a hot blade; he had done it for one of the castlers who had been bitten by a racinghound. The bleeding had stopped that time, so perhaps Tollerman — but the thought was so horrible that she was nearly sick.

Not for worlds would she go into that thicket and

visit the ghastly clearing, but she found the faint tracks she needed and followed them.

There was a manor in the distance; perhaps he had come from there? Even so, she could scarcely present herself at the door in her ragged state. She winced, remembering that Trader Mohr had tried to turn her away when she arrived in Fielding; if she had looked shabby then, she must look much worse now.

Enough of that! She must intercept Tollerman where neither the soulbinder nor anyone else would hear, so she waited where she was. Time didn't matter ... but, yes, it did, for Tollerman was surely in agony now. Had he really suffered twice because of her interfering? Or was it only the first time still? She hoped it was the first time, but she remembered every time herself ... She clasped the gem of time and closed her eyes, then brought a picture into her mind. Tollerman and the hound in moonlight, somewhere between the manor and the place where she was standing.

The light changed against her eyelids, and she blinked them open. It was certainly moonlight, and there were the boy and the hound. Fearing they would go right past her, Allyso began to run, putting herself in their path.

Tollerman changed course to avoid a collision. Allyso darted after him and caught at his arm. 'Tollerman, wait! I need to talk to you.'

It had been a strange night altogether. Tollerman had expected to make his way to the thicket in plenty of time to meet the healer, but he seemed to have been walking for longer than he'd planned. He shivered as if a dragon had passed over his cradle. When he clicked his fingers for Zara, she danced to him and smiled up in the moonlight, her tongue lolling in the comical way it had. Her mismatched eyes seemed merry; Zara loved to go out, and she was delighting in this expedition.

Tollerman began to run. He was making better time now, but he jumped violently as a shadow emerged from the edge of the thicket. Too small to be the healer. He thought at first it was one of his cousins coming to spy on him. He changed course, but the figure grabbed his arm.

Tollerman pulled away. It was not a cousin after all, but a ragged stranger child.

'If you've come to beg alms,' he said quickly, 'you'd best go to the manor.' His voice rang strangely in his ears as he hurried on, but he tossed a few more words over his shoulder. 'You could sleep in the barn, and go to the kitchens tomorrow.'

The child scurried round in front of him, catching at him again. 'I don't want alms, Tollerman.'

'Then go away.'

She ignored his tone and lengthened her stride to keep pace. 'You *have* to listen to me.' She stooped, abruptly, and scooped the dancing hound into her arms. 'What's her name?'

He paused, glanced towards the moon, then at the thicket. 'I call her Zara,' he said unwillingly. 'Put her down. I have to go.'

'She's lovely,' said the child. 'Is she a Spellhound?'

'She's a Merryhound.' He turned on her, exasperated. 'I have no time to talk about hounds, and children like you should be abed. Get home to your mother, or you'll be whipped.'

'I am not a child,' said the girl, 'and I have no mother, and worse than a whipping will happen if you don't listen to me this time.'

She would not go away, so he decided to humour her. 'Well? have your say and be quick.'

'You are called Tollerman of Musson, and you are on your way to see a woman. You probably think she's a healer.'

'How do you —'

'You are going to give her the bauble you wear around your neck.'

Startled, he lifted his hand, but the talisman was hidden under his tunic.

'It's a gem,' she said, 'a crystal, and the soulbinder will use it to maze you.'

Her voice was emphatic, and she was making him uneasy. The light was poor but, as far as he could see, she was a total stranger. Of course she was wrong. The talisman was not a crystal. 'I have no time for this gibbering,' he said, and held out his arms. 'Give Zara to me.'

The girl backed away. 'That dame is evil. She will kill your hound and ruin you and much more besides.'

Tollerman began to walk away. He hoped Zara would struggle free if he seemed about to leave her, but the girl came up beside him, persistent as an applefly.

'She will cut out your tongue!' she panted. 'She will make you serve her and use you as a tool.'

Zara began to bark excitedly, and Tollerman stopped dead. 'Hush!' he said. 'Do you want to rouse up the cottagers?'

'I will, if it will stop you going to that soulbinder. I tell you, she will kill your hound without a heartbeat's pause!'

She sounded overwrought, so Tollerman thought it best to soothe her before she really did rouse up the manor. He was not a prisoner, exactly, but his kinsman had made it plain he was not to leave his chamber after dark. 'Hush now,' he said in what he hoped was a reasonable tone. 'There is no harm in going to visit a healer.'

'She is *not* a healer.' The girl sounded close to tears. 'She is a soulbinder. She is the one who has killed my uncle and your hound and brought Torm to ruin.'

'Why are you saying all this?' asked Tollerman. 'I know nothing about your uncle, but no-one has killed my hound.'

'I saw her,' said the girl. 'I saw her!'

She sounded very certain and Tollerman felt himself wavering. Then he pulled himself together. 'Either you have heard what they say about me and are mocking me,' he said, 'or else you suffer nightmares as bad as mine. Terrible dreams that make you afraid to close your eyes.' He gave her a half-smile, though he doubted she could see his face. 'The healer might help you as well, if you have something to pay.'

'It was no nightmare,' said the girl. 'I tell you, I saw it happen.'

'You are young to be a seer.'

'I'm not. I saw — I mean, I just know some things that will happen. I know about that crystal you wear on a chain ...'

His hand went up again, and this time he drew the talisman free from his collar. He hated to waste this time, but it was one way of quieting her. 'This is a timber-nut, not a crystal,' he said. He dangled it before her. 'So you see, you are wrong. Your vision was of someone else.'

She stamped her foot. 'I saw it, you fleewit!' she snapped. 'You will meet the dame, and she will crack the bauble open and take the crystal out. She will maze you and kill your hound and cut out your tongue, and you will let her do it.'

He was still swinging the chain, but now he caught up the bauble in finger and thumb. He squeezed it and shook it, smiling, although he felt cold and hollow inside. 'No, it is definitely a nut,' he said. 'Carved finely, but I hear the kernel within.'

'That is the crystal,' said the girl stubbornly. 'Break it and you will see.'

'If I break it, I will have nothing to pay for my cure. You will need to spin a better tale than that.'

'Have you ever heard of the Cleave?' she asked abruptly.

'Yes,' he said. 'It is some way south of here.'

'What of the Cloudway?'

'Perhaps.'

'And Torm?'

'Torm. No, I have not heard of Torm.'

He was anxious to be gone. This ragged child was clearly mad, but he hesitated to leave her, even if she would let him go. For one thing, she had Zara in her arms, and for another, he knew how it felt to be brushed aside. And some of the things she said seemed to strike strange echoes in his mind.

'You will help destroy Torm,' she said. 'I saw it happen. And then later I met you on the Cloudway, beside McDaniel Waters.'

'Perhaps it was a dream,' he said more gently. 'Now, will you give me Zara?'

'It hasn't happened yet, for you.' The child seemed puzzled. 'It's odd. I can remember it all, so why don't you?'

Tollerman could think of several answers to that. 'Dreams seem very real,' he said.

'Dreams!' The girl dumped Zara on the ground, and began to scrabble in a journeypack. She took out a tinderflint and struck a flame, scrabbled again and fetched up a writing tablet. '*This* is no dream!' she said, and thrust it and the burning wick towards him. As she did so, the flame illuminated her face. Tollerman stared. It must have been a trick of light, but the child seemed to have gilded skin.

'Look at it, Tollerman! Read what it says.'

He took the tablet and glanced down at the few lines of writing, then tilted it to the light to get a better view. He read the script, and the hollow cold grew worse.

I am Tollerman of Musson.

I am nothing. She took my tongue when she took my father's talism —

He wore a wooden talisman around his neck. It was not a ge —

It is gone.

'Do you recognise the script?' demanded the girl.

'It looks like my own,' he said cautiously, 'but I have never written such foolishness.'

'Then how did it get on this tablet? Please, for your sake and your hound's, stay away from that evil dame.'

Tollerman sighed. He could see the girl was in earnest, and he was at a loss to account for this writing in his own script. He wrote for his lessons, but seldom for any other purpose. There seemed no way the child could have found a sample and copied it to create this.

He blew out the wick and handed the tablet back to its owner. 'Perhaps you should tell me this tale of yours,' he said. He glanced at the moon. 'Tell it briefly.'

The girl sat down, and huddled into her worn mantle. 'My name is Allyso Tormblood,' she said, 'and I am the Heir of Torm. My uncle is — was — Merrit Tormblood and, more than six moons ago, a dame came to Torm and asked for shelter. Merrit was warned against her, but he let her stay. She had a page with her, a page without a tongue. He seemed half-daft, and Merrit said I should make friends with him.' She paused. 'That page was *you*.'

'Six moons ago, I was here at Musson,' said Tollerman.

'It was six moons ago for *me*. Is it Summerclimb now?'

'Yes. First Moon, and tenth day.'

'Then for you it must be about two moonspans in the future. You and the soulbinder will come to Torm on Highsummer Eve, and that will be the beginning of the end for Torm. You will be there for only two or three days, but she will stay until Torm is sucked dry. For you this will all begin tonight, when the soulbinder uses your crystal against you and cuts out your tongue.'

The tale continued for some while. It seemed to have little to do with Tollerman himself, but strangely, that made it seem more probable. If this girl wished to deceive him, wouldn't she have concentrated on *his* role in the saga? Instead, she seemed to know little about what he had done.

'You say this page — I — left the castle after three days,' he said at last, 'and then you met me in the mountains six moons later. What did I do in between those times?'

'How can I know?' she demanded. 'You must have gone to the soulbinder's people. They said she had sent them a message, and you were the only one who could have carried it. You never came back to Torm, so I don't know where you were or what happened to you.' She swallowed. 'It must have been bad. You looked ill enough when you arrived at Torm, but when I found you on the Cloudway you were —'

'What?'

'Like an animal,' she said unhappily. 'Wild, afraid, dirty and starving. You followed me after that, but sometimes you didn't know I was there. And you would sit and rock and whine like a hurt beast.'

Tollerman felt a growing distaste for this tale. He did despair over his nightmares and terrors, but they would never reduce him to the state she suggested.

'Go home now,' she continued. 'Don't let this woman near you. Then it will never need to — oh no, no!' She broke off with a gasp as the healer walked towards them over the grass.

'You are late,' said the healer. Her dark gaze flicked over the girl and hound. 'I told you to come alone for your cure, so there would be no distractions. Why have you brought this wench and hound?'

Tollerman felt his mouth go dry. 'I came to say ... I have changed my mind. I cannot accept your cure.'

'The dreams will drive you mad.' Again her glance darted, and she addressed the girl. 'This lad with whom you dally — do you know he is bound to his bed at times, to keep him from harming others? That he is mad and cursed to suffer for his father's folly?'

'*You* drove him mad,' said the girl. 'You cursed him.'

'It is his father's curse, not mine.' The woman held out her hand. 'Come, Tollerman, give me the talisman as we agreed. That is where the mischief lies.'

Tollerman put his hand over the timber-nut. 'You asked for this to pay for a cure,' he said. 'Now you tell me it is the cause of my nightmares?'

'So I did and so it is,' she said. 'Giving the talisman to me will solve your problem and free you of your dreams.'

The girl, Allyso, was visibly trembling. 'Don't listen to her, Tollerman. She will take that gem and turn it against you.'

He wavered. If he believed the dame, the talisman was the seat of his problem, but if the girl was right, giving it up would bring calamity. 'I will stick to the troubles I have already,' he said at last. 'I know their faces, at least.' And perhaps he could dispose of the talisman later on, in private.

'You will not give me the talisman to save yourself?' The dame sounded cold.

Tollerman shook his head.

'Then do it to save this creature!' The dame scooped up Zara, whipped a knife from her sash and held it against the Merryhound's throat.

CHAPTER TWENTY-FOUR

DARKNESS

SUMMERCLIMB — 1ST MOON OF THE YEAR

OF THE HOUND

ALLYSO expected a curse of the kind that had humbled Merrit, but the dame was using a knife and threats instead. Why did she not employ her strongest weapons?

Tollerman stumbled forward, but the soulbinder tightened her grip on the dancing hound. 'I cannot tell how you fathomed me,' she said, with a venomous glance at Allyso, 'but tell this fool I will kill the hound in a moment. Or perhaps I will merely slit its belly and let it die.'

'She is telling the truth,' said Allyso numbly. 'She has done it before.'

'Give me the talisman,' said the soulbinder. 'Honour our bargain and save your darling here.'

Allyso bit her lip and tasted blood. With the gem of time, she could roll back time, but then the weary explanations would need to begin again. Perhaps she should get away and search out the master of time, who would know how to make the gem more effective? She glanced at Tollerman. The orb had gathered light from the time she had spent in the morning, and now it lent her dragonsight once more. That must give her an advantage, since she could see much better than either of the others.

She reached for Tollerman's arm, and found it was shaking. She hoped he could manage to act if he had the chance.

'Now!' snapped the soulbinder. 'Give the gem to me!'

The hound gave an agonised whine from the pain at her throat, and Allyso boiled with sudden fiery anger. Tollerman had made a bargain he should not keep, but merry little Zara had never deserved to suffer. She should be dancing under the moon, not crying out like this!

The anger rose like water from a spring, and Allyso raised the orb above her head. 'This is the gem of time!' she cried, and the words rushed out of her mouth as if in spate from a river. 'Harm that hound and I send you *out* of time!'

The gem began to glow, and a fan of darkness cut a swathe in the moonlight. Startled, she would have dropped the orb had her fingers not seemed frozen in their grasp.

The soulbinder sneered. 'So a halfling runt plays master of time! Harm me, runt, and the hound is lost as well.'

Allyso turned and swept the beam of darkness over a honeywood sapling. It swelled and grew to a mighty tree. 'How old are you?' asked Allyso. 'How many years could you age until you are nothing but bones?

And it would be *you* that aged and not the Merryhound.' She was trembling now, the fire of anger spreading through her body. Tollerman was staring in horror, and even the soulbinder flung out a hand to ward her away.

Zara snapped at her, and the knife flew wide. Tollerman dived to save his hound.

And still the soulbinder cast no curse, but snatched up her knife instead. She uttered a fearful scream and flung the blade at Allyso. Then all the world went mad.

The soulbinder screamed again, a high thin shriek of terror, and Allyso saw her shredded away like a tatter of leaves in a gale. The honeywood tree grew taller still, towering towards the stars, spreading like a canopy overhead. A sizzle of lightning raced across the sky, thunder rolled and the tree's crown broke with a crack. It fell to earth in a long, shuddering crunch that shook the ground, throwing Allyso down so hard that the breath was driven from her lungs.

The blade keened on through the air.

CHAPTER TWENTY-FIVE

INFERNO

SUMMERCLIMB — 2ND MOON TO 3RD MOON

OF THE YEAR OF THE HOUND

ALLYSO found she was lying on grass, and she blinked at the brightness of the day. She ached all over, limp as a well-wrung cloth.

Tollerman was crouched on the ground some distance away, hunched in the posture she had often seen before. His eyes were wide and fearful, but this time his arms were wrapped around Zara instead of his own thin legs.

'Is she all right?' asked Allyso. Her tongue felt twice its usual size, as if she had been ill.

Zara squirmed from her master's lap and danced over to lick Allyso's cheek. It might have been in gratitude, or it might have been high spirits. Whatever the reason, it made Allyso feel better.

'Why are you staring like that?' she said fretfully to Tollerman.

'You *glowed*,' said Tollerman. 'I s-saw the starlight through you. And then everything went wild. It was like some kind of storm.'

Allyso shivered. It *had* been like a storm but, after the tree had fallen, it had been a storm of silence. Darting lights and streaks of darkness had swirled around her like a host of shooting stars, and the soulbinder's knife had flown like a brand of fire.

'The knife hit you, and then we were suddenly here,' said Tollerman. 'And that tree you made is all over the place.'

'I don't think I made it,' said Allyso doubtfully. Her head was aching with a steady pounding. 'I just *had* to stop her, so I did the first thing that came into my mind. Did you say the knife hit me?'

'I th-think it did.'

Allyso felt herself carefully. 'It must have missed,' she said. 'Or else we came here just a heartbeat before it hit.'

'*Here*? We were here all along.'

'*Now* then, if you prefer it.'

Tollerman was silent for a few breaths, smoothing Zara's fluffy ears, but watching Allyso out of the corner of his eye. 'You really c-can move time?'

'I told you.' She was clutching the gem of time, and she tucked it into her sash, then turned her back on the huge tree she had somehow raised from a sapling. It was, as Tollerman had said, all over the place in pieces. She thought she should probably do something to restore it, but she didn't know how. 'The question is,' she said, 'how far did we move, and where is *she*?'

'You s-said you would s-send her out of time.' Tollerman clutched at Zara's ruff, and the Merryhound turned and licked his hand.

'I know, but I think the gem moved us as well — or instead. She might be half a day behind us or ahead. This might be yesterday or tomorrow or last year.' She sat up cautiously, then tested her legs. They felt very far away, and she was afraid to blink in case she saw the impossible pattern of flashes and shadows once more. 'So you remember what happened?'

'I just told you what I saw.'

'That's odd. You didn't remember the other times.' She shook her head, and wished she hadn't. Her head was pounding, and her eyes seemed unwilling to focus. 'Maybe that means we came forward, not back. Only it *is* still back for me.'

The words seemed garbled to her, and Tollerman stared at her in obvious bewilderment. 'You s-said we came *forward*. How can it be back as well?'

She rose to her feet and stood swaying. 'Watch,' she said. She picked up three dead twigs and laid them out on the ground an uneven distance apart. Then she moved to stand beside the first. 'Now this twig is the time when I was up at Dragon's Gate. I told you about that.'

He nodded.

Allyso turned and walked back several paces to the third twig. 'This is where I met you, and *this* —' she jumped forward to the middle twig — 'is where we might be now. You remember the second and third twigs because you were in both places in the right order. I remember all three because ...' Her voice trailed off as her headache intensified. 'Oh, never mind. I just do.'

'You said I was there as well.' Tollerman pointed to the first twig.

'So you were, but you were older then and that was the way you would have been if you had gone with the soulbinder. You won't ever have to be like that now.' At least, she hoped not.

'I really thought she could cure me,' he said bleakly.

'Is it true what she said about you? That they tie you to the bed?'

'So they say. I never remember much of it. Only the dreams . . .'

'Then how did you get out at night to meet her?'

'They give me a sleeping draught,' he said. 'I swallowed it, but I didn't keep it down.'

Now that she saw him in daylight, she realised he was not as whole and hale as she had thought. He looked less fleewitted than he had at Torm, but his face was hollow, his nails bitten down and his eyes were deeply shadowed.

'That bauble you wear,' she said. 'The crystal inside it is a gem of power. Do you know what that is?'

'I have heard tales,' he said, 'but I thought they were *just* tales.'

'This is no tale,' she said. She touched her sash where the gem of time was nested, and he flinched. 'And that crystal is no tale. You must never let her have it.'

'What if she finds me again? Perhaps I should destroy it, or hide it away.'

'Perhaps,' said Allyso. She sighed. Tollerman seemed uncertain, and she could not be sure the soulbinder would not reappear. If that happened, Tollerman would suffer. Perhaps she should take him home to Torm? But the woman had found Torm once; she might find it again. Tollerman and Zara needed someone stubborn to protect them. Someone who would never give in.

'Go to Seer Wootton at Conners' Hall,' she said. 'Give him the crystal and ask him what you should do.'

'What would he do to me?'

Allyso looked at her branded arm. It still hurt from time to time. 'I don't know,' she said honestly. 'I don't think he would do anything to you, but you might have to do something to yourself.' She paused. 'It couldn't be as bad as what the soulbinder did — would do. And Leonard would never let him hurt Zara. She's fond of hounds. Do you know the way to Singing Tor?'

Tollerman shrugged.

'What about Fielding?'

'That is three days or so from here,' said Tollerman listlessly.

'Then the Tor is probably less. I could show you a map.'

'You will have to come with me,' said Tollerman. 'You know this Wootton, so you could speak for me.'

'He won't remember me.'

Tollerman looked defeated and Allyso sighed again. She had saved him from the soulbinder's knife. Surely he should be able to look after himself while she set her mind to saving Merrit and Torm? But it seemed she could not be free of him yet. And perhaps she should see Wootton anyway, and find out more about the gem of time.

'I'll come with you,' she said.

There was no reason to wait, and plenty of reasons for leaving as quickly as possible, so Allyso and

Tollerman set off towards the north. Tollerman did not return to the manor; he seemed to think his kinsman would be searching for him and would refuse to let him go.

'Then we'd best not walk the main way,' said Allyso. She opened her journeypack and took out the map she had had from Scholar. It seemed odd that she had it still, long before the Winterwane day on which he would give it to her, but the gem of time made oddness a way of life.

They set out along the sideroads, with Zara dancing between them. Allyso was glad the Merryhound had not been harmed, but she was silent as she walked. She was so tired, not only from the frightening time at the thicket, but also from her adventures at Dragon's Gate. She was haunted by the unhappy fear that she would have to return to that place quite soon. She had walked every step of the way from Torm to the Dragon's Gate, so it seemed logical that sometime she must walk back. She had taken a shortcut to this place for this trip into Tollerman's past, but when she returned to her own present she would probably find herself back in the freezing sleet at Cloudway End.

And what about Tollerman? Would *he* be there, crouching on the rocks? The tongueless, half-mad Tollerman had not come back to Musson, and now, since she had foiled the soulbinder's plans, perhaps she was right in thinking *that* Tollerman would never exist. And yet his writing remained.

She would have put her face in her hands and groaned, but she had to keep on walking, stepping out to keep up with Tollerman's longer stride.

They came up to the Conners' Fountain, and struck off towards the top of Singing Tor. Allyso was hungry, but Tollerman seemed too nervous to stop for food, even when Zara sniffed out and dug up some sweetloaves.

'We ought to rest a while,' said Allyso, as night swept over the Tor.

But Tollerman would not. 'I can't sleep in case I dream,' he said. 'I have no sleeping draught with me.'

'Then take the talisman off and give it to me.'

'No.' He lifted his chin. 'It was my father's. Likely that dame was lying, and it has nothing to do with my dreams.'

Allyso doubted that. She had seen the gem in action, had seen with horror what it had done to Tollerman once it was freed from its wooden shell. He had stood there mazed, and let the soulbinder kill his hound and cut out his tongue ... She glanced at Zara, at her gently waving tail. It was brown, but the white tip showed up steadily in the dusk.

'We will keep on walking, then,' she said. 'At least for a little while.'

She climbed on leaden feet, but by the time they reached the top of the Tor, she knew she could go no farther. Mist seemed to be seeping into her brain; she could scarcely see a thing.

'Go ahead if you must,' she told Tollerman. 'I have to sleep. If you meet a Mistra named Leonard, tell her ...' But she and Leonard had not yet met, so she left her request unmade.

She lay down, scarcely even needing her mantle in the Summerclimb weather. She had no idea what Tollerman was doing but before she had had enough sleep, she woke to hear him screaming.

Allyso dragged herself up, cold with fear. She had faced down the soulbinder once; she had no hope she could ever do it again. The sun was already on the rise, and she found she was alone on the Tor. She couldn't see Tollerman, but Zara was racing down towards the stonewood forest. The hound's fluffy ears flew back, her long plume of a tail was carried low. She vanished into the trees, and the cries broke off abruptly. Allyso began to run.

When she reached the forest, she found Tollerman crouched with his face concealed by his arms. If he began to rock and wail — but he raised his head and drew a shuddering breath, then put his cheek for a moment on Zara's head. His face was blanched, and his eyes looked terrible, but Allyso made no comment on that.

'Come,' she said, 'we'll go and find Seer Wootton. If we can.'

She looked for Leonard as they picked their way through the forest. Surely Tollerman's screams should have woken the girl? It seemed to be Leonard's task to deal with strangers.

She found she was looking forward to meeting the apprentice again, though it would do no good to thank her for a kindness that Leonard would not remember.

She even called Leonard's name, but no dark cowled figure appeared to challenge them. And there, before her, she saw the narrow entrance to Conners' Hall.

'That's the way in,' she said to Tollerman. 'Would you like to leave Zara outside? Leonard said Spellhounds hate this place.'

'Zara is not a Spellhound.'

Zara trotted confidently in through the entrance, so Allyso supposed it would be all right. She crept into the gap and found she had dragonsight again. Tollerman stumbled, so she lit the lamp from the lid of the coffer for his use. She ignored the brief white tunics she had seen before. When she encountered the seer again, she meant to have all her belongings close to hand, in case she had made a mistake in coming to him.

Holding the gem of time, she led the way, the light from Tollerman's lantern humming behind her. She heard his hiss of surprise and awe at the giant stonewood trunks, and led the way in the direction she hoped was correct, swapping his lamp for another as it guttered out. The lamps were too high for her to reach, but Tollerman could manage, once she instructed him.

'I wonder what this place was like when the conners were still here?' she murmured, then blinked and reeled as the scene changed before her eyes. Darkness and quiet were replaced by lanterns and babble and colour, as a flurry of bright-clad youths came storming down the hall. For a heartbeat she thought they might pass right through her, but they seemed to see her clearly. They came to a halt and stared with accusing eyes.

'What — ?'

'It just appeared!' cried one.

'A wraith!' exclaimed another, and soon the cry went up.

'A wraith! A wraith! Some fleewit's conjured a wraith!'

The turmoil was increasing when a dark-clad master emerged from a nearby door. He, too, looked hard at Allyso and made an angry gesture. 'Begone, I say. Creature of evil, begone!'

Allyso realised what had happened. She had thought of the place in its populated past, and now she was there. Quickly, she focused her mind on Tollerman and Zara, walking through this very corridor ... and there they were, with Tollerman staring wildly around him.

'Here I am,' she said. Her mouth was dry with fear, and she hastened on, following the trail of lamps until she found the door to Wootton's chamber.

'Stand back,' she told Tollerman, and he snuffed the lantern and retreated into the shadows. He was staring at her, probably worried in case she vanished again.

Allyso rapped and waited, hoping hard that Leonard would come, but it was Seer Wootton who finally opened the door. He was dressed in the same grey robes with the shadowing cowl and seemed exactly as he had been before.

'I have the gem of time, and we need your help,' she said. She was too tired and confused to work out a more tactful greeting.

'And who are you?' He had known her name the last time they had met, but that was because Leonard had told him.

'I am Allyso Tormblood. Is Leonard here?'

'There is no-one of that name here. Is he your companion?'

'Leonard is a young Mistra. She is your apprentice — or maybe your servant.'

'I have no apprentice,' he said. 'And you have no cause to disturb me. Go back where you belong, Allyso Tormblood.'

'That's what I'm trying to do. I have the gem of time,' she said again. 'You were the one who told me how to find it, but you won't remember that. For you it hasn't happened yet.'

'I see.' He sounded grim, but not disbelieving. 'Have you any proof of this future acquaintance of ours?'

'I found my way to your door. I know you have a candle iron and wear a ring with a red stone. And then there is this.' Allyso raised her arm and bared the scar of the candle iron. 'Do you recognise this, Master Wootton?'

He drew her through the door and into the light where he bent and peered at the healing burn. 'I see,' he said, and this time she thought he really did. 'So the Master of Time has arrived! I have been rather expecting you, but I hadn't thought you would be quite so young.'

'I have the gem, but I'm not the Master of Time,' she said.

'You *are* the Master of Time, since you came to me with proof of a future visit. You must have earned the gem, and that makes you its master. Sit down and tell me your tale.'

Just like that?

'I have some companions,' she said. 'Tollerman of Musson and his hound.'

'I believe I caught a glimpse of them, hovering in the shadows. Are they out of their time as well?'

'A little, I think. Perhaps a few days.'

'You *have* been busy, and not, perhaps, very wise. Whom else have you moved?'

'Only a soulbinder ... and a tree.'

'*Only* a soulbinder — and a *tree*?'

'Tollerman has a gem of power,' she said in excuse. 'The soulbinder tried to take it, but I knew what she would do with it, so I had to stop her. Then everything went mad and when — when things settled, the gem had moved us on to now.'

Wootton held up an imperious hand. 'Enough! You must tell this tale in proper order, or else I cannot help.'

'You refused to help, before,' she said. 'You tried to force me to forget what I needed to know.'

Wootton frowned. 'Did I have any reason for that?'

Allyso considered the Keeper of Dragon's Gate. The gemdrake had refused to deal with her until it saw the sear of the candle iron.

'Perhaps you did,' she said, reluctantly, 'but perhaps it was just a lucky coincidence.'

'I shall help you now, in any case. Sit down while I summon your friends.'

Left in the chamber, Allyso looked about her. She was not surprised to find that the banks of candle stubs and the candle iron were missing. She had always thought the room she had seen on her fateful visit had been especially prepared. This seemed to be the same apartment, but now it was spare yet comfortable, furnished with long, low couches and lined with more books than she had ever seen before. She sat down on a low settle and folded her hands, as Wootton returned with Tollerman and Zara.

'Allyso says you have a gem of power?' Wootton was saying.

Tollerman glanced at Allyso for advice.

'You can tell him,' she said. 'He'll either help you or tell you to go away, but he isn't like *her*.'

'Fairly put,' said Wootton, 'if by *her* you mean this soulbinder.'

'I have a talisman that belonged to my father,' said Tollerman wearily. 'Allyso says it is a crystal, and the healer — the soulbinder — wanted it so much she threatened to kill Zara unless I gave it to her.'

'You had it from your father!' Wootton put back his cowl, and Allyso saw his face for the first time. He was rather younger than Merrit, with spiky fair hair and narrow, pale blue eyes and a slender beak of a nose.

'I can see why you wear a cowl,' she said. 'No-one who saw your face would be scared of you. You look like a —'

'Be quiet,' said Wootton. He kept his gaze on Tollerman. 'Your father was cruel to give you this, my lad.'

'He died before I was born, so I don't know what he was like,' said Tollerman. 'He always wore it, so my kinsman gave it to me.'

'The soulbinder used it to maze him,' added Allyso. 'She said it was a curse, and that it was giving him bad dreams that would drive him mad.'

'She may well have been right. Show me this talisman,' said Wootton.

Tollerman glanced at Allyso again. She nodded, so he lifted the talisman over his head and handed it to Wootton. The seer took it gingerly and ran his fingers over the carving.

'The shell is a real timber-nut. What is it like inside?'

Allyso described it as well as she could. She had seen it often on the soulbinder's hand, but had never examined it closely.

'That does sound like a gem of power,' said Wootton. 'It's curious to find one trapped in wood, and breaking it out might be very dangerous. We need wiser counsel on this. Fetch me the rock from the door and set it on this coffer.'

The rock he had asked for was a jagged piece of dull grey matter, bigger than a dragonpod. It smelled slightly of sulphur and was so greasy to the touch that Allyso rubbed her fingers on her mantle when she had set it in place.

Wootton glanced at Tollerman. 'Be silent, lad, until you are asked to speak,' he warned. 'There could be danger here for you.' He laid his hand on the rock for a moment, and the ring on his finger flashed with sullen fire. 'Keeper?' he said. He repeated the word twice more, and rapped on the rock with his knuckles.

The rock stirred, swelling like an unbaked loaf. A faint voice emerged from within. 'Who calls the Keeper, and with what cause?'

'I am Wootton, the Seer of Conners' Hall, also Master of Truth. I need to speak with you.'

The rock turned dark and from it bloomed the gemdrake: the keeper of Dragon's Gate. It was tiny now; Allyso could have held it in her hands, but it swung its snout towards her, arrogant as ever. 'A halfling child! Beware, halfling, else I burn you to the bone.'

Wootton rapped impatiently on the coffer. 'It is not the master of time who needs your attention, Keeper. It is the lad.'

The gemdrake peered at Tollerman. 'A sorry scrut,' it remarked. 'Is he worth my attention?'

'That's what we need to fathom. He was left this talisman by his father.' Wootton swung the talisman down to the gemdrake's level. 'Within this shell is a gem of power, but we need to know which one.'

The gemdrake oriented on the timber-nut and gazed at it hungrily. 'That is the gem of dreams,' it said. 'Blinded and bound as it is, I know my own. Let me set it free.'

Wootton swung the chain again. 'Who is its master, Keeper?'

The gemdrake's gaze followed the swinging talisman. 'He who was master of dreams is far beyond dreaming now.' Its voice was almost crooning.

'Then why was the gem not returned to the Crystalium Caverns?'

'Blinded and bound, blinded and bound, so how could it find its way home?' The gemdrake snorted a tiny belch of flame, and Allyso's eyes watered from the acrid smoke. 'Let me burn it free.'

'What about this lad?' asked Wootton. 'He has worn the gem for years without knowing what it was. It seems to have done him considerable harm.'

'He had no right! He has not paid! He should have fetched it home.'

'Tollerman was up on the Cloudway,' said Allyso, coughing. 'Perhaps he was trying to take it home?'

Then she recalled that the maimed Tollerman had not had the gem at all. It was this younger Tollerman who had it, and he had never been on the Cloudway to Dragon's Gate. Stumbling, she explained this to the gemdrake. 'So why would he have been on the Cloudway?' she asked. 'Since he didn't have the gem?'

'He would have been seeking his dreams,' said the gemdrake. 'Once he had lost the gem, he would be forced to seek until he found them.'

'I *hate* the dreams!' cried Tollerman. 'Why would I seek them when I want to be rid of them?'

Wootton held up a warning hand, but the gemdrake fixed its gaze on Tollerman. 'So the scrut can speak for himself! Then I'll tell you, scrut, it is too late for you to be rid of the harm.' It said this rather smugly. 'You kept the gem too long, without the proper payment.'

'How could he know?' asked Allyso. 'Nobody told him what it was.'

The gemdrake ignored her. 'Gems of power are not to be taken lightly, scrut. Wear it and dream yourself mad, take it off and become an empty husk. The choice is all you have left.'

'I can't *bear* the dreams,' pleaded Tollerman. 'I *want* to lose them.'

'Lose your dreams if you like,' said the gemdrake. 'And then who knows what might move into your empty mind? There are worse things than nightmares, scrut. At least you wake from those.'

'Now, that's enough!' said Allyso crossly. 'You waste your time and everyone else's with these riddles, Keeper. And do you know, you're sounding more and more like a figure from some fleewitted hearthside tale. You gave *me* the gem of time to use as a light while I looked for the gem of time. You could just as well have told me what it was.'

'You could just as well have asked,' said the gemdrake swiftly. Its lofty tone had changed, and it gave her glare for glare. 'And how should I recall what

I have not yet done? Let me loose my gem of dreams and look on it once more.'

'When the soulbinder wore it as a ring, she used it to maze folk,' said Allyso. 'That gem is evil, and it should be destroyed.'

The gemdrake hissed with displeasure and spurted a jet of flame in her direction.

'Evil minds find evil purpose,' said Wootton. 'A knife is not evil; it might be used to cut your throat, but also to prepare food or to harvest grain. Like a knife, a gem of power works to its master's wishes. How can it be blamed for the harm it does?'

'It has done harm to Tollerman,' said Allyso. 'Someone gave him the gem when he was a little child, and he has paid the price for having it.'

Wootton gave her a midwinter smile. 'There speaks the very new Master of Time. You could, if you chose, roll back time and take the gem from the child before the harm is done. You could then return it to the Crystalium Caverns.'

Tollerman's eyes widened, and he opened his mouth as if to speak.

Allyso broke in: 'I never thought! But how *can* I do that? I'm younger than Tollerman, and if I go to the time when he was a baby, I won't exist.'

'But you are Master of Time,' said Wootton. 'You will grow a day older for every day you live, whether you spend that day in your present, your past or your future. You will age day by day, but you will never grow younger. If you travel with a companion, you will share your gift. If you travel alone and meet that person in the past, you will find his younger self, who will not know you.'

'I see,' said Allyso. 'I think.' She traced the scar on her arm. 'If I were younger now than when I met you before, I wouldn't have this brand.'

'When did we meet, by your reckoning?' asked Wootton.

'It was in Winterwane, the eleventh moon, eleventh day. You will remember me when I arrive. *Did* you remember me, I wonder? Leonard could not have done, since she isn't here now, but you must have remembered me when I arrived.'

'You will not *arrive*,' said Wootton. 'You will be here when Winterwane comes. It will take many moonspans for me to teach you the knowledge you need to properly master that gem.'

'I can't stay here. I have to save my uncle and Torm.'

'Perhaps,' said Wootton, 'you should tell me the whole —!' His words broke off with a cry, as the gemdrake took advantage of his distraction and blew a ball of flame at the talisman.

'Agh,' said the gemdrake contentedly, watching the tiny inferno. 'My gem is unbound and unblinded. My gem of dreams is freed.'

Tollerman had started to his feet as his talisman burned. Now, as the flames died down, he crumpled quietly to the floor.

'The Master of Dreams has fainted,' observed the gemdrake. 'I think this one will do quite well. He *has* paid a price. The price of being unworthy has been so high that it has finally made him worthy after all.' It began to laugh, a rusty, smoky sound that died away as it drew itself back to the heart of the rock.

Wootton lifted the boy back on the couch, then soothed the anxious Zara. 'It is as well the boy has had a Merryhound,' he said. 'She is better than any potion for cheering the mind.'

'Tollerman isn't very cheerful,' said Allyso sharply.

'He would be worse if she hadn't found him. Probably totally mad.' Wootton smiled a little. 'Merryhounds have a way of finding those in need of their company.'

'You said you were the Master of Truth,' said Allyso.

'Yes.' Wootton raised his hand and let the bloodstone wink. 'It is not the role I would have chosen, but here I am.'

'Does that mean you answer questions truthfully?'

'It does, and most who ask would rather hear something different.' Wootton smiled sourly. 'I would rather say something different, mostly. And so, Master of Time, I can tell you with more truth than courtesy that I shall be most uncomfortably busy with two of you children to train.'

'You don't train me,' snapped Allyso. 'I have too much to do. And why are you so helpful all of a sudden? When I came before, you were very harsh. I had to brand my arm to learn what I needed.'

Wootton sighed. 'The gems of power are cruel, Master of Time. Their masters have to be able to master themselves, their desires and their fears. They must search their yesterdays and look beyond tomorrow. You will learn a lot about yourself, by taking this role.'

'I have *not* taken any role,' said Allyso. 'I am Allyso of Torm, not the master of time or anything else. I need this gem to undo the horrible things that happened at Torm. Then the Keeper can have it back. Or you can look after it.'

'Tell me about Torm,' said Wootton.

Allyso told him the tale she had told to Tollerman, again omitting any word of the well-way.

'What do you plan to do now?' he asked when she had finished.

'I will be waiting when the soulbinder comes to Torm,' she said. 'I will make sure Merrit turns her away.' She frowned, remembering how she had erred at the thicket. 'I may need to try more than once before I get it right.'

'Rending time is not to be done so lightly.'

'I won't be doing it lightly. I just need to make things right with a single simple change. If Merrit refuses the soulbinder, then Torm won't starve and Merrit won't be cursed. Then the Lords won't try to take over Torm. And if they stay at their own castles, they can protect themselves from the Tenth Castle if they come. And Scholar and Tace will stay at home at Zimmerhanzel instead of going to Ankoor, and then I can bring the gem back here to you or take it to the Keeper at Dragon's Gate ...' She faltered.

'You see, it is not such a single, simple thing,' said Wootton.

'No,' she said. 'I see that now. If the soulbinder can't get into Torm, the Lords won't lay the siege. That means I won't need to escape from Torm by — by the secret way I used. And *that* means I will never come here to you, and so I will never find the gem of time. And if I never find the gem of time, how can I give it *back*?'

'It is obvious that you cannot,' said Wootton.

Allyso stared at him, feeling the blood blanch from her face. 'Does that mean I *can't* undo it? That after all this, I can't save Torm and Merrit?'

'It means,' said Wootton, 'that you need do nothing more. It means you must have done the thing already.'

Allyso groaned. 'Oh, please, I don't understand.'

'You have already made the change that was needed,' said Wootton. 'The soulbinder woman has not got the gem of dreams. Instead, you have restored it to its master, and brought them both safely to me.'

'She will still come to Torm, and she might still curse Merrit!'

'Without the gem of power, the dame is nothing more dangerous than a kitchen crone. No doubt she could slit your belly or feed you poison but, without the gem, she cannot turn others to do her will.'

'She can't curse Merrit without the gem of dreams?'

'She can curse herself hoarse and do no more harm than any spiteful crone.'

'Then it's going to be all right!' The cloud that had hung over Allyso seemed to be lifting. She might have hugged Seer Wootton if he had been just a little less formal. Instead, she picked up Zara and hugged her, then danced a joyful little jig.

She could go home to Torm, and take up her life, and never face such terrible choices again.

But could it be so simple? 'If it's already done,' she said, 'I can leave the gem with you right now and go straight back to Torm. That means I will live through several moons again, until I catch up with the time I left Cloudway End. Won't that make me older than I should be? And in the wrong place?'

'Use the gem of time,' said Wootton. 'Go back to your home at a time you remember well. You cannot have grown very much during a siege, so I think your folk will accept you.'

'And what about the gem if I use it again? What happens to it afterwards?'

'If you refuse to be Master of Time, it must go back to the Crystalium Caverns. You have seen the havoc a gem can wreak if out of the proper hands.'

'How am I to get it back to Dragon's Gate? Merrit won't let me go off by myself, and I'd still have to get back home again.'

Wootton shrugged. 'That I cannot say. Why not take up the challenge and use what you have earned?'

Another set of choices, just when she had thought she was rid of them! '*That's* no answer!' she said. 'That would be even worse. I want my life back, Master Wootton. I want to put it right and then forget that any of this happened.' She paced across the cave. 'What if I hide the gem of time in the safest place I know? Then, when I am older, I can take it back to the caverns. Would that do?'

Wootton said nothing, but spread his hands. 'I cannot advise you on this.'

'Then it will have to do.' She bit her lip. She didn't much like Seer Wootton, but he had helped her in his fashion. 'Thank you,' she said.

Wootton nodded. 'What is it you think I look like?' he asked curiously. 'You began to say it when I took off my hood, but I cut you off.'

'You look like a strawcap hen,' she said. 'Gill keeps a flock at Torm. They're the silliest things, forever flapping about. The soldiers ate them all, but I suppose they're all alive again now.'

Wootton's pale blue eyes widened, and he looked less than pleased.

'They're very handsome hens,' assured Allyso. 'They have ruffled crests and slender beaks like yours.'

She took the gem of time and held it in her hands. No point in thinking of any time since the siege began, so she fixed her mind on the day that Dagg and Mohr had arrived at Castle Torm. It had been a stormy day, she recalled, and Mohr and his cat had been especially pleased to escape the drenching rain. She had watched them arrive from her perch at the top of the tower ...

'If you change your mind,' said Wootton, 'you can come back here. Think about it, Allyso.'

'I am *not* going to change my mind,' she said. 'Goodbye.'

And she was leaning on the watchtower, and Dagg and Mohr were plodding towards the gates. Her mantle was drenched, which was all to the good, for it gave her an excuse to change into her everyday clothing.

Her turret room was exactly as she recalled, but it seemed the room of a child. She washed and made herself tidy, then dressed in her green Summerclimb tunic before going out to find Merrit greeting his guests. He was whole and hale and hospitable as ever.

'*Merrit*!' Tears started from her eyes, but Merrit simply smiled.

'There you are, Allyso! Just in time. Go and ask Gill to roast some sweetloaves — the Traders will be here for supper.'

CHAPTER TWENTY-SIX

TALE

HIGHSUMMER — 3ND MOON OF THE YEAR TO

MIDWINTER — 11TH MOON OF THE YEAR

OF THE HOUND

IT was very strange to be back at Torm, to see Merrit striding about in his usual fashion. Allyso took her message and soon Gill was busy in the kitchen, roasting sweetloaves with her usual efficiency, while Gregory lingered in the hope of hearing tales from Trader Mohr.

At supper, Allyso ate in silence. The others might accept her, but she knew she was not the same as the girl they thought they knew. She scarcely dared to say anything for fear of revealing something they would wonder about.

The sweetloaves were puffed and golden, and reminded her of Tace and also of Leonard. She supposed the Spellhound was safe with its master at Zimmerhanzel, but what about Leonard? Would she ever be Wootton's apprentice now that Tollerman had arrived at the Conners' Hall? And what about Scholar and Tollerman and Zara? They had all changed her life in some way, but if she had to live the same moonspans over again, wouldn't she also have to forget the whole adventure? So she might, if it weren't for the gem of time.

Forgetting seemed the best and the neatest way for this to end so, after the castle was sleeping, she took the gem out to the wellyard and let herself into the well. It was cool enough, but Highsummer had taken away the ghastly chill she had known before.

She remembered her terror when she'd entered the well-way, but a dip in a well was little to someone who had braved the Cleave and the Cloudway, had faced the Keeper, the candle iron and thicket. She managed to find the tunnel on her second dive, swam through to the rocky rampart and heaved herself up to the ledge.

She put the gem in the tunnel, twisted about and squirmed back through the underwater course until she reached the well.

She regained her turret room without discovery but, despite her exhaustion, it took her a very long time to fall asleep. Wootton had told her Torm was saved, yet she still feared tomorrow.

But Highsummer Eve passed by without a ripple. Mohr and Dagg stayed on, and Mohr told his tales. Highsummer Day swung over into Summerwane. It was all the way it should have been, but she needed to be sure. She had made a change in time, but had it been enough?

'Was a dame driven out of Clair while you were there?' she asked the Traders as they cracked timber-nuts out in the wellyard some days later. She winced as a shell came open, almost expecting it to reveal a gem of power.

'Why do you ask, Mistra Allyso?' asked Dagg.

Mistra Allyso! He *would* say that! But she remembered how Dagg had offered her a home, and managed to smile. 'It was something I heard,' she said. 'Something about an Ankoorian soulbinder leaving Clair.'

'We met an Ankoorian healer there,' said Mohr doubtfully. 'She offered to soothe a trifling rash on my arm, but I rather misliked her mien, so I told her no.'

'The salve was good enough,' said Dagg. 'It was the dame who was a sorry figure.'

Allyso shivered. So the woman was in Clair. But without the gem of dreams, she was nothing but a dubious healer.

'She was seeking a lad, she said,' continued Dagg, 'An afflicted lad who needed her care. She was asking everyone where he might be found.'

'We could believe that tale, or not!' said Mohr. 'It is good to be wary of Ankoorian strangers just now. The Tenth Castle is growing strong.'

Merrit laughed. 'Those fleewits are seeking land to take as their own! Let them come to McAnerin, I say, and we will give them a lesson. Torm and her folk are proof against any rabble.' He turned to Allyso. 'There is a lesson, Heir of Torm. Good folk all together can always hold out against the bad.'

'But what if one of these Tenth Castle people slipped in through our gates?' said Allyso. 'What would happen then, if she — or he — made trouble between the castlers?'

'The folk of Torm know better than that.'

'But what if it *did* happen?'

Merrit raised a brow. 'Who has been putting these notions in your mind?' He glanced at Mohr.

'What would you do if someone came?' she persisted. 'Would you send her away?'

'I would want him under my eye,' said Merrit. 'I like to know what is happening on my lands.' He ruffled her hair. 'Get Gill to crop this mass tomorrow. You look like a shaggy halfling.'

'A what?'

'Halfling — half keyre, like small Lord Torm.'

The bell jangled in the watchtower, and Merrit went to see what Berneathy wanted. He came back grumbling. 'My porter is getting timid. These tales of the Tenth Castle have turned his courage to milk, so I have just admitted a sorry stranger he would have turned away.'

Allyso felt sick, but the stranger Merrit had mentioned was a man. He was not a welcome guest, but he did nothing worse than steal a silver talisman from Mohr's pack. The cat, Greyson, saw the theft and wailed a fearsome warning. Berneathy and Gregory arrived to seize the man, and brought him to Merrit for justice.

'This is no way to repay our hospitality, sleightmaster,' Merrit said mildly. 'Give the trinket back to Trader Mohr. If you want it so badly, I'm sure you may make him an offer.'

The sleightmaster spat at his feet. 'The Tenth Castle is rising! When it marches you'll find some hospitality all right, my Lord of Torm.'

Allyso tried to feel better, for this event, although unpleasant, had never happened before. It seemed to prove that time had taken a different stream. She tried to accept each new day as if it were *really* new, but she saw, in every face among the castlers, how thin was the skin of trust and friendliness. And of course, she had the scar of the candle iron.

That bothered her most of all.

The moons wore on and nothing seemed quite right. Even her tunics and leggings would not sit well. Gill made her more, with tucks in the bodice and larger hems than before.

Midwinter passed, and Winterwane began. The Tenth Moon was nearly over when Allyso saw the High Traders, Templeton and Walton, arrive. She remembered, with a sick feeling, how they had been struck down before, but this time all was well. Their cart was unmolested, and they did good trade among the castlers. Merrit bought a mantle-pin from Walton, and then a fine bronze dagger from Templeton.

'Is there anything you would like, Allyso?' he asked. 'You are near fourteen now; have you found a taste for jewels?'

'If we have nothing to tempt you now, young Mistra,' said Templeton, 'we will bring new stock home from Western Port Fair.'

'Western Port Fair ...' said Allyso. 'Is that in Ankoor, Trader Templeton?'

'It is the finest fair in all of that bleak country,' said Walton.

'Isn't it dangerous in Ankoor? Because of the Tenth Castle?'

'The rogues are on the move, it is true,' said Templeton, 'but they'll not molest honest Traders.'

Allyso wasn't so sure of that. 'Do be careful,' she said. 'They are — they sound dangerous.'

Merrit laughed. 'Allyso, you are growing as timid as Berneathy! These High Traders have trodden the route to Western Port since long before you were born. Honest folk have nothing to fear from noisy fools.'

'They might have spears or arrows. They might cast curses or spells.'

'You never used to be so fearful,' said Merrit. He ruffled Allyso's hair. 'It seems my heir is too concerned for your safety to choose a trinket now.'

Templeton smiled. 'We will take care, young Mistra, and we thank you for your concern.'

The High Traders went on their way, and the Tenth Moon passed into the Eleventh. Everything seemed well, and Allyso knew she had almost finished her moons of living twice. She wished she could enjoy the relief, but the gem in the well-way was never far from her mind.

What would happen if she left it there too long? Would it turn on her as the gem of dreams had turned on Tollerman? But how could she get it to the Caverns? Merrit would *never* let her go.

She was sitting in the wellyard kicking the coping when Merrit settled beside her. She tried to smile in welcome, but Merrit turned and looked at her closely.

'What's amiss with you, Allyso? You hardly seem yourself.'

She shrugged.

'Gill thinks it nothing but your age, but Hilz recommends a tonic.'

Allyso shook her head. Gill had cropped her hair, but now it was flopping into her eyes. She was lifting her hand to flick it away when Merrit grasped her wrist.

'How did you come by that scar?'

She blinked at him, for no-one at Torm had ever noticed the brand.

'Have you been playing torture games with Gregory? I'll have his hide if so!'

'Of *course* not!' she flashed. 'Why would I ever do that?'

'To prove you are brave, perhaps, or to add some excitement to life,' said Merrit. 'I did such things when I was a growing lad. And you are certainly growing, Allyso. I think perhaps you need some occupation.'

'I can read and write and I know my figuring. I help Gill in the kitchens.'

'Did you burn your arm in the kitchens? Ah, here come Hilz and Gill. We might ask their opinion, and Gregory's as well, I think. Gill, would you call your son?'

Allyso knew that Merrit must have arranged this confrontation, but making a fuss would only make things worse. She offered her arm so Hilz could examine it.

'Very strange,' said Hilz. 'Has someone been mazing you?'

'It looks like a rite-mark to me,' said Gill. 'As if she's been branded to some cause or calling. Better have a Spellhound in, just to be certain.'

Merrit tugged at his own bronze hair. '*Must* you mumble such stuff, Gill? You may be a good cook, but your head is stuffed with more stupid notions than a strawcap is with eggs. Spellhounds are nothing but fancy superstition. Breed a hound with a copper coat and charge a golden fee, and there you have a Spellhound — and a fool for its master.'

Gill stared at him, hurt, and that seemed to exasperate Merrit even more. 'I seem surrounded by fools!' he exclaimed. 'Hilz looks wise and speaks of *mazing*, Berneathy wants to bar the gates against the most harmless stranger, you prate of superstition —'

Gregory scowled and put his arm about his mother's shoulders.

'As for you, my lad,' said Merrit, 'I think you know more about this scar of Allyso's than you say. She would never have done it herself!'

'You're wrong!' snapped Allyso. She felt the bubble of rage inside her, and recognised it as the shadow of the rage she had felt near the thicket when the soulbinder threatened Zara. 'You're *wrong*,' she said again. 'You're wrong about Gill and Berneathy and Healer Hilz, and you're wrong about Spellhounds, too. You're wrong about so much, but you never listen to sense, and you never see what's plain before you. Gregory would never hurt me. He's my *friend*.'

'Then tell us how you got that brand,' said Merrit.

Gill and Gregory were staring at her, Healer Hilz was quietly mixing salve. Merrit looked angry and puzzled and even hurt.

'If I tell you,' she said, 'you won't believe a word.'

'Try us,' said Merrit.

If she hadn't been so angry, she might have concocted a story of an accident at the village forge. But she *was* angry and, after a moment, she realised why. 'You have no right to tell Gill the things she believes are silly superstition,' she said. 'She's right about some things. Spellhounds *do* have powers, and even *you* believe in the gem of time!'

Merrit laughed. 'The gem of time is nothing but a hearth-tale.'

'You believe in it,' persisted Allyso. 'When there is nothing else to believe in, and no hope of help, you will believe in that.'

'Nonsense!'

'You do,' she said. 'You did. And so I'll tell you the story ... It started on Highsummer Eve when the soulbinder came ...'

She had told parts of the tale before, to the Traders, to Tollerman and to Wootton; now she told the whole saga to Merrit and the others. The only part she left out was her escape through the well-way, just as she had left it out when telling her tale to the others. It was easy enough to hedge the point; she explained how Healer Hilz had offered disguise, and simply said she'd escaped the castle by night.

As the tale continued, Merrit's expression lightened. 'That's quite a turn you have for tale-spinning,' he said, when Allyso paused for breath. 'You have left me fading away from a curse while you fled with the soldier's hound. Now tell how I rallied and rescued Torm from these wicked invaders!' He chuckled. 'My neighbours Sheels and Toombs would be amazed to be cast in the role of besiegers. And what a clever ruse those blight-wards were!'

'You never rallied,' said Allyso. 'Scholar said you were dead. And not only you ...' She pressed her hands to her eyes, remembering what Scholar had refused to say. 'And Scholar said he went home to Zimmerhanzel and found that the Tenth Castle brutes had taken over it and Hasselsjo and killed many of the castlers there.'

'But you had left this Scholar, had you not? How did he tell you what happened later? Had he a messenger bird?'

'We met again later,' said Allyso. 'While he was finding it out, I had gone to seek the gem of time. I went to Fielding and asked help from Trader Dagg and Trader Mohr ... I went on to Singing Tor and met a girl named Leonard ...'

The tale continued, but instead of becoming easier to tell, it became more and more difficult. Her voice was shaking as she neared the end, and she was afraid she was going to cry.

'And so,' said Merrit more gently, 'let me guess the ending. You used the gem one last time to return yourself to Torm at a point before these fantastic happenings, and that explains why the rest of us remember nothing about the siege.'

Allyso blinked. 'How did you know?'

'It was obvious,' said Merrit with a hint of apology. 'If I had been spinning a tale, I would have crafted it so. It is the only ending that makes sense. With the knowledge sponged from everyone's minds but your own, there is no proof.'

'But that's *wrong*,' said Gregory, scowling. 'In a tale there should be proof.'

'No proof,' said Merrit again, 'because if there were, we would be forced to accept the tale, and that we could never do.'

'I *told* you,' said Allyso. 'I said you would never believe me. But there is proof after all. There is my brand, and if you went to Conners' Hall, you would find Tollerman with Seer Wootton. How could I know that if my tale is all made up?'

'Ah yes, the mysterious seer who lives in the depths of the hill. Who will remember nothing, I suspect.'

'He will remember meeting me with Tollerman. And I have the gem of time.'

'And may we see this gem?'

'I hid it in — in a place I promised to keep a secret.' Since the secret of Torm could not be told to Gill and Gregory, she shook her head again.

'I suppose,' said Merrit with amusement, 'this tale is meant to teach me a lesson or two. Does it mean that you want adventures, I wonder?'

She lifted her face from her hands. 'I *certainly don't* want adventure, but I shall have to go to the Dragons-Gate. I could give the gem to the Keeper, and then things would be normal again.'

The bell in the watchtower jangled.

'I suppose,' said Merrit, 'I should see to that, before Berneathy sends them away.'

He went off, leaving Allyso with Gill and Gregory and Healer Hilz, who handed her the salve he had mixed. 'Rub this on the scar,' he said. 'It will soften it a little.'

Gill looked troubled. 'Gregory, show me your arms. I want to be sure you haven't been burning yourself, too!'

'I *told* you what happened,' said Allyso. 'Every word was *true*!' But she saw the doubt in their faces and began to doubt herself.

'Come, Gregory,' said Gill. 'I need more wood for the ovens ...'

BEGINNING

WINTERWANE — 11TH MOON TO 12TH MOON

OF THE YEAR OF THE HOUND

WHEN the others had gone, Allyso looked at her scar. It was white and shiny, in the manner of a long-healed wound. She remembered the ghastly hiss as she touched the candle iron, but the pain had gone. She turned and peered into the well. Had she really hidden the gem of time down there?

Needing to be certain, she took off her mantle and slid feet-first into the well. It was cold as fear, but she ducked down under the water, found the tunnel and pulled herself inside.

Her elbows jammed against the sides and she had to push herself along with her toes. Her lungs seemed close to bursting when she reached the end and dragged herself up to the ledge.

She could not get into the upper tunnel.

She twisted and squirmed, kicking desperately, but her shoulders were jammed and her chest pressed painfully into the stone. It was that new, unfamiliar pain that told her what had happened. She had grown too big for the well-way!

Her mind whirled as she hung there, shaking with cold, her legs in the water, her shoulders jammed in the rock. She *must* reach the gem of time. Let her touch it with so much as a fingertip, and she could send herself back six moonspans or so to Summerwane ... But she wouldn't get any smaller, so that was no help at all.

Stupid, *stupid*, to hide it in the well-way! And to think she had been proud to be growing at last!

'I never wanted to *keep* it!' she gasped, as she scrabbled at the stone. 'I wanted to keep it safe!'

'Who calls the Keeper, and with what cause?'

The voice came gusting out of the rocks, far away but familiar. Familiar, too, was the sulphur smell and the oily touch of soot.

'*Keeper*?'

'Who calls the Keeper, and with what cause?'

'It's Allyso!' she gasped. 'I really need your help.'

There was a silence and she strained her ears, hearing only the drip of water and the furious thump of her heart.

'Who calls the Keeper, and with what cause? Speak, or I will burn you beyond the bone!'

Allyso sighed. 'You know me, Keeper. I am the Master of Time.'

There was a pause, filled with echoes and the chuckle of fire within the stone. 'I remember you,' said the gemdrake's voice. 'You are the halfling, the brat who dared to challenge me when I freed the gem of dreams. You are the one who twirled the tail of time.'

'Yes,' said Allyso. Her teeth were chattering and not only with cold. 'What are you doing here at Torm? Why are you not at the Caverns?'

'I have told you this before. I live in the rock and I am of the rock. I come when I am called. And how I punish those who call me lightly!'

'I need your help,' she said again. 'I hid the gem of time down here, but now I want to return it to the Crystalium Caverns, and I have grown too big to reach it.'

The ghost of a laugh came gurgling from the tunnel, and suddenly the well-way lit with a gust of dragonfire. And there, glowing, just before her, Allyso saw the orb.

'Take it,' said the gemdrake. 'You know what you must do.'

'I will bring it back to the caverns,' she said.

'Too late for that, Master of Time. You have taken up the challenge and made a beginning.' The gemdrake's voice was fading, and the light was growing dim. 'See that you take your chance before the shadows fall on Torm.'

'But the shadows are gone,' said Allyso. 'The soulbinder has no power!'

'She was one. Others will come, and will Torm's Lord stand against them?'

Allyso took the gem and abruptly her shoulders came free, and she knew she was alone. She slithered very suddenly down from the ledge.

By sunfall, she was back in her chamber, drying her hair and pondering her options. She could show the gem to Merrit, but that would lead to further complications. If he tried to use it and made mistakes, if he tried to send someone else to return it to the caverns ... And she knew that nothing had really changed. Merrit was just the same as ever, fearing nothing and no-one and laughing at the fears of others. Even if she used the gem of time again, the trouble would remain. And she realised she was afraid to use it. What if she made things worse?

And yet, the Keeper had said she had taken up the challenge ... It had called her Master of Time.

She put on her reinbeast mantle, since her other one was damp. It was too short for her now, and very shabby, but its familiarity gave her comfort.

Someone tapped on the door. 'Allyso? Come out. We have some guests for the night.'

She opened the door and saw Merrit waiting, his expression both wry and wary. 'Who is it?' she asked nervously.

'It is Scholar of Zimmerhanzel,' said Merrit. 'A coincidence, is it not? He played quite a role in your tale!'

Scholar, *here*? 'But he won't remember me!' she said.

'He has a hound with him,' said Merrit. 'Also a young Mistra, one of the Hasselsjo brood. Come along and help me make them welcome.'

She followed obediently, clutching the gem of time inside her sleeve, her heart thudding as it had thudded in the well.

At first she hardly recognised Scholar. He had been dusty and careworn when she had known him before, and now he was clean and dressed in reinbeast weave. He was also gaunt and hollow-eyed, as if he'd been ill. He greeted her politely, but with a certain shock in his eyes. The Mistra with him was a little more forthright: '*This* is the Heir of Torm?'

Allyso felt awkward, but before she could say anything in reply, the Spellhound at Scholar's feet gave a whine of pleasure and wagged her whip of a tail.

'Tace!' cried Allyso, and knelt and held out her arms.

The hound came sedately over, and thrust her muzzle into Allyso's mantle.

'Tace!' Scholar sounded startled and amused, and the Mistra with him laughed.

'You said the hound would never go to a stranger without your instruction. That just goes to show how far I should trust the word of Zimmerhanzel!'

'Be quiet, Tegwen,' snapped Scholar.

'So,' said Merrit, 'we have the heirs of Zimmerhanzel and Hasselsjo come to call. You two have never met my heir before?'

Scholar shook his head and his companion smiled. 'I doubt it,' she said, 'but then, why should I remember?'

If that was an insult, thought Allyso, it was prettily delivered. And Tegwen of Hasselsjo *was* a pretty girl, with a proud, high-coloured face and a wilful mouth.

'What is this all about, Merrit?' asked Allyso. 'Is it to do with what I told you? Have you brought these two to make a fool of me? I told you Master Scholar would not remember me, and I have never met this Mistra at all.'

Merrit put a hand on her shoulder, then rubbed the Spellhound's ears. 'I would never do that to you, Allyso. When have you ever known me cruel?'

'Then why are they here?' she asked. 'It cannot be a coincidence.'

Tegwen yawned. 'That is easily explained, my child. My Aunt Misty is the herb-warden to Castle Curran in western McAnerin. Herbal lore is a useful skill to have for any person. Master Scholar is escorting me and will join me in my studies. We started rather later than we'd hoped and so we decided to overnight at Torm. Lord Merrit's hospitality is famed throughout the north.'

'I see,' said Allyso. She stared at Tegwen Hasselsjo. The girl's explanation sounded reasonable, but she must remember that anyone from Hasselsjo or Zimmerhanzel might be an enemy. To be sure, Lords Toombs and Sheels had not attacked Torm this time around, but they had been willing to do so once and she supposed they would be willing again, if the opportunity arose. Did their heirs mean trouble? Had they come to spy? Or had the lords sent the heirs *away* from trouble this time? Scholar had helped her before, but that had been on Tace's account, not hers.

'How long do you mean to stay at Curran?' she asked.

Tegwen shrugged. 'I believe the harvest lasts for two moonspans.'

'And how do you get there?'

'We travel down to the Conners' Wayside Fountain,' said Scholar. 'The track turns west towards Curran not far from there.'

So, they were passing the Conners' Fountain! If she could get there, she could slip away in the night and make for Conners' Hall. Wootton would take her in, and he would teach her how to properly master the gem of time.

She stroked Tace, hoping the Spellhound was still her friend. 'Herbal lore sounds interesting,' she said casually. 'I wish *I* could see western McAnerin.'

'There's not a lot to see there,' said Tegwen.

'I have never been to Curran.'

'Nor have I,' said Scholar. 'I suppose you *could* come with us, if Lord Merrit would agree?'

Allyso was torn between triumph and fear, but she managed a gasp of apparent delight. '*Could* I, Merrit? I do have much to learn.'

'You are a little young to go off like this,' said Merrit. He glanced at Scholar. 'She is just fourteen, young Zimmerhanzel. Do you really want her company as well as that of Mistra Hasselsjo?'

Tegwen Hasselsjo laughed. 'I believe Lord Merrit thinks we are fond of one another!' she said. 'Tell him we are not!'

Scholar shrugged. 'We are not close friends, Lord Merrit, but since I am escorting Tegwen to her studies, I might as well take another Mistra as well. Perhaps they could talk together on the journey and give me some peace.'

'I would really like to go,' said Allyso. She tried to sound eager rather than desperate, but she was aware that all three guests were watching her closely. Scholar's mismatched eyes were very intent and for a moment she shrank away. If these two *wanted* her to come, did that mean trouble?

'Perhaps ...' she began, but Scholar gave her a tiny nod.

'Come if you please,' he said. 'It makes no difference to us.'

Allyso glanced at Tace, who was panting gently and wagging her tail. If Tace thought it was safe — Allyso made up her mind. 'I would like to go, if Mistra Tegwen's kin will not object.'

Merrit laughed. 'Mistra Misty has always been fond of young company. She'll not mind one more pupil.'

'Then I shall travel with you,' said Allyso. 'At least,' she added under her breath, 'for a while.'

The evening passed in a flurry of activity. She fetched her journey-pack, the one she had had from Trader Mohr. Recalling the difficulties she had faced on the journey before, she took food from the buttery, packed spare leggings and tunics and added the knife she had had from Gregory. Gill helped her, but seemed flustered and uncertain, though the presence of Scholar's Spellhound seemed to reassure her a little.

'Stay with the hound, Allyso, and no harm will come to you,' she said, as she hugged Allyso goodbye the next morning.

'Learn what you can, and bring me some supplies of any new herbs you note,' said Healer Hilz.

And Gregory said wistfully, 'I wish I could come with you.'

Allyso wished he could, but she had her own plans, and Gregory would make it difficult to make her move.

Having said her farewells, she put on her strongest boots and presented herself to the others. Scholar nodded with seeming approval, and Merrit chuckled. 'Anyone would think you were off on a quest instead of merely a ride to Castle Curran.'

'A *ride*?'

'You are travelling in comfort,' said Merrit. 'It seems that Mistra Misty has sent a garner.' He laughed at Allyso's expression. 'You could hardly have thought two castle heirs could travel unescorted and afoot?'

The garnerbeast was huge and placid, covered with heavy, iron-grey wool. It wore a long double-sided saddle on its high back, and it was so tall that Merrit had to hoist Allyso up to reach the stirrup. Once on board, she perched sideways, sitting back to back with Tegwen, with her heels in the saddle groove.

'What about Tace?' she asked, but it seemed that the saddle had a suitable place for Spellhounds, too.

The garner set off at a tireless striding pace, making three or four times the speed Allyso had made on foot. She felt insecure, but she did spare one hand to wave to Merrit. He waved back, casually, then turned towards the gates.

Torm receded from sight, and Allyso had plenty of time to wonder if she had made a horrible mistake. The gem of time was in her journeypack, and she dared not think of it too often, just in case it plunged her into time. It had been bad enough when she had had to explain herself to Tollerman. The idea of ending up in the wrong time with two castle heirs, a Spellhound and a garnerbeast was not to be considered.

They spent the night in a wayside house, where Tegwen complained of the lumpy bed, and were off again soon after sunlift.

As Scholar helped her back onto the garnerbeast, Allyso wondered again at his gaunt looks. She had assumed, this second time around, that Scholar was safely at Zimmerhanzel with his father and Tace, but now she had time to wonder if he had merely swapped one terrible adventure in that time for a different one in this. She had, as the gemdrake put it, *twisted the tail of time*, but had time decreed that Scholar must still pass some kind of trial? Did no-one ever escape?

Her back prickled as she remembered Merrit's casual wave as she left. Merrit lived, but he hadn't learned so that still lay ahead.

She wanted to ask Scholar how he had spent the last few moons, but no tactful phrasing came to mind until they neared the Conners' Fountain.

'It was kind of Tegwen's aunt to send her garnerbeast,' she said abruptly. 'How long have you been planning this journey?'

'This is not my aunt's garner,' said Tegwen.

'Merrit said it was.'

'Lord Merrit *assumed* it was. He is a fool. Everyone says he is easily taken in —'

'Shut *up*, Tegwen!' snapped Scholar, and Tace gave a warning growl.

'All right. But she has to know soon.'

'Know *what*?' Allyso looked down in sudden apprehension, but the ground was moving by at a speed that made jumping seem unwise. She thought, if she could bear to wait, she would let this pair do whatever they planned, and when she knew their scheme, she would turn back time and use her knowledge to overturn it. 'What are you going to do to me?' she demanded.

'Nothing!' said Scholar. 'We're taking you to meet someone we know.'

'*Not* the Mistra Misty?'

'No. Well, at least, not this time.'

'We never *said* we were going to Curran this time,' said Tegwen.

'But —'

'You think back,' said Tegwen smugly. 'Neither of us ever said a thing that wasn't true. I said I had a herb-warden aunt, which I do. Scholar said he was escorting me to our studies, which he is.'

'Where are we really going, then?'

Scholar swivelled to face her. 'We are taking you to see someone we know. This will be impossible for you to believe, but she says you are the Master of Time.'

Allyso scowled at him. 'So I am,' she said.

Scholar looked relieved. 'If you know that, then you may also know the rest of it. She says that the time is coming when McAnerin could be lost without your power.'

Not *again*, thought Allyso. And then she realised what else Scholar had said. '*She*? What is your friend's name?'

'Her name is Leonard,' said Tegwen, 'but I wouldn't call her a friend. She comes from some other place, and she thinks she knows everything. Wootton says —'

Allyso found she was clenching her hands. 'Shut *up*, Tegwen!' she said, echoing Scholar. 'Maybe we should have left you dead!'

'What?' Tegwen's face was blank with shock.

'Never mind,' said Allyso. 'You died before, that's all, so Scholar said. The soldiers killed you when they invaded Hasselsjo.'

'*Scholar* said? I am *not* dead! What would Scholar know?'

'I don't understand this, either,' said Scholar. 'But here's the Conners' Fountain. West to Curran or east to Conners' Hall?'

'West!' snapped Tegwen. 'I want no part of this!'

'East,' said Allyso. 'I have to go to be trained by Seer Wootton.'

Tace wagged her tail and peered past Allyso, happily snuffing the air.

'East it is,' said Scholar, and turned the garnerbeast towards the Tor.